Margaret Cevendish Duchess of Newcastle

# The lives of William Cavendishe, Duke of Newcastle, and of his wife Margaret

Margaret Cevendish Duchess of Newcastle

**The lives of William Cavendishe, Duke of Newcastle, and of his wife Margaret**

ISBN/EAN: 9783744726917

Printed in Europe, USA, Canada, Australia, Japan

Cover: Foto ©Raphael Reischuk / pixelio.de

More available books at **www.hansebooks.com**

# THE LIVES OF
# WILLIAM CAVENDISHE,

## DUKE OF NEWCASTLE,

### AND OF HIS WIFE,

## MARGARET DUCHESS OF NEWCASTLE.

### WRITTEN BY THE THRICE NOBLE AND

### ILLUSTRIOUS PRINCESS,

## MARGARET, DUCHESS OF NEWCASTLE.

### EDITED WITH A PREFACE AND OCCASIONAL

### NOTES BY

## MARK ANTONY LOWER, M.A., Etc.

### LONDON:
# JOHN RUSSELL SMITH,
### 36, SOHO SQUARE.
### 1872.

# Preface.

AMONG the curiofities of biogra-phical and autobiographical lite-rature of the feventeenth cen-tury, there are but few which exceed in intereft the two mentioned in the title-page of this book.  By way of introduc-tion, it is neceffary to quote their titles in full. The firft is—

" The Life of the Thrice Noble, High, and puiffant Prince, WILLIAM CAVENDISHE, Duke, Marquefs, and Earl of NEWCASTLE, Earl of Ogle; Vifcount Mansfield; and Baron of *Bolfover*, of *Ogle*, *Bothal*, and *Hepple:* Gentleman of His Majefties Bed-Chamber; one of His Majefties moft Honourable Privy Council; Knight of the Moft Noble Order of the Garter; His Majefties Lieutenant of

the County and Town of *Nottingham;* and
Juſtice in Ayre, *Trent North:* who had the
honour to be Governour to our moſt Glorious
King, and Gracious Soveraign, in his Youth,
when He was Prince of *Wales;* and ſoon
after was made Captain General of all the
Provinces beyond the River of *Trent,* and
other Parts of the Kingdom of *England,* with
Power, by a ſpecial Commiſſion to make
Knights.—Written by the thrice Noble, Illuſ-
trious, and Excellent Princeſs, MARGARET,
Ducheſs of Newcaſtle, His [ſecond] Wife.—
London, Printed by *A. Maxwell* in the year
1667."

The title of the ſecond work is—

" A True Relation of the Birth, Breeding, and Life of MARGARET CAVENDISH,
Ducheſs of Newcaſtle." [Written by herſelf.]

The latter was not publiſhed in a ſeparate
form, but it appears in a ſcarce and curious
folio, called " 𝕹atures 𝕻ictures drawn by
FANCIES PENCIL to the Life. Written by
the thrice Noble, Illuſtrious, and Excellent
Princeſs, THE LADY MARCHIONESS OF NEW-
CASTLE.—*In this Volume there are ſeveral
feigned ſtories of Natural Deſcriptions, as Comi-*

*cal, Tragical, and Tragi-comical, Poetical, Ro-
mantical, Philofophical, and Hiftorical, both in
Profe and Verfe, fome all Profe, fome mixt, partly
Profe and partly Verfe. Alfo there are fome
Morals, and fome Dialogues, but they are as
the advantage Loaves of Bread as a Baker's
Dozen; and a true Story at the latter End,
wherein there is no feinins."*—London: Printed
by J. Martin, and J. Alleftrye at the Bell in
Saint Pauls Church-yard, 1656.[1]

The latter work (or rather part of a work)
was printed as a brochure by Sir Egerton
Brydges at his private prefs at Lee Priory,
with a "critical preface," &c., in 1814.
This reprint is one of the worft ever given
to the world, the typography being fhamefully
incorrect. In the prefent re-impreffion the
punctuation and capital letters have been
carefully attended to, fo that I truft it will
be found a faithful copy of the quaint original.

It is fcarcely neceffary to add to thefe
remarks any biographical notices of the Duke
and Duchefs. The hufband was undoubtedly

---

[1] *Nature's Pictures,* p. 368.

a true Nobleman, and whatever opinion the prefent age may hold concerning his political views, there can be no doubt that loyalty to his pupil, afterwards Charles II., influenced him in a direction which, but for that, might have been different. We forgive errors in our own children and friends which we fhould not excufe in other people—the errors, I mean, of *partiality*.

As to MARGARET, the Duchefs, and authorefs of thefe two biographies, Sir Egerton Brydges makes fome excellent remarks. "That the Duchefs was deficient in a cultivated judgment," he fays; " that her knowledge was more multifarious than exact; and that her powers of fancy and fentiment were more active than her powers of reafoning, I will admit; but that her productions, mingled as they are with great abfurdities, are wanting either in talent or virtue, or even in genius, I cannot concede. . . . . ' I fear my ambition,' fays the Duchefs, ' inclines to vainglory; for I am very ambitious; yet 'tis neither for beauty, wit, titles, wealth, or power, but as they are Steps to raife me to Fancies Tower, which is to live by Remem-

brance in after Ages. . . . . I was addicted
from my Childhood to Contemplation, rather
then Converfation; to Solitarinefs rather then
Society; to Melancholy rather then Mirth;
to write with the Pen then to work with my
Needle."

She further adds: " My Difpofition is more
inclining to Melancholy than Merry; but
not crabbed or peevifh Melancholy, but foft,
melting, folitary, and contemplating Melancholy, and I am apt to weep rather than
laugh." For other features of her character
the reader muft feek in the body of her auto-
biography, and I feel certain that no modern
reader, on a candid perufal of her writings,
will concur in attributing to her the nickname
which her jealous (female?) contemporaries
gave her—" *Mad Madge of Newcaftle!* "

" The labours of no modern authorefs,"
fays Dyce, in his *Britifh Poetefſes*, " can be
compared as to quantity with thofe of the
indefatigable Duchefs of Newcaftle, who filled
nearly twelve volumes folio with plays, poems,
orations, philofophical difcourfes, &c. Her
writings fhow that fhe poffeffed a mind of
confiderable power and activity, with much

imagination, but not one particle of judgment or taste." But this is by far too sweeping a criticism—eccentric she doubtless was, and perhaps John Evelyn's dictum will not be disputed when he says, in a few brief words, after he had paid the Duke and Duchess a visit at their town-house in Clerkenwell Close; "I was much pleased with the extraordinary fanciful habit, garb and discourse of the Duchess."

When in the country, the Duke and Duchess resided chiefly at Welbeck Abbey in Nottinghamshire, and at Bolsover Castle in Derbyshire, seats about six or seven miles apart. There is a portrait of her Grace, in a kind of theatrical costume, now at Welbeck Abbey, and another (a very fine one) at Wentworth Castle, Yorkshire, which has been engraved, after a painting by Abraham Van Diepenbach of Antwerp, a pupil of Rubens. This picture has been attributed by mistake to Sir Peter Lely.

The Duchess died in London, and was buried near the Duke in Westminster Abbey, January 7th, 1674. A fine monument in the north transept bears the following inscription :—

HERE LYES THE LOYALL DUKE OF NEWCASTLE,
AND HIS DUTCHESS HIS SECOND WIFE, BY WHOM HE
HAD NO ISSUE: HER NAME WAS MARGARETT LUCAS,
YONGEST SISTER TO THE LORD LUCAS, OF COL-
CHESTER; A NOBLE FAMILIE, FOR ALL THE BROTHERS
WERE VALIANT, AND ALL THE SISTERS VIRTUOUS.
THIS DUTCHESS WAS A WISE, WITTIE, AND LEARNED
LADY, WHICH HER MANY BOOKES DO WELL TESTIFIE;
SHE WAS A MOST VIRTUOUS AND A LOVEING AND
CAREFULL WIFE, AND WAS WITH HER LORD ALL
THE TIME OF HIS BANISHMENT AND MISERIES, AND
WHEN HE CAME HOME NEVER PARTED FROM HIM
IN HIS SOLITARY RETIREMENTS.

I have not enlarged this preface as I might have done, becaufe all the main incidents of the lives of the Duke and Duchefs will be found in the text of the two biographies in-cluded in this volume, and in the occafional notes which I have added in the courfe of my editorfhip.   M. A. L.

## POSTSCRIPT.

MR. HALLIWELL, in his "Letters of the Kings of England," prints feveral from Charles the Firft to the Duke of Newcaftle. The firft is dated from Shrewfbury, 23rd September, 1642. "This is to tell you that this rebellion is grown to that height, that I muſt not look what opinion men are of who at the time [are] willing and able to ſerve me. Therefore, I do not only permit, but command you to make uſe of all my loving ſubjects' ſervices, without examining their conſciences (more than their loyalty to me) as you ſhall find moſt to conduce to the upholding of my juſt regal power.—So I reſt, Your moſt aſſured faithful friend,

"CHARLES R."

The next letter is dated from Oxford, November 2, 1642, in which he ſays: "Newcaſtle. Your letters are ſo really faithful and lucky in my ſervice, that though I pretend not to thank you in words, yet I cannot but tell you . . . . of the ſenſe I have of them." The king goes on to ſtate that he has ſent the Duke £4,000 for war expenſes, and concludes with "Your moſt aſſured conſtant friend, CHARLES R."

In the third letter the King thanks Newcaſtle (then Earl) for his eminent ſervices, and avers that he ſhall look upon him as "a principal inſtrument in keeping the crown on my head." In this letter the King informs

the Earl that he has given orders for a commiſſion "to command all the countries beyond Trent." This letter is dated from
Oxford, December 15, 1642.

The next is alſo dated from Oxford, a few
days later, December 29, 1642. The King
thanks the Earl for ſending for the Queen
with "earneſtnefs," and regrets that he cannot ſend him more arms, at the ſame time
wondering that as there were 12,000 of the
trained bands in the Earl's diſtrict, he ſhould
find any lack of weapons. It concludes with :
" I pray you let me hear from you as oft as
you may."

The fifth letter bears date Oxford, April 5,
1644, and contains ſtrong expreſſions refpecting the Scots. The King ſays : " Remember
all courage is not in fighting : conſtancy in a
good cauſe being the chief, and the defpiſing
of ſlanderous tongues and pens being not the
leaſt ingredient."

The next is of little importance. It is
dated from Oxford, April 11, 1644, and refers
to the Scots' invaſion.

The ſeventh letter is addreſſed to Newcaſtle under his new title of Marquis, in final

teftimony of his great fervices after the dif-
comfiture of the royal forces in the North. It
is dated from " Our court at Oxford 28. Nov.
1644," and is full of praifes and gratitude, and
addreffed : " To our right trufty and entirely
beloved councillor, William, Marquis of Newcaftle."

# THE
# LIFE
## OF THE

Thrice Noble, High and Puiſſant PRINCE,

# William Cavendiſhe,

Duke, Marqueſs, and Earl of *Newcaſtle*; Earl of *Ogle*; Viſcount *Mansfield*; and Baron of *Bolſover*, of *Ogle*, *Bothal* and *Hepple*: Gentleman of His Majeſties Bed-chamber; one of His Majeſties moſt Honourable Privy-Councel; Knight of the moſt Noble Order of the Garter; His Majeſties Lieutenant of the County and Town of *Nottingham*; and Juſtice in Ayre *Trent-North*: who had the honour to be Governour to our moſt Glorious King, and Gracious Soveraign, in his Youth, when He was Prince of *Wales*; and ſoon after was made Captain General of all the Provinces beyond the River of *Trent*, and other Parts of the Kingdom of *England*, with Power, by a ſpecial Commiſſion, to make Knights.

---

WRITTEN

*By the thrice Noble, Illuſtrious, and Excellent Princeſs,*
MARGARET, *Ducheſs of* Newcaſtle,
*His 2d Wife.*

---

*LONDON,*

Printed by *A. Maxwell*, in the Year 1667.

# To His moſt Sacred Majeſty
# Charles the Second,

By the Grace of God, of *England*, *Scotland*, *France* and *Ireland* King, Defender of the Faith, *&c.*

*May it pleaſe Your Majeſty,*

 HAVE, in confidence of your Gracious acceptance, taken the boldneſs, or rather the preſumption, to dedicate to Your Majeſty this ſhort Hiſtory (which is as full of Truths, as words) of the Actions and Sufferings of Your moſt Loyal Subject, my Lord and Huſband (by Your Majeſties late favour) Duke of *Newcaſtle;* who when Your Majeſty was Prince of *Wales*, was Your moſt careful Governour, and honeſt Servant. Give me therefore leave to relate here, that I have

heard him often ſay, He loves Your Royal Perſon ſo dearly, that He would moſt willingly, upon all occaſions, ſacrifice his Life and Poſterity for Your Majeſty: whom that Heaven will ever bleſs, is the Prayer of

*Your moſt Obedient, Loyal,*

*humble Subject*

*and Servant,*

Margaret Newcaſtle.

# To His Grace the Duke of Newcaſtle.

My Noble Lord,

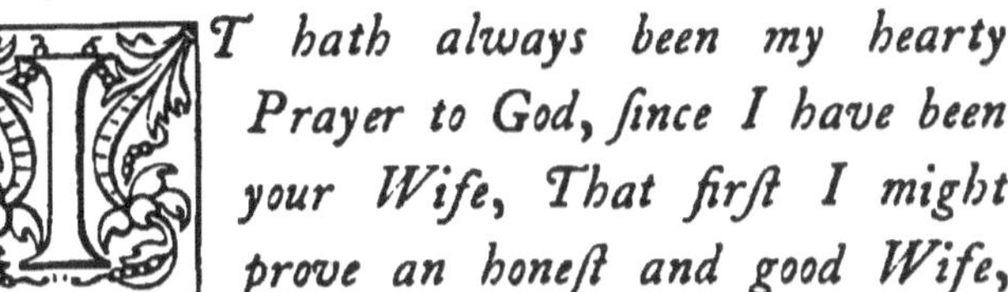*T hath always been my hearty Prayer to God, ſince I have been your Wife, That firſt I might prove an honeſt and good Wife,* whereof your Grace muſt be the onely *Judg:* Next, That God would be pleaſed to enable me to ſet forth and declare to after-ages, the truth of your loyal actions and endeavours, for the ſervice of your King and Country; For the accompliſh-ing of which deſign, I have followed the beſt and trueſt Obſervations of your Secretary* John Rol-leſton, *and your Lordſhips own Relations, and have accordingly writ the Hiſtory of your Lord-ſhips Life, which although I have endeavoured to render as perſpicuous as ever I could, yet one

*thing I find hath much darkned it; which is,
that your Grace commanded me not to mention
any thing or paſſage to the prejudice or diſgrace
of any Family or particular perſon (although they
might be of great truth, and would illuſtrate
much the actions of your Life) which I have
dutifully performed to ſatisfie your Lordſhip,
whoſe Nature is ſo Generous, that you are as
well pleaſed to obſcure the faults of your Enemies,
as you are to divulge the vertues of your Friends;
And certainly, My·Lord, you have had as many
Enemies, and as many Friends, as ever any one
particular perſon had; and I pray God to forgive
the one, and proſper the other: Nor do I ſo much
wonder at it, ſince I, a Woman, cannot be ex-
empt from the malice and aſperſions of ſpightful
tongues, which they caſt upon my poor Writings,
ſome denying me to be the true Authoreſs of them;
for your Grace remembers well, that thoſe Books
I put out firſt, to the judgment of this cenſorious
Age, were accounted not to be written by a
Woman, but that ſome body elſe had writ and
publiſh'd them in my Name; by which your
Lordſhip was moved to prefix an Epiſtle before
one of them in my vindication, wherein you aſſure
the world upon your honour, That what was*

written and printed in my name, was my own ;
and I have also made known, that your Lordship
was my onely Tutor, in declaring to me what
you had found and observed by your own experience ; for I being young when your Lordship
married me, could not have much knowledg of the
world ; But it pleased God to command his Servant Nature to indue me with a Poetical and
Philosophical Genius, even from my Birth ; for
I did write some Books in that kind, before I
was twelve years of Age, which for want of
good method and order, I would never divulge.
But though the world would not believe that
those Conceptions and Fancies which I writ,
were my own, but transcended my capacity, yet
they found fault, that they were defective for
want of Learning ; and on the other side, they
said I had pluckt Feathers out of the Universi-
ties ; which was a very preposterous judgment.
Truly, My Lord, I confess that for want of
Scholarship, I could not express my self so well as
otherwise I might have done, in those Philosophical Writings I publish'd first ; but after I
was returned with your Lordship into my Native
Country, and led a retired Country life, I applied
my self to the reading of Philosophical Authors,

*of purpose to learn those names and words of Art that are used in Schools; which at first were so hard to me, that I could not understand them, but was fain to guess at the sense of them by the whole context, and so writ them down as I found them in those Authors, at which my Readers did wonder, and thought it impossible that a Woman could have so much Learning and Understanding in Terms of Art, and Scholastical Expressions; so that I and my Books are like the old Apologue mention'd in Æsop, of a Father, and his Son, who rid on an Ass through a Town when his Father went on Foot, at which sight the People shouted and cried shame, that a young Boy should ride, and let his Father, an old man, go on Foot: whereupon the old Man got upon the Ass, and let his Son go by; but when they came to the next Town, the People exclaimed against the Father, that he a lusty man should ride, and have no more pity of his young and tender child, but let him go on foot: Then both the Father and his Son got upon the Ass, and coming to the third Town, the People blamed them both for being so unconscionable as to over-burden the poor Ass with their heavy weight: After this both Father and Son went on foot, and led the Ass; and when they came to the fourth Town, the People railed as much at them as ever the former had done, and called them both Fools, for going on foot, when they had a Beaſt able to carry them. The old Man, ſeeing he could not pleaſe Mankind in any manner, and having received ſo many ble-miſhes and aſperſions, for the ſake of his Aſs, was at laſt reſolved to drown him when he came to the next bridg. But I am not ſo paſſionate to burn my Writings for the various humours of Mankind, and for their finding fault, ſince there is nothing in this world, be it the nobleſt and moſt commendable action whatſoever, that ſhall eſcape blameleſs. As for my being the true and onely Authoreſs of them, your Lordſhip knows beſt, and my attending Servants are witneſs that I have had none but my own Thoughts, Fancies and Speculations to aſſiſt me; and as ſoon as I have ſet them down, I ſend them to thoſe that are to tranſcribe them, and fit them for the Preſs; whereof ſince there have been ſeveral, and amongſt them ſuch as onely could write a good hand, but neither underſtood Orthography, nor had any Learning (I being then in baniſhment with your Lordſhip, and not able to maintain learned Secre-taries) which hath been a great diſadvantage to my poor works, and the caufe that they have been printed fo falfe, and fo full of Errors; for befides that, I want alfo the fkill of Scholarfhip and true writing, I did many times not perufe the Copies that were tranfcribed, left they fhould difturb my following Conceptions; by which neglect, as I faid, many Errors are flipt into my Works, which yet I hope Learned and Impartial Readers will foon rectifie, and look more upon the fenfe, then carp at words. I have been a Student even from my Childhood; and fince I have been your Lordfhips Wife, I have lived for the moft part a ftrict and retired Life, as is beft known to your Lordfhip, and therefore my Cenfurers cannot know much of me, fince they have little or no acquaintance with me: 'Tis true, I have been a Traveller both before and after I was married to your Lordfhip, and fometimes fhew my felf at your Lordfhips Command in Publick places or Affemblies; but yet I converfe with few. Indeed, My Lord, I matter not the Cenfures of this Age, but am rather proud of them; for it fhews that my Actions are more then ordinary, and according to the old Proverb,* It is better to be Envied, then Pitied: *for I know well, that it is meerly out of fpight and malice, whereof this present Age is so full, that none can escape them, and they'l make no doubt to stain even Your Lordships Loyal, Noble and Heroick Actions, as well as they do mine, though yours have been of War and Fighting, mine of Contemplating and Writing: Yours were performed publickly in the Field, mine privately in my Closet: Yours had many thousand Eye-witnesses, mine none but my Waiting-maids. But the Great God that hath hitherto bless'd both Your Grace and me, will, I question not, preserve both our Fames to after Ages, for which we shall be bound most humbly to acknowledg his great Mercy; and I my self, as long as I live, be*

Your Graces Honest Wife,

and Humble Servant

*M. NEWCASTLE.*

# The Preface.

WHEN I firſt Intended to write this Hiſtory, knowing my ſelf to be no Scholar, and as ignorant of the Rules of writing Hiſtories, as I have in my other Works acknowledg'd my ſelf to be of the Names and Terms of Art; I deſired my Lord, That he would be pleaſed to let me have ſome Elegant and Learned Hiſtorian to aſſiſt me; which requeſt his Grace would not grant me ; ſaying, That having never had any Aſſiſtance in the writing of my former Books, I ſhould have no other in the writing of his Life, but the Informations from himſelf, and his Secretary, of the chief Tranſactions and Fortunes occurring in it, to the time he married me.  I humbly anſwer'd, That without a learned Aſſiſtant,

the Hiſtory would be defective: But he replied, That Truth could not be defective.   I
ſaid again, That Rhetorick did adorn Truth:
And he anſwer'd, That Rhetorick was fitter
for Falſhoods then Truths.  Thus I was
forced by his Graces Commands, to write
this Hiſtory in my own plain Style, without
elegant Flouriſhings, or exquiſit Method, re-
lying intirely upon Truth, in the expreſſing
whereof, I have been very circumſpect; as
knowing well, that his Graces Actions have
ſo much Glory of their own, that they need
borrow none from any bodies Induſtry.

Many Learned Men, I know, have publiſhed Rules and Directions concerning the
Method and Style of Hiſtories, and do with
great noiſe, to little purpoſe, make loud exclamations againſt thoſe Hiſtorians, that keeping cloſe to the Truth of their Narrations,
cannot think it neceſſary to follow ſlaviſhly
ſuch Inſtructions; and there is ſome Men of
good Underſtandings, as I have heard, that
applaud very much ſeveral Hiſtories, meerly
for their Elegant Style, and well-obſerv'd
Method; ſetting a high value upon feigned
Orations, myſtical Deſigns, and  fancied

Policies, which are, at the beſt, but pleaſant Romances. Others approve, in the Relations of Wars, and of Military Actions, ſuch tedious Deſcriptions, that the Reader, tired with them, will imagine that there was more time ſpent in Aſſaulting, Defending, and taking of a Fort, or a petty Gariſon, then *Alexander* did employ in conquering the greateſt part of the World : which proves, That ſuch Hiſtorians regard more their own Eloquence, Wit and Induſtry, and the knowledg they believe to have of the Actions of War, and of all manner of Governments, than of the truth of the Hiſtory, which is the main thing, and wherein conſiſts the hardeſt taſk, very few Hiſtorians knowing the Tranſactions they write of, and much leſs the Counſels, and ſecret Deſigns of many different Parties, which they confidently mention.

Although there be many ſorts of Hiſtories, yet theſe three are the chiefeſt : 1. a General Hiſtory. 2. A National Hiſtory. 3. A Particular Hiſtory. Which three ſorts may, not unfitly, be compared to the three ſorts of Governments, Democracy, Ariſtocracy, and Monarchy. The firſt is the Hiſtory of the

known parts and people of the World; The
fecond is the Hiftory of a particular Nation,
Kingdom or Commonwealth. The third is
the Hiftory of the life and actions of fome
particular Perfon. The firft is profitable for
Travellers, Navigators and Merchants; the
fecond is pernicious, by reafon it teaches fubtil
Policies, begets Factions, not onely between
particular Families and Perfons, but alfo between whole Nations, and great Princes,
rubbing old fores, and renewing old Quarrels,
that would otherwife have been forgotten.
The laft is the moft fecure; becaufe it goes
not out of its own Circle, but turns on its
own Axis, and for the moft part, keeps within
the Circumference of Truth. The firft is
Mechanical, the fecond Political, and the
third Heroical. The firft fhould onely be
written by Travellers, and Navigators; The
fecond by Statefmen; The third by the Prime
Actors, or the Spectators of thofe Affairs and
Actions of which they write, as *Cæfars* Com-
mentaries are, which no Pen but of fuch an
Author, who was alfo Actor in the particular
Occurrences, private Intrigues, fecret Counfels, clofe Defigns, and rare Exploits of War

he relates, could ever have brought to so high Perfection.

This Hiſtory is of the Third ſort, as that is ; and being of the Life and Actions of my Noble Lord and Huſband, who hath informed me of all the particular paſſages I have recorded, I cannot, though neither Actor, nor Spectator, be thought ignorant of the Truth of what I write ; Nor is it inconſiſtent with my being a Woman, to write of Wars, that was neither between *Medes* and *Perſians,* *Greeks* and *Trojans,* *Chriſtians* and *Turks;* but among my own Countreymen, whoſe Cuſtoms and Inclinations, and moſt of the Perſons that held any conſiderable Place in the Armies, was well known to me ; and beſides all that (which is above all) my Noble and Loyal Lord did act a chief Part in that fatal Tragedy, to have defended (if humane power could have done it) his moſt Gracious Soveraign, from the fury of his Rebellious Subjects.

This Hiſtory being (as I have ſaid) of a particular Perſon, his Actions, and Fortunes ; it cannot be expected, that I ſhould here Preach of the beginning of the World ; nor ſeem to expreſs underſtanding in the Politicks, by tedious moral Difcourfes, with long Obferva-tions upon the feveral forts of Government that have been in *Greece* & *Rome*, and upon others more modern ; I will neither endeavour to make fhow of Eloquence, making Speeches that never was fpoken, nor pretend to great fkill in War, by making Mountains of Mole-hills, and telling Romanfical Falfhoods for Hiftorical Truths ; and much lefs will I write to amufe my Readers, in a myftical and alle-gorical Style, of the difloyal Actions of the oppofite Party, of the Treacherous Cowardife, Envy and Malice of fome Perfons, my Lords Enemies, and of the ingratitude of fome of his feeming Friends ; wherein I cannot better obey his Lordfhips Commands to conceal thofe things, then in leaving them quite out, as I do, with fubmiffion to his Lordfhips de-fire, from whom I have learn'd Patience to overcome my Paffions, and Difcretion to yield to his Prudence.

Thus am I refolved to write, in a natural plain ftyle, without Latin Sentences, moral Inftructions, politick Defigns, feigned Ora-tions, or envious and malicious Exclamations, this fhort Hiftory of the Loyal, Heroick and

Prudent Actions of my Noble Lord, as alfo of his Sufferings, Loffes, and ill-Fortunes, which in honour and Confcience I could not fuffer to be buried in filence; nor could I have undertaken fo hard a tafk, had not my love to his Perfon, and to Truth, been my Encourager and Supporter.

I might have made this Book larger, in tranfcribing (as is ordinary in Hiftories) the feveral Letters, full of Affection, and kind promifes he received from His Gracious Soveraign, *Charles* the Firft, and from his Royal Confort, in the time he was in the Actions of War, as alfo fince the War, from his dear Soveraign and Mafter, *Charles* the Second; But many of the former Letters having been loft, when all was loft; I thought it beft, feeing I had not them all, to print none. As for Orations, which is another way of fwelling the bulk of Hiftories; it is certain, that My Lord made not many; chufing rather to fight, then to talk; and his Declarations having been printed already, it had been fuperfluous to infert them in thefe Narrations.

This Book would however, have been a great Volume, if his Grace would have given

me leave to publiſh his Enemies Actions ;
But being to write of his own onely, I do it
briefly and truly; and not as many have done,
who have written of the late Civil War, with
but few ſprinklings of Truth, like as Heat-
drops upon a dry barren Ground; knowing
no more of the Tranſactions of thoſe Times,
then what they learned in the Gazets, which,
for the moſt part, (out of Policy to amuſe and
deceive the People) contain nothing but Falſhoods and Chimeraes; and were ſuch Para-
ſites, that after the Kings Party was overpowred, the Government among the Rebels
changing from one Faction to another, they
never miſs'd to exalt highly the Merits of the
chief Commanders of the then prevailing ſide,
comparing ſome of them to *Moſes*, and ſome
others to all the great and moſt famous Heroes,
both Greeks and Romans; wherein, unawares,
they exceedingly commended my Noble Lord;
for if thoſe Ring-leaders of Factions were ſo
great men as they are reported to be, by thoſe
Time-ſervers, How much greater muſt his
Lordſhip be, who beat moſt of them, except
the Earl of *Eſſex*, whoſe employment was
never in the Northern parts, where all the

reft of the greateft ftrength of the Parliament was fent, to oppofe my Lord's Forces, which was the greateft the Kings Party had any where.

Good Fortune is fuch an Idol of the World, and is fo like the golden Calf worfhipped by the Ifraelites, that thofe Arch-Rebels never wanted Aftrologers to foretel them good fuccefs in all their Enterprifes, nor Poets to fing their Praifes, nor Orators for Panegyricks; nay, which is worfe, nor Hiftorians neither, to record their Valour in fighting, and Wifdom in Governing. But being, fo much as I am, above bafe Profit, or any Preferment whatfoever, I cannot fear to be fufpe&ted of Flattery, in declaring to the World the Merits, Wealth, Power, Loyalty, and Fortunes of My Noble Lord, who hath done great A&tions, fuffered great Loffes, endured a long Banifhment, for his Loyalty to his King and Countrey; and leads now, like another *Scipio*, a quiet Countrey-life. If notwithftanding all this, any fhould fay, That thofe who write Hiftories of themfelves, and their own a&tions, or of their own Party, or inftru&t and inform thofe that write them, are partial to themfelves; I anfwer, That it is very improbable, Worthy Perfons, who having done Great, Noble and Heroick Exploits, deferving to be recorded, fhould be fo vain, as to write falfe Hiftories; but if they do, it proves but their Folly; for Truth can never be concealed, and fo it will be more for their difgrace, then for their Honour or Fame. I fear not any fuch blemifhes in this prefent Hiftory, for I am not confcious of any fuch Crime as Partiality or Falfhood, but write it whileft My Noble Lord is yet alive, and at fuch a time where Truth may be declared, and Falfhood contradicted; and I challenge any one (although I be a Woman) to contradict any thing that I have fet down, or prove it to be otherwife then Truth; for be there never fo many Contradictions, Truth will conquer all at laft.

Concerning My Lords Actions in War, which are comprehended in the firft Book, the relation of them I have chiefly from my Lords Secretary Mr. *Rollefton*, a Perfon that has been an Eye-witnefs thereof, and accompanied My Lord as Secretary in his Army, and gave out all his Commiffions; his honefty and worth is unqueftionable by all that know him. And as for the Second Book, which contains My Lords Actions and Sufferings, during the time of his Exile, I have fet down fo much as I could poffibly call to mind, without any particular Expreffion of time, onely from the time of his Banifhment, or rather (what I can remember) from the time of my Marriage, till our return into *England*. To the end of which I have joined a Computation of My Lord's Loffes, which he hath fuffered by thofe unfortunate Warres. In the third Book I have fet down fome particular Chapters concerning the Defcription of his Perfon, his Natural Faculties, and Perfonal Vertues, *&c.* And in the laft, fome Effayes and Difcourfes of My Lords, together with fome Notes and Remarques of mine own; which I thought moft convenient to place by themfelves at the end of this Work, rather then to intermingle them with the Body of the Hiftory.

It might be fome prejudice to my Lord's Glory, and the credit of this Hiftory, not to take notice of a very confiderable thing I have heard, which is, That when his Lordfhip's Army had got fo much Strength and Reputation, that the Rebellious Parliament finding themfelves overpower'd with it, rather then to be utterly ruin'd, (as was unavoidable) did call the *Scots* to their Affiftance, with a promife to reward fo great a Service, with the Four Northern Counties of *Northumberland*, *Cumberland*, *Weftmerland*, and the Bifhoprick of *Durham*, which I have not mention'd in the Book.

And it is moft certain, That the Parliaments Forces were never Powerful, nor their Commanders or Officers Famous, until fuch time as my Lord was overpower'd; neither could Loyalty have been overpower'd by Rebellion, had not Treachery had better Fortune then Prudence.

When I fpeak of my Lord's Pedigree, where *Thomas* Earl of *Arundel*, Grandfather to the now Duke of *Norfolk*, is mention'd, they have left out *William* Vifcount *Stafford*, one of his Sons, who did marry the Heir of the laft Baron *Stafford*, defcended from the Dukes of *Buckingham*; which was fet down in my Original Manufcript.

Some of thofe Omiffions, and very probably others, are happened, partly for want of timely Information, and chiefly by the death of my Secretary, who did copy my Writings for the Prefs, and dy'd in *London*, attending that Service, afore the Printing of the Book was quite finifh'd. And as I hope of your Favour to be excus'd for omitting thofe things in the Book; fo I expect of your Juftice to be approv'd in putting them here, though fomewhat unfeafonably.

Before I end this Preface, I do befeech my Readers not to miftake me when I fpeak of my Lord's Banifhment, as if I would conceal that he went voluntarily out of his Native Country; for it is moft true, that his Lordfhip prudently perceiving all the King's Party loft, not onely in *England*, but alfo in *Scotland* and *Ireland*; and that it was impoffible to withftand the Rebels, after the fatal overthrow of his Army; his Lordfhip, in a poor and mean condition quitted his own Countrey, and went beyond Sea; foon after which, the Rebels. having got an Abfolute Power, and granted a general Pardon to all thofe that would come in to them, upon compofition, at the Rates they had fet down, his Lordfhip, with but few others, was excepted from it, both for Life and Eſtate, and did remain thus baniſh'd till His Majeſties happy Reſtauration.

I muſt alſo acknowledg, That I have committed great Errors in taking no notice of Times as I ſhould have done in many places of this Hiſtory: I mention in one place the Queen Mothers being in *France*, when my Lord went thither, but do not ſay in what year that was: Nor do I expreſs when His Majeſty (our now Gracious Soveraign) came in, and went out again ſeveral times from that Kingdom, which has happen'd for want of Memory, and I deſire my Readers to excuſe me for it.

No body can certainly be more ready to find faults in this Work, then I am to confeſs them; being very conſcious that I have, as I told my Lord I ſhould, committed many for want of Learning, and chiefly of ſkill in writing Hiſtories: But having, according to his Lordſhips Commands, written his Actions and Fortunes truly and plainly, I have reaſon to expect, that whatſoever elſe ſhall be found amiſs, will be favourably pardoned by the candid Readers, to whom I wiſh all manner of happineſs.

# An Epiſtle to Her Grace the Duchefs of Newcaſtle.

May it pleaſe your Grace,

 *HAVE been taught, and do believe, That Obedience is better then Sacrifice; and know, that both are due from me to your Grace; and ſince I have been ſo long in obeying your Commands, I ſhall not preſume to uſe any Arguments for my excuſe, but rather chuſe ingeniouſly to confeſs my fault, and beg your Graces Pardon. And becauſe forgiveneſs is a Glory to the ſupreameſt Powers, I will hope that your Grace by that great example will make it yours. And now I humbly take leave to repreſent to your Grace, as faithfully and truly as my memory will ſerve me, all my Obſervations of the moſt memorable Actions, and honourable Deportments of*

*His Grace, my moſt Noble Lord and Maſter,*
William *Duke of* Newcaſtle, *in the Execution
and Performance of the Truſts and high Employments committed and commended to his care
and charge by three Kings of* England; *that is
to ſay, King* James, *King* Charles *the Firſt, of
ever bleſſed Memory; and our Gracious King,*
Charles *the Second; under whom he hath had
the happineſs to live, and the honour to ſerve
them in ſeveral capacities: And becauſe I humbly
conceive, that it is not within the intention of
your Graces Commands, that I ſhould give you a
particular Relation .of His Graces High Birth,
his Noble and Princely Education and Breeding,
both at home and abroad; his Natural Faculties, and Perſonal Vertues; his Juſtice, Bounty,
Charity, Friendſhip; his Right Approved Courage, and True Valour, not grounded upon, or
govern'd by Paſſion, but Reaſon; his Magnificent manner of living and ſupporting his Dignity,
teſtified by his great Entertainments of their Majeſties, and his private Friends, upon all fit occaſions, beſides his ordinary and conſtant Houſekeeping and Attendants; ſome for Honour, and
ſome for buſineſs, wherein he exceeded moſt of his
Quality; and that he was, and is an incom-*

*parable Mafter to his Servants, is fufficiently teftified by all or moft of the chiefeft of them, living and dying in His Graces Service, which is an Argument that they thought themfelves as happy therein, as the World could make them; nor of his well-chofen Pleafures, which were principally Horfes of all forts, but more particularly Horfes of Mannage;* [1] *His Study and Art of the true ufe of the Sword; His Magnificent Buildings. Thefe are his chiefeft Delights, wherein his Grace fpared for no coft nor charge, which are fufficiently manifefted to the World; for other Delights, as thofe of running Horfes, Hawking, Hunting, &c. His Grace ufed them meerly for focieties fake, and out of a generous and obliging Nature to pleafe others, though his know ledg in them excelled, as well as in the other. And yet notwithftanding thefe his large and vaft*

---

[1] *Mannage*, from the Fr. *menager*, to carry on, to conduct; hence a careful houfewife is called " a good manager," and a carelefs one " a bad manager." Manage, as applied to horfes, fignifies the graceful government of a horfe. Shakefpeare has—

" Speak terms of *manage* to the bounding fteed," and Young has—

" They vault from hunters to the *managed* fteed."

*expences, before his Grace was called to the Court, he encreafed his Revenue by way of Purchafe to a great value; and when he was called to the Court, he was then free from Debts, and, as I have heard, fome Thoufands of Pounds in his Purfe. Thefe Particulars, and as many more of this kind as would fwell a Volume, I could enumerate to your Grace; but that they are fo well known to your Grace, it would be a Prefumption in me, rather then a Service, to give your Grace that trouble; and therefore I humbly forbear, and proceed, according to my Intention, to give your Grace a faithful account of Your Graces Commands, as becomes*

May it pleafe your Grace,

     Your Graces moft humble,

         and moft obedient Servant,

            *John Rollefton.*

The

# Life of the Moſt Illuſtrious
Prince, William Duke of
Newcaſtle.

•

*THE FIRST BOOK.*

SINCE my chief intent in this preſent Work, is to deſcribe the Life and Actions of My Noble Lord and Huſband, *William, Duke of Newcaſtle*, I ſhall do it with as much Brevity, Perſpicuity and Truth, as is required of an Impartial Hiſtorian. The Hiſtory of his Pedigree I ſhall refer to the Heralds, and partly give you an account thereof at the latter end of this work; onely thus much I ſhall now mention, as will be requiſite for the better underſtanding of the following diſcourſe.

His Grandfather by his Fathers ſide was

B

Sir *William Cavendiſh*, Privy Counſellour and Treaſurer of the Chamber to King *Henry* the Eighth, *Edward* the Sixth, and Queen *Mary*. His Grandfather by his Mother was *Cuthbert* Lord *Ogle*, an ancient Baron. His Father Sir *Charles Cavendiſh* was the youngeſt ſon to Sir *William*, and had no other Children but three Sons, whereof My Lord was the Second; but his elder Brother dying in his Infancy, left both his Title and Birth-right to My Lord, ſo that My Lord had then but one onely Brother left, whoſe name was *Charles* after his Father, whereas My Lord had the name of his Grandfather.

Theſe two Brothers were partly bred with *Gilbert* Earl of *Shrewſbury* their Uncle in Law, and their Aunt *Mary*, Counteſs of *Shrewſbury*, *Gilbert's* Wife, and Siſter to their Father; for there interceded an intire and conſtant Friendſhip between the ſaid *Gilbert*, Earl of *Shrewſbury*, and My Lord's Father, Sir *Charles Cavendiſh*, cauſed not onely by the marriage of My Lord's Aunt, his Fathers Siſter, to the aforeſaid *Gilbert*, Earl of *Shrewſ-bury*, and by the marriage of *George*, Earl of *Shrewſbury*, *Gilbert's* Father, with My Lord's

Grandmother, by his Fathers fide; but Sir *Charles Cavendifh*, My Lord's Father, and *Gilbert*, Earl of *Shrewfbury*, being brought up and bred together in one Family, and grown up as parts of one body, after they came to be beyond Children, and travelled together into foreign Countries, to obferve the Fafhions, Laws, and Cuftoms of other Nations, con-tracted fuch an intire Friendfhip which lafted to their death: neither did they out-live each other long, for My Lord's Father, Sir *Charles Cavendifh*, lived but one year after *Gilbert* Earl of *Shrewfbury*.

But both My Lords Parents, and his Aunt and Uncle in Law, fhewed always a great and fond love to My Lord, endeavouring, when He was but a Child, to pleafe him with what he moft delighted in. When He was grown to the Age of fifteen or fixteen, he was made Knight of the *Bath*, an ancient and honour-able Order, at the time when *Henry*, King *James*, of blefled Memory, His eldeft Son was created Prince of *Wales:* and foon after he went to travel with Sir *Henry Wotton*,[1]

---

[1] Sir Henry Wotton. See the Biographical Dic-tionaries for accounts of this diftinguifhed perfon, and alfo his " Life " by Walton.

who was fent as Ambaſſador Extraordinary to the then *Duke* of *Savoy;* which Duke made very much of My Lord, and when he would be free in Feaſting, placed Him next to him-felf. Before My Lord did return with the Ambaſſador into *England,* the faid Duke pro-fer'd My Lord, that if he would ſtay with him, he would not onely confer upon him the beſt Titles of Honour he could, but alfo give him an honourable Command in War, although My Lord was but young, for the Duke had then fome defigns of War. But the Ambaf-fador, who had taken the care of My Lord, would not leave Him behind without his Parents confent.

At laſt, when My Lord took his leave of the Duke, the Duke being a very generous perfon, prefented Him with a *Spaniſh* Horfe, a Saddle very richly embroidered, and with a rich Jewel of Diamonds.

Some time after My Lord's return into *England,* *Gilbert* Earl of *Shrewſbury* died, and left My Lord, though he was then but young, and about Twenty two years of age, his Executor ; a year after, his Father Sir *Charles Cavendiſh,* died alfo. His Mother, being then a Widow, was defirous that My Lord fhould marry: in obedience to whofe Commands, he chofe a Wife both to his own good liking, and his Mothers approving; who was Daughter and Heir to *William Baffet* of *Blore* Efq.; a very honourable and ancient Family in *Stafford-fhire*, by whom was added a great part to His Eftate, as hereafter fhall be mentioned. After My Lord was married, he lived, for the moft part, in the Country, and pleafed Himfelf and his neighbours with Hofpitality, and fuch delights as the Country afforded; onely now and then he would go up to *London* for fome fhort time to wait on the King.

About this time King *James*, of bleffed memory, having a purpofe to confer fome Honour upon My Lord, made him Vifcount *Mansfield*, and Baron of *Bolfover;* and after the deceafe of King *James*, King *Charles* the Firft, of bleffed Memory, conftituted him Lord Warden of the Forreft of *Sherewood*, and Lieutenant of *Nottingham-fhire*, and reftored his Mother *Catharine*, the fecond Daughter of *Cuthbert* Lord *Ogle*, to her Fathers Dignity, after the death of her onely Sifter *Jane* Countefs of *Shrewfbury*, publickly declaring, that it was her Right; which Title after the death of his Mother, defcended alfo upon My Lord, and his Heirs General, together with a large Inheritance of 3,000 l. a year, in *Northumberland.*

About the fame time, after the deceafe of *William,* late Earl of *Devonfhire,* his Noble Coufin German, My Lord was by his faid Majefty made Lord Lieutenant of *Derbyfhire;* which truft and honour, after he had enjoyed for feveral years, and managed it, like as all other offices put to his Truft, with all poffible care, faithfulnefs and dexterity, during the time of the faid Earls Son, *William,* the now Earl of *Devonfhire,* his Minority, as foon as this fame Earl was come to age, and by Law made capable of that truft, he willingly and freely refign'd it into his hands, he having hitherto kept it onely for him, that he and no body elfe might fucceed his Father in that dignity.

In thefe, and all other both publick and private imployments, My Lord hath ever been careful to keep up the Kings Rights to the uttermoft of his power, to ftrengthen thofe mentioned Counties with Ammunition, and to adminifter Juftice to every one; for he refufed no man's Petition, but fent all that came to him, either for relief or juftice, away from him fully fatisfied.

Not long after his being made Lieutenant of *Nottingham-fhire*, there was found fo great a defect of Armes and Ammunition in that County, that the Lords of the Council being advertifed thereof, as the manner then was, His Majefty commanded a levy to be made upon the whole County for the fupply thereof; whereupon the fum of 500 l. or thereabout, was accordingly levied for that purpofe, and three Perfons o<sup>f</sup> Quality, then Deputy Lieutenants, were defired by My Lord to receive the money, and fee it difpofed; which being done accordingly, and a certain account rendred to My Lord, he voluntarily ordered the then Clerk of the Peace of that County, That the fame account fhould be recorded amongft the Seffions Roles, and be publifhed in open Seffions, to the end that the Country might take notice how their monies were difpofed of, for which act of Juftice My Lord was highly commended.

Within fome few years after, King *Charles*

the Firſt, of bleſſed Memory, His Gracious
Soveraign, in regard of His true and faithful
ſervice to his King and Country, was pleaſed
to honour him with the Title of *Earl of Newcaſtle*, and *Baron of Bothal* and *Heple;* which
Title he graced ſo much by His Noble Actions and Deportments, that ſome ſeven years
after, which was in the Year 1638, His Majeſty called him up to Court, and thought Him
the fitteſt Perſon whom He might intruſt with
the Government of His Son *Charles*, then
Prince of *Wales*, now our moſt Gracious
King, and made him withal a Member of
the Lords of His Majeſties moſt honourable
Privy Council; which, as it was a great
Honour and Truſt, ſo He ſpared no care and
induſtry to diſcharge His Duty accordingly;
and to that end, left all the care of governing
his own Family and Eſtate, with all Fidelity
attending His Maſter not without conſiderable
Charges, and vaſt Expences of his own.

In this preſent Employment He continued
for the ſpace of three Years, during which
time there happened an Inſurrection and Rebellion of His Majeſties diſcontented Subjects
in *Scotland*, which forced His Majeſty to raiſe

an Army, to reduce them to their Obedience,
and His Treafury being at that time exhaufted
he was neceffitated to defire fome fupply and
affiftance of the Nobleft and Richeft of his
Loyal Subjects; amongft the reft, My Lord
lent His Majefty 10000 l. and raifed Himfelf
a Voluntier-Troop of Horfe, which confifted
of 120 Knights and Gentlemen of Quality,
who marched to *Berwick* by His Majefties
Command, where it pleafed His Majefty to
fet this mark of Honour upon that Troop,
that it fhould be Independent, and not commanded by any General Officer, but onely by
his Majefty Himfelf;[1] The reafon thereof
was upon this following occafion.

His Majefties whole body of Horfe, being
commanded to march into *Scotland* againft
the Rebels, a place was appointed for their
Rendezvous; Immediately upon their meet-
ing, My Lord fent a Gentleman of Quality of

---

[1] We have feveral King's or Queen's "Own Regiments." Query, if this troop was not the origin of that
title? Loyal men, if rich enough, frequently raifed
troops or regiments of foldiers and prefented them to
the fovereign.

his Troop[1] to His Majesties then General of the Horse, to know where his Troop should march; who returned this answer, That it was to march next after the Troops of the General Officers of the Field. My Lord conceiving that his Troop ought to march in the Van, and not in the Rear, sent the same Messenger back again to the General, to inform him, That he had the honour to march with the Princes Colours, and therefore he thought it not fit to march under any of the Officers of the Field; yet nevertheless the General ordered that Troop as he had formerly directed. Whereupon, My Lord thinking it unfit at that time to dispute the business, immediately commanded his Cornet[2] to take off the Princes Colours from his staff, and so marched in the place appointed, choosing rather to march without his Colours flying, then to lessen his Masters dignity by the command of any subject.

Immediately after the return from that expedition to his Majesties Leaguer, the General

---

[1] Sir *William Carnaby*, Kt.

[2] Mr. *Gray*, Brother to the Lord *Gray* of the North.

made a complaint thereof to his Majefty; who being truly informed of the bufinefs, commended my Lords difcretion for it, and from that time ordered that Troop to be commanded by none but himfelf. Thus they remain'd upon duty, *without receiving any payment or allowance from His Majefty,*[1] until His Majefty had reduced his Rebellious Subjects, and then My Lord returned with honour to his Charge, *viz.* The Government of the Prince.

At laft when the whole Army was difbanded, then, and not before, my Lord thought it a fit Time to exact an account from the faid General for the affront he pafs'd upon him, and fent him a Challenge; the place and hour being appointed by both their Confents, where and when to meet, My Lord appear'd there with his Second,[2] but found not his Oppofite: After fome while his Oppofite's Second came all alone, by whom my Lord perceiv'd that their Defign had been difcover'd to the King by

---

[1] In both the copies now before me the words in italic have been carefully obliterated with ink. Why?

[2] Francis Palmes.

fome of his Oppofite's Friends, who prefently caufed them both to be confined until he had made their Peace.

My Lord having hitherto attended the Prince, his Mafter, with all faithfulnefs and duty befitting fo great an Employment, for the fpace of three years, in the beginning of that Rebellious and unhappy Parliament, which was the caufe of all the ruines and misfortunes that afterwards befell this Kingdom, was privately advertifed, that the Parliaments Defign was to take the Government of the Prince from Him, which he apprehending as a difgrace to Himfelf, wifely prevented, and obtained the Confent of His late Majefty, with His Favour, to deliver up the Charge of being Governor to the Prince, and retire into the Countrey; which he did in the beginning of the Year 1641, and fetled himfelf, with his Lady, Children and Family, to his great fatisfaction, with an intent to have continued there, and refted under his own Vine, and managed his own Eftate; but he had not enjoyed himfelf long, but an Exprefs came to him from His Majefty, who was then unjuftly and unmannerly treated by the faid Parliament,

to repair with all poffible fpeed and privacy to
*Kingfton* upon *Hull*, where the greateft part of
His Majefties Ammunition and Arms then
remained in that Magazine, it being the moft
confiderable place for ftrength in the Northern
parts of the Kingdom.

Immediately upon the receipt of thefe His
Majefties Orders and Commands, my Lord
prepared for their execution, and about
Twelve of the Clock at night, haftned from
his own houfe when his Familie were all at
their reft, fave two or three Servants which
he appointed to attend him. The next day
early in the morning he arrived at *Hull*, in
the quality of a private Gentleman, which
place was diftant from his houfe forty miles ;
and none of his Family that were at home,
knew what was become of him, till he fent
an Exprefs to his Lady to inform her where
he was.

Thus being admitted into the Town, he fell
upon his intended Defign, and brought it to
fo hopeful an iffue for His Majefties Service,
that he wanted nothing but His Majefties
further Commiffion and Pleafure to have
fecured both the Town and Magazine for

His Majesties ufe : and to that end by a fpeedy Exprefs[1] gave His Majefty, who was then at *Windfor*, an account of all his Tranfactions therein, together with his Opinion of them, hoping His Majefty would have been pleafed either to come thither in Perfon, which He might have done with much fecurity, or at leaft have fent him a Commiffion and Orders how he fhould do His Majefty further Service.

But inftead thereof he received Orders from His Majefty to obferve fuch Directions as he fhould receive from the Parliament then fitting : Whereupon he was fummoned perfonally to appear at the Houfe of Lords, and a Committee chofen to examine the Grounds and Reafons of his undertaking that Defign ; but my Lord fhewed them his Commiffion, and that it was done in obedience to His Majefties Commands, and fo was cleared of that Action.

Not long after, my Lord obtained the freedom from His Majefty to retire again to his Countrey Life, which he did with much

---

[1] Capt. Mazine.

alacrity: He had not remained many months there, but His Majesty was forced by the fury of the said Parliament, to repair in Person to *York*, and to send the Queen beyond the Seas for her safety.

No sooner was His Majesty arrived at *York* but he sent his Commands to my Lord to come thither to him; which, according to his wonted custom and loyalty, he readily obeyed, and after a few days spent there in Consultation, His Majesty was pleased to Command him to *Newcastle* upon *Tyne*, to take upon him the Government of that Town, and the four Counties next adjoining; that is to say, *Northumberland, Cumberland, Westmerland*, and the Bishoprick of *Durham*; which my Lord did accordingly, although he wanted Men, Money and Ammunition, for the performance of that design; for when he came thither he neither found any Military provision considerable for the undertaking that work, nor generally any great encouragement from the people in those parts, more then what his own interest created in them: Neverthelefs, he thought it his duty rather to hazard all, then to neglect the Commands of His Soveraign; and refolved to fhew his Fidelity, by nobly fetting all at ftake, as he did, though he well knew how to have fecured himfelf, as too many others did, either by Neutrality or adhering to the Rebellious Party; but his Honour and Loyalty was too great to be ftained with fuch foul adherencies.

As foon as my Lord came to *Newcaftle*, in the firft place he fent for all his Tenants and Friends in thofe parts, and prefently raifed a Troop of Horfe confifting of 120, and a Regiment of Foot, and put them under Command, and upon duty and exercife in the Town of *Newcaftle*; and with this fmall beginning took the Government of that place upon him; where with the affiftance of the Towns-men, particularly the Mayor,[1] (whom by the power of his Forces, he continued Mayor for the year following, he being a perfon of much truft and fidelity, as he approved himfelf) and the reft of his Brethren, within few days he fortified the Town, and raifed men daily, and put a Garrifon of Soldiers into *Tinmouth*-Caftle, ftanding upon the River *Tyne*, betwixt *New-*

---

[1] Sir *John Marlay*, Kt.

*caſtle* and the Sea, to ſecure that Port, and armed the Soldiers as well as he could: And thus he ſtood upon his Guard, and continued them upon Duty; playing his weak Game with much Prudence, and giving the Town and Country very great ſatisfaction by his noble and honourable Deportment.

In the mean time, there happend a great mutiny of the Trainband Souldiers of the Biſhoprick at *Durham*, ſo that my Lord was forced to remove thither in Perſon, attended with ſome forces to appeaſe them ; where at his arrival (I mention it by the way, and as a merry paſſage) a jovial Fellow uſed this ex-preſſion, That he liked my Lord very well, but not his Company (meaning his Soldiers.)

After my Lord had reduced them to their obedience and duty, he took great care of the Church Government in the ſaid Biſhoprick (as he did no leſs in all other places committed to his Care and Protection, well knowing that Schiſm and Faction in Religion is the Mother of all or moſt Rebellions, Wars and Diſtur-bances in a State or Government) and con-ſtituted that Learned and Eminent Divine the then Dean of *Peterborough*, now Lord-Biſhop of *Durham*,[1] to view all Sermons that were to be Preached, and suffer nothing in them that in the least reflected against His Majesties Person and Government, but to put forth and add whatsoever he thought convenient, and punish those that should trespass against it. In which that worthy Person used so much care and industry, that never the Church could be more happily govern'd then it was at that present.

Some short time after, my Lord received from Her Majesty the Queen, out of *Holland* a small supply of Money, *viz.* a little barrel of Ducatoons, which amounted to about 500 l. *Sterling;* which my Lord distributed amongst the Officers of his new raised Army, to encourage them the better in their service ; as also some Armes, the most part whereof were consigned to his late Majesty ; and those that were ordered to be conveyed to his Majesty, were sent accordingly, conducted by that onely Troop of Horse, which my Lord had newly raised, with orders to return again to him ; but it seems His Majesty liked the Troop so

---

[1] Dr. Coosens.

well, that he was pleafed to command their ftay to recruit his own Army.

About the fame time the King of *Denmark* was likewife pleafed to fend His Majefty a Ship, which arrived at *Newcaftle*, laden with fome Ammunition, Armes, Regiment Pieces, and *Danifh* Clubs;[1] which my Lord kept for the furnifhing of fome Forces which he intended to raife for His Majefties fervice; for he perceiving the flames increafe more and more in both the Houfes of Parliament then fitting at *Weftminfter*, againft his Majefties Perfon and Government; upon Confultation with his Friends and Allies, and the intereft he had in thofe Northern parts, took a refolution to raife an Army for His Majefties fervice, and by an exprefs acquainted His Majefty with his defign; who was fo well pleafed with it, that he fent him Commiffions for that purpofe, to conftitute him General of all the Forces raifed and to be raifed in all the parts of the Kingdom, *Trent-North*, and moreover in the feveral Counties of *Lincoln, Nottingham,*

---

[1] Danifh Clubs were war-maces originally ufed by the Danes inftead of fwords.

*Derby, Lancashire, Cheshire, Leicester, Rutland, Cambridg, Huntington, Norfolk, Suffolk,* and *Essex,* and Commander in Chief for the same; as also to impower and authorize him to confer the honour of Knighthood upon such Persons as he should conceive deserved it, and to coin Money and Print[1] whensoever he saw occasion for it. Which as it was not onely a great Honour, but a great Trust and Power; so he used it with much discretion and wisdom, onely in such occurrencies, where he found it tending to the advancement of His Majesties Service, and conferr'd the honour of Knight-hood sparingly, and but on such persons whose Valiant and Loyal Actions did justly deserve it, so that he Knighted in all to the number of Twelve.

Within a short time, my Lord formed an

---

[1] This is an early instance of making Knights by Deputy. I am not aware that the power still exists, except in the case of the Lord Lieutenant of Ireland. As to the coining of money, not of royal mintage, we have many instances during the Civil Wars; and the so-called "siege pieces," for the payment of soldiers, and other uses, are not uncommon. They are generally of silver, and very rudely executed.

Army of 8000 Foot, Horfe and Dragoons, and
put them into a condition to march in the
beginning of *November*, 1642. No fooner was
this effected, but the Infurrection grew high
in *York-fhire*, in fo much, that moft of His
Majefties good fubjects of that County, as
well the Nobility as Gentry, were forced for
the prefervation of their perfons, to retire to
the City of *York*, a walled Town, but of no
great ftrength ; and hearing that my Lord had
not onely kept thofe Counties in the Northen
parts generally faithful to his Majefty, but
raifed an Army for His Majefties Intereft, and
the protection of his good fubjects; thought it
convenient to employ and authorife fome perfons of Quality to attend upon my Lord, and
treat with him on their behalf, that he would
be pleafed to give them the affiftance of his
Army, which my Lord granted them upon
fuch Terms as did highly advance His Majefties Service, which was my Lords chief
and onely aim.

Thus my Lord being with his Army invited
into *York-fhire*, He prepared for it with all the
fpeed that the nature of that bufinefs could
poffibly permit ; and after he had fortified the

Town of *Newcaſtle*, *Tynmouthcaſtle*, *Hartle-pool* (a Haven Town) and ſome other neceſſary Gariſons in thoſe parts, and Mann'd, Victuall'd and order'd their conſtant ſupply, He thought it fit in the firſt place, before he did march, to manifeſt to the World by a Declaration in Print, the reaſons and grounds of his under-taking that deſign; which were in General, for the preſervation of His Majeſties Perſon and Government, and the defence of the Orthodox Church of *England*; where He alſo ſatisfied thoſe that murmur'd for my Lords receiving into his Army ſuch as were of the Catholick Religion, and then he preſently marched with his Army into *York-ſhire* to their aſſiſtance, and within the time agreed upon, came to *York*, notwithſtanding the Enemies Forces gave him all the interruption they poſſibly could, at ſeveral paſſes; whereof the chief was at *Pierce-bridg*, at the entering into *York-ſhire*, where 1500 of the Enemies Forces, Commanded in chief by Col. *Hotham*, were ready to interrupt my Lord's Forces, ſent thither to ſecure that paſſe, conſiſting of a Regiment of Dragoons, commanded by Colo-nel *Thomas Howard*, and a Regiment of Foot,

Commanded by Sir *William Lambton*, which they performed with fo much Courage, that they routed the Enemy, and put them to flight, although the faid Col. *Howard* in that Charge loft his life by an unfortunate fhot.

The Enemy thus miffing of their defign, fled until they met with a conjunction of their whole Forces at *Tadcafter*, fome eight miles diftant from *York*, and my Lord went on without any other confiderable Interruption. Being come to *York*, he drew up his whole Army before the Town, both Horfe and Foot, where the Commander in Chief, the then Earl of *Cumberland*, together with the Gentry of the Country, came to wait on my Lord, and the then Governor of *York*, Sir *Thomas Glemham*, prefented him with the Keys of the City.

Thus my Lord marched into the Town with great joy, and to the general fatisfaction both of the Nobility and Gentry, and moft of the Citizens; and immediately without any delay, in the later end of *December* 1642, fell upon Confultations how he might beft proceed to ferve his King and Country; and particularly, how his Army fhould be maintained and paid, (as he did alfo afterwards in every Country wherefoever he marched) well knowing, that no Army can be governed without being conftantly and regularly fupported by provifion and pay. Whereupon it was agreed, That the Nobility and Gentry of the feveral Counties, fhould felect a certain number of themfelves to raife money by a regular Tax, for the making provifions for the fupport and maintenance of the Army, rather than to leave them to free-quarter, and to carve for themfelves; and if any of the Soldiers were exorbitant and diforderly, and that it did appear fo to thofe that were authorifed to examine their deportment, that prefently order fhould be given to repair thofe injuries out of the moneys levied for the Soldiery; by which means the Country was preferved from many inconveniences, which otherwife would doubtlefs have followed.

And though the feafon of the year might well have invited my Lord to take up his Winter-quarters, it being about *Chriftmas;* yet after he had put a good Garifon into the City of *York,* and fortified it, upon intelligence that the Enemy was ftill at *Tadcafter,* and had fortified that place, he refolved to march thither. The greateft part of the Town ftands on the Weft fide of a River not fordable in any place near thereabout, nor allowing any paffage into the Town from *York*, but over a Stone-bridge, which the Enemy had made im-paffable by breaking down part of the Bridg, and planting their Ordnance upon it, and by raifing a very large and ftrong Fort upon the top of a Hill, leading Eaftward from that Bridg towards *York*, upon defign of commanding the Bridg and all other places fit to draw up an Army in, or to plant Cannon againft them.

But notwithftanding all thefe Difcourage-ments, my Lord after he had refrefh'd his Army at *York*, and recruited his provifions, ordered a march before the faid Town in this manner: That the greateft part of his Horfe and Dragoons fhould in the night march to a Pafs at *Weatherby*, five miles diftant from *Tadcafter*, towards North-weft, from thence under the Command of his then Lieutenant General of the Army, to appear on the Weft fide of *Tadcafter* early the next morning, by which time my Lord with the reft of his

Army refolved to appear at the Eaft-fide of the faid Town; which intention was well defign'd, but ill executed; for though my Lord with that part of the Army which he commanded in perfon, that is to fay, his Foot and Cannon, attended by fome Troops of Horfe, did march that night, and early in the morning appear'd before the Town on the Eaft fide thereof, and there drew up his Army, planted his Cannon, and clofely and orderly befieged that fide of the Town, and from ten in the morning till four a Clock in the afternoon, battered the Enemies Forts and Works, as being in continual expectation of the appearance of the Troops on the other fide, according to his order; yet (whether it was out of Neglect or Treachery that my Lords Orders were not obeyed) that days Work was rendred ineffectual as to the whole Defign.

However the vigilancy of My Lord did put the Enemy into fuch a Terror, that they forfook that Fort, and fecretly fled away with all their Train that very night to another ftrong hold not far diftant from *Tadcafter*, called *Cawood*-Caftle, to which, by reafon of its low and boggy Scituation, and foul and narrow Lanes and paſſages, it was not poſſible for my Lord to purſue them without too great an hazard to his Army; whereas had the Lieutenant General performed his Duty, in all probability the greateſt part of the principal Rebels in *York-ſhire* would that day have been taken in their own trap, and their further miſchief prevented. My Lord, the next morning, inſtead of ſtorming the Town (as he had intended), entred without interruption, and there ſtayed ſome few days to refreſh his Army, and order that part of the Country.

In *December,* 1642, My Lord thought it fit to march to *Pomfret,*[1] and to quarter his Army in that part of the Country which was betwixt *Cawood* and ſome Gariſons of the Enemy, in the weſt part of *York-ſhire, viz. Hallifax, Bradford, Leeds, Wakefield, &c.,* where he remained ſome time to recruit and enlarge his Army, which was much leſſened by erecting of Gariſons, and to keep thoſe parts in order and obedience to His Majeſty; And after he had thus ordered his Affairs, He was enabled to give Protection to thoſe parts

---

[1] Pontefract.

of the Country that were moſt willing to embrace it, and quarter'd his Army for a time in ſuch places which he had reduced. *Tadcaſter*, which ſtood upon a Paſs, he made a Gariſon, or rather a ſtrong Quarter, and put alſo a Gariſon into *Pomfret* Caſtle, not above eight Miles diſtant from *Tadcaſter*, which commanded that Town, and a great part of the Country.

During the time that his Army remained at *Pomfret*, My Lord ſetled a Gariſon at *Newark* in *Nottingham-ſhire*, ſtanding upon the River *Trent*, a very conſiderable paſs, which kept the greateſt part of *Nottingham-ſhire*, and part of *Lincoln-ſhire*, in obedience ; and after that he returned, in the beginning of *January*, 1642, back to *York*, with an intention to ſupply Himſelf with ſome Ammunition, which He had ordered to be brought from *Newcaſtle*: A Convoy of Horſe that were imployed to conduct it from thence, under the Command of the Lieutenant General of the Army, the Lord *Ethyn*, was by the Enemy at a paſs, called *Yarum-bridg*, in *York-ſhire*, fiercely encountred ; in which encounter My Lord's Forces totally routed

them, flew many, and took many Prifoners,
and moft of their Horfe Colours, confifting
of Seventeen Cornets ; and fo march'd on to
*York* with their Ammunition, without any
other Interruption.

My Lord, after he had received this Ammunition, put his Army into a condition to
march, and having intelligence that the Queen
was at Sea, with intention to land in fome
part of the Eaftriding of *York-fhire*, he directed
his March in *February*, 1642, into thofe parts,
to be ready to attend Her Majefties landing,
who was then daily expected from *Holland*.
Within a fhort time, after it had pleafed God
to protect Her Majefty both from the fury of
Wind and Waves, there being for feveral
days fuch a Tempeft at Sea that Her Majefty,
with all her Attendance, was in danger to be
caft away every minute ; as alfo from the fury
of the Rebels, which had the whole Naval
Power of the Kingdom then in their Hands,
fhe arrived fafely at a fmall Port in the Eaft
riding of *York-fhire* called *Burlington* Key,
where Her Majefty was no fooner landed, but
the Enemy at Sea made continual fhot againft
her Ships in the Port, which reached not

onely Her Majesties landing, but even the House where she lay (though without the least hurt to any), so that she her self, and her Attendants, were forced to leave the same, and to seek Protection from a Hill near that place, under which they retired; and all that while it was observed that Her Majesty shewed as much Courage as ever any person could do; for Her undaunted and Generous spirit was like her Royal Birth, deriving it self from that unparrallell'd King, Her Father, whose Heroick Actions will be in perpetual Memory whilest the World hath a being.

My Lord finding Her Majesty in this condition, drew his Army near the place where she was, ready to attend and protect Her Majesties Person, who was pleased to take a view of the Army as it was drawn up in order; and immediately after, which was in *March*, 1643, took Her journey towards *York*, whither the whole Army conducted Her Majesty, and brought her safe into the City. About this time, Her Majesty having some present occasion for Money, My Lord presented Her with 3000 l. *Sterling*, which she graciously accepted of, and having spent fome time there in Confultation about the prefent affairs, fhe was pleafed to fend fome Armes and Ammunition to the King, who was then in *Oxford;* to which end, my Lord ordered a Party, confifting of 1500, well Commanded, to conduct the fame, with whom the Lord *Percy*, who then had waited upon Her Majefty from the King, returned to *Oxford;* which Party His Majefty was pleafed to keep with him for his own Service.

Not long after, My Lord, who always endeavoured to win any place or perfons by fair means, rather then by ufing of force, reduced to His Majefties obedience a ftrong Fort and Caftle upon the Sea, and a very good Haven, call'd *Scarborough*-Caftle, perfwading the Governour thereof, who heretofore had oppofed his Forces at *Yarum*-bridg, with fuch rational and convincible Arguments, that he willingly rendred himfelf, and all the Garifon, unto His Majefties Devotion; By which prudent Action My Lord highly advanced His Majefties Intereft; for by that means the Enemy was much annoyed and prejudiced at Sea, and a great part in the Eaft-riding of *York-fhire* kept in due obedience.

After this, My Lord having received Intelligence that the Enemies General of the Horfe[1] had defigned to march with a Party from *Cawood* Caftle, whither they were fled from *Tadcafter*, as before is mentioned to fome Garifons which they had in the Weft of *York-fhire*; prefently order'd a party of Horfe, Commanded by the General of the Horfe, the Lord *George Goring*,[2] to attend the Enemy in their March, who overtook them on a Moor, call'd *Seacroft-Moor*, and fell upon their Rear, which caufed the Enemy to draw up their Forces into a Body; to whom they gave a Total rout (although their number was much greater) and took about 800 Prifoners, and 10 or 12 Colours of Horfe, befides many that were flain in the charge; which Prifoners were brought to *York*, about 10 or 12 miles diftant from that fame place.

Immediately after, in purfuit of that Victory, My Lord fent a confiderable Party into the

---

[1] Sir *Thomas Fairfax.*

[2] Created Earl of Norwich, 1644. His fon General George Goring, who died before him, was alfo an eminent leader in the loyalift caufe.

Weſt of *York-ſhire*, where they met with about 2000 of the Enemies Forces, taken out of their ſeveral Gariſons in thoſe parts, to execute ſome deſign upon a Moor called *Tankerly-Moor*, and there fought them, and routed them ; many were ſlain, and ſome taken Priſoners.

Not long after, the Remainder of the Army that were left at *York*, marched to *Leeds*, in the Weſt of *York-ſhire*, and from thence to *Wakefield*, being both the Enemies Quarters, to reduce and ſettle that part of the Country : My Lord having poſſeſſed himſelf of the Town of *Wakefield*, it being large, and of great compaſs, and able to make a ſtrong quarter, order'd it accordingly ; and receiving Intelligence that in two Market-Towns Southweſt from *Wakefield, viz. Rotherham* and *Sheffield*, the Enemy was very buſie to raiſe Forces againſt his Majeſty, and had fortified them both about four miles diſtant from each other, hoping thereby to give protection and encouragement to all thoſe parts of the Country which were populous, rich and rebellious, he thought it neceſſary to uſe his beſt endeavours to blaſt thoſe their wicked deſigns in the bud; and thereupon took a reſolution in *April* 1643, to march with part of his Army from *Wakefield* into the mentioned parts, attended with a convenient Train of Artillery and Ammunition, leaving the greateſt part of it at *Wakefield* with the remainder of his Army, under the Care and Conduct of his General of the Horſe, and Major General of the Army,[1] which was ſo conſiderable, both in reſpect of their number and proviſion, that they did, as they might well, conceive themſelves Maſter of the Field in thoſe parts, and ſecure in that quarter, although in the end it proved not ſo, as ſhall hereafter be declared, which muſt neceſſarily be imputed to their invigilancy and careleſsneſs.

My Lord firſt marched to *Rotheram*, and finding that the Enemy had placed a Gariſon of Soldiers in that Town, and fortified it, he drew up his Army in the morning againſt the Town, and ſummon'd it; but they refuſing to yield, my Lord fell to work with his Can-

-------------------------------------------------------------

[1] In both the copies which I have before me a ſidenote to explain the * has been ſmudged with ink for the purpoſe of obliteration; but I can make out the words "The Lord Goring and Sir Francis Mackworth, Knight."

non and Muſket, and within a ſhort time took it by ſtorm, and enter'd the Town that very night; ſome Enemies of note that were found therein, were taken Priſoners; and as for the common Soldiers, which were by the Enemy forced from their Allegiance, he ſhew'd ſuch Clemency to them, that very many willingly took up Arms for his Majeſties Service, and proved very faithful and.loyal Subjeᶜts, and good Soldiers.

After my Lord had ſtayed two or three dayes there, and order'd thoſe parts, he march'd with his Army to *Sheffield*, another Market-Town of large extent, in which there was an ancient Caſtle; which when the Enemies.Forces that kept the Town, came to hear of, being terrified with the fame of my Lords hitherto Viᶜtorious Army, they fled away from thence into *Derbyſhire*, and left both Town and Caſtle (without any blow) to my Lords Mercy; and though the people in the Town were moſt of them rebelliouſly affeᶜted, yet my Lord ſo prudently ordered the buſineſs, that within a ſhort time he reduced moſt of them to their Allegiance by love, and the reſt by fear, and recruited his Army daily;

he put a Garifon of Soldiers into the Caftle, and fortified it in all refpects, and conftituted a Gentleman of Quality[1] Governour both of the Caftle, Town and Country ; and finding near that place fome Iron Works, he gave prefent order for the cafting of Iron Cannon for his Garifons, and for the making of other Inftruments and Engines of War.

Within a fhort time after, my Lord receiving Intelligence that the Enemy in the Garifons near *Wakefield* had united themfelves, and being drawn into a body in the night time, had furprifed and enter'd the Town of *Wakefield*, and taken all or moft of the Officers and Soldiers, left there, Prifoners, (amongft whom was alfo the General of the Horfe, the Lord *Goring*, whom my Lord afterwards redeem'd by Exchange) and poffeffed themfelves of the whole Magazine, which was a very great lofs and hinderance to my Lords defigns, it being the Moity of his Army, and moft of his Ammunition, he fell upon new Counfels, and refolved without any delay to march from thence back towards *York*, which was in *May* 1643, where

----

[1] Sir *Will. Savil* Kt. and Bar.

after he had refted fome time, Her Majefty being refolved to take Her Journey towards the Southern parts of the Kingdom, where the King was, defigned firft to go from *York* to *Pomfret*, whither my Lord ordered the whole Marching Army to be in readinefs to conduct Her Majefty, which they did, he himfelf attending Her Majefty in perfon. And after Her Majefty had refted there fome fmall time, fhe being defirous to proceed in Her intended Journey, no lefs then a formed Army was able to fecure Her Perfon: Wherefore my Lord was refolved out of his fidelity and duty to fupply Her with an Army of 7000 Horfe and Foot, befides a convenient Train of Artillery, for Her fafer Conduct; chufing rather to leave himfelf in a weak condition (though he was even then very near the Enemies Garifons in that part of the Country) then fuffer Her Majefties Perfon to be expofed to danger. Which Army of 7000 men, when Her Majefty was fafely arrived to the King, He was pleafed to keep with him for His own Service.

After Her Majefties departure out of *York-fhire*, my Lord was forced to recruit again his Army, and within a fhort time, *viz.* in *June*,

1643, took a refolution to march into the Enemies Quarters, in the Weftern parts; in which march he met with a ftrong ftone houfe well fortified, call'd *Howley*-Houfe, wherein was a Garifon of Soldiers, which my Lord fummon'd; but the Governour difobeying the fummons, he batter'd it with his Cannon, and fo took it by force; the Governour having quarter given him contrary to my Lord's Orders, was brought before my Lord by a Perfon of Quality, for which the Officer that brought him received a check; and though he refolved then to kill him, yet my Lord would not fuffer him to do it, faying, It was inhumane to kill any man in cold blood. Hereupon the Governour kiff'd the Key of the Houfe door, and prefented it to my Lord; to which my Lord return'd this anfwer: *I need it not*, faid he, *for I brought a Key along with me, which yet I was unwilling to ufe, until you forced me to it.*

At this Houfe my Lord remained five or fix days, till he had refrefhed his Soldiers; and then a refolution was taken to march againft a Garifon of the Enemies call'd *Bradford*, a little but a ftrong Town; in the way

he met with a strong interruption by the
Enemy drawing forth a vast number of Mufquetiers, which they had very privately gotten
out of *Lancashire*, the next adjoining County
to thofe parts of *York-shire*, which had fo eafie
an accefs to them at *Bradford*, by reafon the
whole Country was of their Party, that my
Lord could not poffibly have any conftant intelligence of their defigns and motions; for
in their Army there were near 5000 Mufquetiers, and 18 Troops of Horfe, drawn up in a
place full of hedges, called *Atherton-moor*, near
to their Garifon at *Bradford*, ready to encounter my Lords Forces, which then con-
tained not above half fo many Mufquetiers as
the Enemy had; their chiefeft ftrength confifting in Horfe, and thefe made ufelefs for
a long time together by the Enemies Horfe
poffeffing all the plain ground upon that Field;
fo that no place was left to draw up my Lords
Horfe, but amongft old Coal-pits : Neither
could they charge the Enemy, by reafon of a
great ditch and high bank betwixt my Lord's
and the Enemies Troops, but by two on a
breaft, and that within Mufquet fhot; the
Enemy being drawn up in hedges, and con-

tinually playing upon them, which rendred the
fervice exceeding difficult and hazardous.

In the mean while the Foot of both fides
on the right and left Wings encounter'd each
other, who fought from Hedg to Hedg, and
for a long time together overpower'd and got
ground of my Lords Foot, almoft to the in-
vironing of his Cannon; my Lords Horfe
(wherein confifted his greateft ftrength) all
this while being made, by reafon of the
ground, incapable of charging; at laft the
Pikes of my Lords Army having had no employment all the day, were drawn againft the
Enemies left wing, and particularly thofe of
my Lords own Regiment, which were all
ftout and valiant men, who fell fo furioufly
upon the Enemy, that they forfook their
hedges, and fell to their heels: At which very
inftant my Lord caufed a fhot or two to be
made by his Cannon againft the Body of the
Enemies Horfe, drawn up within Cannon
fhot, which took fo good effect, that it difor-
dered the Enemies Troops; Hereupon my
Lord's Horfe got over the Hedg, not in a
body (for that they could not), but difperfedly
two on a breaft; and as foon as fome confi-

derable number was gotten over, and drawn up, they charged the Enemy, and routed them; fo that in an inftant there was a ftrange change of Fortune, and the Field totally won by my Lord, notwithftanding he had quitted 7000 Men, to conduct Her Majefty, befides a good Train of Artillery, which in fuch a Conjuncture would have weakned *Cæfars* Army. In this Victory the Enemy loft moft of their Foot, about 3000 were taken Prifoners, and 700 Horfe and Foot flain, and thofe that efcaped fled into their Garifon at *Bradford,* amongft whom was alfo their General of the Horfe [Sir Thos. Fairfax.]

After this My Lord caufed his Army to be rallied, and marched in order that night before *Bradford,* with an intention to ftorm it the next morning; but the Enemy that were in the Town, it feems, were fo difcomfited, that the fame night they efcaped all various ways, and amongft them the faid General of the Horfe, whofe Lady being behind a Servant on Horfe-back, was taken by fome of My Lord's Soldiers, and brought to his Quarters, where fhe was treated and attended with all civility

and refpect, and within few days fent to *York*
in my Lords own Coach, and from thence
very fhortly after to *Kingftone* upon *Hull*,
where fhe defired to be, attended by my
Lords Coach and Servants.

Thus my Lord, after the Enemy was gone,
entred the Town and Garifon of *Bradford*,
by which Victory the Enemy was fo daunted,
that they forfook the reft of their Garifons,
that is to fay, *Hallifax*, *Leeds* and *Wakefield*,
and difperfed themfelves feverally, the chief
Officers retiring to *Hull*, a ftrong Garifon of
the Enemy; and though my Lord, knowing
they would make their efcape thither, as
having no other place of refuge to refort to,
fent a Letter to *York* to the Governour of
that City, to ftop them in their paffage; yet
by neglect of the Poft, it coming not timely
enough to his hands, his Defign was fruftrated.

The whole County of *York*, fave onely
*Hull*, being now cleared and fetled by my
Lords Care and Conduct, he marched to the
City of *York*, and having a competent num-
ber of Horfe well armed and commanded, he
quarter'd them in the Eaft-riding, near *Hull*,

there being no vifible Enemy then to oppofe them : In the mean while my Lord receiving News that the Enemy had made an Invafion into the next adjoining County of *Lincoln*, where he had fome Forces, he prefently difpatched[1] his Lieutenant General of the Army away with fome Horfe and Dragoons, and foon after marched thither himfelf with the body of the Army, being earneftly defired by his Majefties Party there. The Forces which my Lord had in the fame County, commanded by the then Lieutenant General of the Horfe, Mr. *Charles Cavendifh*, fecond Brother to the now Earl of *Devonfhire*, though they had timely notice, and Orders from my Lord to make their retreat to the Lieutenant-General of the Army, and not to fight the Enemy; yet the faid Lieutenant-General of the Horfe being tranfported by his Courage (he being a Perfon of great Valour and Conduct), and having charged the Enemy, unfortunately loft the field, and himfelf was flain in the Charge, his Horfe lighting in a bogg : Which news being brought to my Lord when he was on his

---

[1] The Lord *Ethyn.*

March, he made all the haſt he could, and was no ſooner joined with his Lieutenant General, but fell upon the Enemy, and put them to flight.

The firſt Gariſon my Lord took in *Lincoln-ſhire* was *Gainſborrough*, a Town ſtanding upon the River *Trent*, wherein (not long before), had been a Gariſon of Soldiers for His Ma-jeſty, under the Command of the then Earl of *Kingſtone*, but ſurpriſed, and the Town Taken by the Enemies Forces, who having an intention to conveigh the ſaid Earl of *Kingſtone* from thence to *Hull* in a little Pinnace, met with ſome of my Lords Forces by the way, commanded by the Lieutenant of the Army, who being deſirous to reſcue the Earl of *Kingſtone*, and making ſome ſhots with their Regiment Pieces, to ſtop the Pin-nace, unfortunately ſlew him and one of his Servants.

My Lord drawing near the mentioned Town of *Gainſborrough*, there appear'd on the top of a Hill above the Town, ſome of the Enemies Horſe drawn up in a body; whereupon he immediately ſent a party of his Horſe to view them; who no ſooner came within their ſight, but they retreated fairly fo long as they could well endure; but the purfuit of my Lords Horfe caufed them prefently to break their ranks, and fall to their heels, where moft of them efcaped, and fled to *Lincoln*, another of their Garrifons. Hereupon my Lord fummon'd the Town of *Gainfborough*; but the Governour thereof refufing to yield, caufed my Lord to plant his Cannon, and draw up his Army on the mention'd Hill; and having play'd fome little while upon the Town, put the Enemy into fuch a terror, that the Governour fent out, and offer'd the furrender of the Town upon fair terms, which my Lord thought fit rather to embrace, then take it by force; and though according to the Articles of Agreement made between them, both the Enemies Arms and the Keys of the Town fhould have been fairly delivered to my Lord; yet it being not performed as it was expected, the Arms being in a confufed manner thrown down, and the Gates fet wide open, the Prifoners that had been kept in the Town began firft to plunder; which my Lords Forces feeing, did the fame, although it was againft my Lords will and orders.

After my Lord had thus reduced the Town, and put a good Garifon of Soldiers into it, and better fortified it, he marched before *Lincoln*, and there he entred with his Army without great difficulty, and plac'd alfo a Garifon in it, and raifed a confiderable Army, both Horfe, Foot and Dragoons, for the prefervation of that County, and put them under Commanders, and conftituted a Perfon of Honour[1] Commander in Chief, with intention to march towards the South, which if it had taken effect, would doubtlefs have made an end of that War; but he being daily importuned by the Nobility and Gentry of *York-fhire*, to return into that County, efpecially upon the perfwafions of the Commander in Chief of the Forces left there, who acquainted my Lord that the Enemy grew fo ftrong every day, being got together in *Kingftone* upon *Hull*, and annoying that Country, that his Forces were not able to bear up againft them; alledging withall, that my Lord would be fufpected to betray the Truft repofed in him, if he came not to fuccour and affift them; he went back

---

[1] The *Lord Widdrington.*

with his Army for the protection of that fame
Country; and when he arrived there, which
was in *Auguſt*, 1643, he found the Enemy of
fo fmall confequence, that they did all flie
before him. About this time His Majefty
was pleafed to honour my Lord for His true
and faithful Service, with the Title of *Marqueſs of Newcaſtle.*

My Lord being returned into *York-ſhire*,
forced the Enemy firft from a Town called
*Beverly,* wherein they had a Garifon of Soldiers; and from thence, upon the entreaty of
the Nobility and Gentry of *York-ſhire*, (as
before is mentioned) who promifed him Ten
thoufand men for that purpofe, though they
came fhort of their performance, marched
near the Town of *Kingſtone* upon *Hull,* and
befieged that part of the Garifon that bordered
on *York-ſhire,* for a certain time; in which
time the Enemy took the courage to fally out
of the Town with a ftrong party of Horfe and
Foot very early in the morning, with purpofe
to have forced the Quarters of a Regiment of
my Lords Horfe, that were quarter'd next the
Town; but by the vigilancy of their Commander Sir *Marmaduke Langdale,* afterwards

Lord *Langdale*, his Forces being prepared for their reception, they received fuch a Welcome as coft many of them their Lives, moft of their Foot (but fuch as were flain) being taken Prifoners; and thofe of their Horfe that efcaped, got into their Hold at *Hull*.

The Enemy thus feeing that they could do my Lords Army no further damage on that fide of the River in *York-fhire*, endeavoured by all means (from *Hull*, and other confederate places in the Eaftern parts of the Kingdom) to form a confiderable party to annoy and difturb the Forces raifed by my Lord in *Lincoln-fhire*, and left there for the protection of that County; where the Enemy being drawn together in a body, fought my Lords Forces in his abfence, and got the honour of the day near *Hornby* Caftle in that County; which lofs, caufed partly by their own rafhnefs, forced my Lord to leave his defign upon *Hull*, and to march back with his Army to *York*, which was in *October*, 1643, where he remained but a few dayes to refrefh his Army, and receiving intelligence that the Enemy was got into *Derbyfhire*, and did grow numerous there, and bufie in feducing the people, that Country being under my Lords Command, he refolved to direct his March thither in the beginning of *November*, 1643, to fupprefs their further growth ; and to that end quarter'd his Army at *Chefterfield*, and in all the parts thereabout, for a certain time.

Immediately after his departure from *York* to *Pomfret*, in his faid March into *Derbyfhire*, the City of *York* fent to my Lord to inform him of their intention to chufe another Mayor for the year following, defiring his pleafure about it : My Lord, who knew that the Mayor for the year before, was a perfon of much Loyalty and Difcretion, declared his mind to them, That he thought it fit to continue him Mayor alfo for the year following ; which it feems they did not like, but refolved to chufe one which they pleafed, contrary to my Lords defire. My Lord perceiving their intentions, about the time of the Election, fent orders to the Governour of the City of *York*, to permit fuch Forces to enter into the City as he fhould fend ; which being done accordingly, they upon the Day of the Election repaired to the Town-Hall, and with their Arms ftaid there until they had continued the said Mayor according to my Lords desire.[1]

During the time of my Lords stay at *Chesterfield* in *Derbyshire*, he ordered some part of his Army to march before a strong House and Garison of the Enemies, call'd *Wingfield Mannor*, which in a short time they took by storm. And when my Lord had raised in that County as many Forces, Horse and Foot, as were supposed to be sufficient to preserve it from the fury of the Enemy, he armed them, and constituted an Honourable Person[2] Commander in Chief of all the Forces of that County, and of *Leicestershire;* and so leaving it in that condition, marched in *December* 1643, from *Chesterfield* to *Bolsover* in the same County, and from thence to *Welbeck* in *Nottinghamshire*, to his own House and Garison, in which parts he staid some time, both to

---

[1] Perhaps as notable an instance of intimidation at an election as was ever known ! We have still in many free (?) boroughs the objectionable and thoroughly feudal custom, for the steward of the Lord to dictate to the householders what constables they must choose for the year.

[2] The Lord of *Loughborrough*.

refresh his Army, and to settle and reform some diforders he found there, leaving no visible Enemy behind him in *Derbyshire*, save onely an inconsiderable party in the Town of *Derby*, which they had fortified, not worth the labour to reduce it.

About this time the report came, that a great Army out of *Scotland*, was upon their march towards the Northern parts of *England*, to assist the Enemy against His Majesty, which forced the Nobility and Gentry of *Yorkshire* to invite my Lord back again into those parts, with promise to raise for his service, an Army of 10000 men; My Lord (not upon this proffer, which had already heretofore deceived him, but out of his Loyalty and duty to preserve those parts which were committed to his care and protection) returned in the middle of *January* 1643. And when he came there, he found not one man raised to assist him against so powerful an Army, nor an intention of raising any; Wherefore he was necessitated to raise himself, out of the Countrey, what forces he could get, and when he had settled the affairs in *York-shire* as well as time and his present condition would permit, and consti-

tuted an honourable Perfon[1] Governor of
*York* and Commander in chief of a very confiderable party of horfe and foot for the defence
of the County (for Sr. *Thomas Glemham* was
then made Colonel General, and marched
into the Field with the Army) he took his
march to *Newcaftle* in the beginning of
*February* 1643, to give a ftop to the *Scots*
army.

Prefently after his coming thither with
fome of his Troups, before his whole army
was come up, he received intelligence of the
*Scots* Armie's near approach, whereupon he
fent forth a party of horfe to view them, who
found them very ftrong, to the number of
22000 Horfe and Foot well armed and commanded : They marched up towards the
Town with fuch confidence, as if the Gates
had been open'd for their reception; and the
General of their Army feem'd to take no
notice of my Lords being in it, for which
afterwards he excufed himfelf; but as they
drew near, they found not fuch entertainment
as they expeƈted; for though they affaulted a

---

[1] The Lord *Bellafis.*

Work that was not finifhed, yet they were beaten off with much lofs.

The Enemy being thus ftopt before the Town, thought fit to quarter near it, in that part of the Country; and fo foon as my Lords Army was come up, he defigned one night to have fallen into their Quarter; but by reafon of fome negle&t of his Orders in not giving timely notice to the party defigned for it, it took not an effe&t anfwerable to his expecta-tion. In a word, there were three Defigns taken againft the Enemy, whereof if one had but hit, they would doubtlefs have been loft ; but there was fo much Treachery, Jugling and Falfhood in my Lord's own Army, that it was impoffible for him to be fuccefsful in his Defigns and Undertakings. However, though it failed in the Enemies Foot-Quarters, which lay neareft the Town ; yet it took good effe&t in their Horfe-Quarters, which were more remote ; for my Lord's Horfe, Commanded by a very gallant and worthy Gentleman[1] falling upon them, gave them fuch an Alarm, that all they could do, was to draw

---

[1] The Lord *Langdale*.

into the Field, where my Lord's Forces charged them, and in a little time routed them totally, and kill'd and took many Prifoners, to the number of 1500.

Upon this the Enemy was forced to draw their whole Army together, and to quarter them a little more remote from the Town, and to feek out inacceffible places for their fecurity, as afterwards appear'd more plainly; for fo foon as my Lord had prepared his Army for a March, he drew them forth againft the *Scots*, which he found quarter'd upon high Hills clofe by the River *Tyne*, where they could not be encounter'd but upon very difadvantagious terms; befides, that day proved very ftormy and tempeftuous, fo that my Lord was neceffitated to withdraw his Forces, and retire into his own Quarters.

The next day after, the *Scots* Army finding ill harbour in thofe quarters, marched from hill to hill into another part of the Bifhoprick of *Durham*, near the Sea coaft, to a Town called *Sunderland*; and thereupon my Lord thought fit to march to *Durham*, to ftop their further progrefs, where he had contrived the bufinefs fo, that they were either forced to fight or ſtarve within a little time.  The firſt was offered to them twice, that is to ſay, at *Penſher-hills* one day, and at *Bowden-hills* another day in the Biſhoprick of *Durham :* But my Lord found them at both times drawn up in ſuch places, as he could not poſſibly charge them ; wherefore he retired again to *Durham*, with an intention to ſtreighten their Quarters, and to wait upon them, if ever they left their Holds and inacceſſible places.  In the mean time it hapned that the Earl of *Montroſs* came to the ſame place, and having ſome deſign for his Majeſties ſervice in *Scotland*, deſired My Lord to give him the aſſiſtance of ſome of his Forces; and although My Lord ſtood then in preſent need of them, and could not coveniently ſpare any, having ſo great an Army to oppoſe ; yet out of a deſire to advance His Majeſties ſervice as much as lay in his power, he was willing to part with 200 Horſe and Dragoons to the ſaid Earl.

The *Scots* perceiving My Lords vigilancy and care, contented themſelves with their own quarters, which could not have ſerv'd them long, but that a great misfortune befel My Lords Forces in *York-ſhire ;* for the Governour whom he had left behind with fufficient Forces for the defence of that Country, although he had orders not to encounter the Enemy, but to keep himfelf in a defenfive pofture; yet he being a man of great valour and courage, it tranfported him fo much that he refolved to face the Enemy, and offering to keep a Town that was not tenable,[1] was utterly routed, and himfelf taken Prifoner, although he fought moft gallantly.

So foon as my Lord received this fad Intelligence, he upon Confultation, and upon very good Grounds of Reafon, took a refolution not to ftay between the two Armies of the Enemies, *viz.* the *Scots* and the *Englifh*, that had prevailed in *York-fhire*; but immediately to march into *York-fhire* with his Army, to preferve (if poffible) the City of *York* out of the Enemies hands: which retreat was ordered fo well, and with fuch excellent Conduct, that though the Army of the *Scots* marched clofe upon their Rear, and fought them every day of their retreat, yet they gained feveral Paffes for their

---

[1] *Selby* in *Yorkfhire*.

fecurity, and entred fafe and well into the City of *York*, in *April* 1643.

My Lord being now at *York*, and finding three Armies againſt him, *viz.* the Army of the *Scots*, the Army of the *Engliſh* that gave the defeat to the Governour of *York*, and an Army that was raiſed out of aſſociate Counties, and but little Ammunition and Proviſion in the Town; was forced to ſend his Horſe away to quarter in ſeveral Counties, *viz. Derbyſhire*, *Nottinghamſhire*, *Leiceſterſhire*, for their ſub-ſiſtance, under the Conduct of his Lieutenant-General of the Horſe, My dear Brother Sir *Charles Lucas*, himſelf remaining at *York*, with his Foot and Train for the defence of that City.

. In the mean time, the Enemy having cloſely beſiedged the City on all ſides, came to the very Gates thereof, and pull'd out the Earth at one end, as thoſe in the City put it in at the other end; they planted their great Cannons againſt it, and threw in Granadoes at pleaſure: But thoſe in the City made ſeveral ſallies upon them with good ſucceſs. At laſt, the General of the aſſociate Army of the Enemy, having cloſely beleaguer'd the North

fide of the Town, fprung a Mine under the
wall of the Mannor-yard, and blew part of it
up; and having beaten back the Town-Forces
(although they behaved themfelves very gallantly) enter'd the Mannor-houfe with a great
number of their men, which as foon as my
Lord perceived, he went away in all hafte,
even to the amazement of all that were by,
not knowing what he intended to do; and
drew 80 of his own Regiment of Foot, called
the White-Coats, all ftout and valiant Men, to
that Poft, who fought the Enemy with that
courage, that within a little time they killed
and took 1500 of them; and My Lord gave
prefent order to make up the breach which
they had made in the wall; Whereupon the
Enemy remain'd without any other attempt in
that kind, fo long, till almoft all provifion for
the fupport of the foldiery in the City was
fpent, which neverthelefs was fo well ordered
by my Lords Prudence, that no Famine or
great extremity of want enfued.

My Lord having held out in that manner
above two Months, and withftood the ftrength
of three Armies; and feeing that his Lieutenant-General of the Horfe whom he had

ſent for relief to His Majeſty, could not ſo ſoon obtain it (although he uſed his beſt endeavour) for to gain yet ſome little time, began to treat with the Enemy; ordering in the mean while, and upon the Treaty, to double and treble his Guards. At laſt after three Months time from the beginning of the Siege, His Majeſty was pleaſed to ſend an Army, which joining with my Lords Horſe that were ſent to quarter in the aforeſaid Countreys, came to relieve the City, under the Conduct of the moſt Gallant and Heroick Prince *Rupert*, his Nephew; upon whoſe approach near *York*, the Enemy drew from before the City, into an entire Body, and marched away on the Weſtſide of the River *Owſe*, that runs through the City, His Majeſties Forces being then of the Eaſt-ſide of that River.

My Lord immediately ſent ſome perſons of Quality to attend His Highneſs, and to invite him into the City to conſult with him about that important Affair, and to gain ſo much time as to open a Port to march forth with his Cannon and Foot which were in the Town, to join with His Highneſs's Forces; and went himſelf the next day in perſon to wait on His

Highnefs ; where after fome Conferences, he declared his Mind to the Prince, defiring His Highnefs not to attempt any thing as yet upon the Enemy ; for he had intelligence that there was fome difcontent between them, and that they were refolved to divide themfelves, and fo to raife the Siege without fighting: Befides, my Lord expected within two dayes, Collonel *Cleavering,* with above three thoufand men out of the North, and two thoufand drawn out of feveral Garifons, (who alfo came at the fame time, though it was then too late). But His Highnefs anfwered my Lord, That he had a Letter from His Majefty (then at *Oxford*) with a pofitive and abfolute Command to fight the Enemy ; which in Obedience, and according to his Duty he was bound to perform. Whereupon my Lord replied, That he was ready and willing for his part, to obey his Highnefs in all things, no otherwife then if His Majefty was there in Perfon Himfelf ; and though feveral of my Lords Friends advifed him not to engage in Battel, becaufe the Command (as they faid) was taken from Him : Yet my Lord anfwer'd them, That happen what would, he would not fhun to fight, for he had no other ambition but to live and dye a Loyal Subject to His Majesty.

Then the Prince and my Lord conferr'd with several of their Officers, amongst whom there were several Disputes concerning the advantages which the Enemy had of Sun, Wind and Ground. The Horse of His Majesties Forces, was drawn up in both Wings upon that fatal Moor call'd *Heſſom-Moor;* and my Lord aſk'd His Highneſs what Service he would be pleas'd to command him; who return'd this Anſwer, That he would begin no action upon the Enemy, till early in the morning; deſiring my Lord to repoſe himſelf till then. Which my Lord did, and went to reſt in his own Coach that was cloſe by in the Field, until the time appointed.

Not long had My Lord been there, but he heard a great noiſe and thunder of ſhooting, which gave him notice of the Armies being engaged: Whereupon he immediately put on his Arms, and was no ſooner got on Horſeback, but he beheld a diſmal ſight of the Horſe of His Majeſties right Wing, which out of a panick fear had left the Field, and run away with all the ſpeed they could; and though my

Lord made them stand once, yet they immediately betook themselves to their heels again, and killed even those of their own party that endeavoured to stop them ; the Left Wing in the mean time, Commanded by those two Valiant Persons, the Lord *Goring*, and Sir *Charles Lucas*, having the better of the Enemies Right Wing, which they beat back most valiantly three times, and made their General retreat, in so much that they founded Victory.

In this Confusion my Lord (accompanied onely with his Brother Sir *Charles Cavendish*, Major *Scot*, Capt. *Mazine*, and his Page) hastning to see in what posture his own Regiment was, met with a Troop of Gentlemen-Voluntiers, who formerly had chosen him their Captain, notwithstanding he was General of an Army ; to whom my Lord spake after this manner : *Gentlemen*, said he, *You have done me the Honour to chuse me your Captain, and now is the fittest time that I may do you service ; wherefore if you'l follow me, I shall lead you on the best I can, and shew you the way to your own Honour.* They being as glad of my Lords Profer, as my Lord was of their Readiness, went on with the greatest Courage ; and passing through Two Bodies of Foot, engaged with each other not at forty yards diſtance, received not the leaſt hurt, although they fired quick upon each other; but marched towards a *Scots* Regiment of Foot, which they charged and routed; in which Encounter my Lord himſelf kill'd Three with his Pages half-leaden Sword, for he had no other left him; and though all the Gentlemen in particular, offer'd him their Swords, yet my Lord refuſed to take a Sword of any of them. At laſt, after they had paſs'd through this Regiment of Foot, a Pike-man made a ſtand to the whole Troop; and though my Lord charg'd him twice or thrice, yet he could not enter him; but the Troop diſpatched him ſoon.

In all theſe Encounters my Lord got not the leaſt hurt, though ſeveral were ſlain about him; and his White-Coats ſhew'd ſuch an extraordinary Valour and Courage in that Action, that they were kill'd in Rank and File: And here I cannot but mention by the way, That it is remarkable, that in all actions and undertakings where My Lord was in Perſon himſelf, he was always Victorious, and proſpered in the execution of his deſigns; but whatfoever was loft or fucceeded ill, happen'd in his abfence, and was caufed either by the Treachery, or Negligence and Carelefnefs of his Officers.

My Lord being the laft in the Field, and feeing that all was loft, and that every one of His Majefties Party made their efcapes in the beft manner they could; he being moreover inquired after by feveral of his Friends, who had all a great love and refpect for my Lord, efpecially by the then Earl of *Craford* (who lov'd my Lord fo well that he gave 20*s*. to one that affured him of his being alive and fafe, telling him, that that was all he had) went towards *York* late at night, accompanied onely with his Brother, and one or two of his fervants; and coming near the Town, met His Highnefs Prince *Rupert*, with the Lieutenant General of the Army, the Lord *Ethyn*; His Highnefs afked My Lord how the bufinefs went? To whom he anfwered, That all was loft and gone on their fide.

That night my Lord remained in *York*; and having nothing left in his power to do his Majefty any further fervice in that kind; for he had neither Ammunition, nor Money to raife more Forces, to keep either *York*, or any other Towns that were yet in His Majesties Devotion, well knowing that thofe which were left could not hold out long, and being alfo loath to have afperfions caft upon him, that he did fell them to the Enemy, in cafe he could not keep them, he took a Refolution, and that juftly and honourably, to forfake the Kingdom ; and to that end, went the next morning to the Prince, and acquainted him with his Defign, defiring His Highnefs would be pleafed to give this true and juft report of him to his Majefty, that he had behaved himfelf like an honeft man, a Gentleman, and a Loyal fubject. Which requeft the Prince having granted, my Lord took his leave ; and being conducted by a Troop of Horfe, and a Troop of Dragoons to *Scarborough*, went to Sea, and took fhipping for *Hamborough* ; the Gentry of the Country, who alfo came to take their leaves of My Lord, being much troubled at his departure, and fpeaking very honourably of him, as furely they had no reafon to the contrary.

The

# Life of the Moſt Illuſtrious
# Prince, William Duke of
# Newcaſtle.

*THE SECOND BOOK.*

HAVING hitherto faithfully related the life of My Noble Lord and Huſband, and the chief Actions which He performed during the time of his being employed in His Majeſties Service for the Good and Intereſt of his King and Country, until the time of his going out of *England*, I ſhall now give you a juſt account of all that paſſed during the time of his baniſh-ment, till the return into his native Country.

My Lord being a Wiſe Man, and foreſeeing well what the loſs of that fatal Battle upon *Heſſom-moor*, near *York*, would produce, by which not onely thofe of His Majefties Party in the Northern parts of the Kingdom, but in all other parts of His Majefties Dominions both in *England*, *Scotland*, and *Ireland* were loft and undone, and that there was no other way, but either to quit the Kingdom, or fubmit to the Enemy, or die, he refolved upon the former, and preparing for his journey, afked his Steward, How Much Money he had left? Who anfwer'd, That he had but 90*l.* My Lord not being at all ftartled at fo fmall a Summ, although his prefent defign required much more, was refolved too feek his Fortune, even with that litle; and thereupon having taken leave of His Highnefs Prince *Rupert*, and the reft that were prefent, went to *Scarborough* (as before is mentioned) where two Ships were prepared for *Hamborough* to fet fail within 24 hours, in which he embarqued with his Company, and arrived in four days time to the faid City, which was on the 8*th* of *July*, 1644.

In one of thefe Ships was my Lord, with his two Sons, *Charles* Vifcount *Mansfield*, and Lord *Henry Cavendifh*, now Earl of *Ogle*; as alfo Sir *Charles Cavendifh*, My Lord's Brother;

the then Lord Bifhop of *London-derry*, Dr. *Bramhall*; the Lord *Falconbridg*, the Lord *Widdrington*, Sir *William Carnaby*, who after died at *Paris*, and his Brother Mr. *Francis Carnaby*, who went prefently in the fame Ship back again for *England*, and foon after was flain by the Enemy, near *Sherborne* in *York-fhire*, befides many of my Lord's and their fervants. In the other Ship was the Earl of *Ethyne*, Lieutenant General of My Lord's Army, and the Lord *Cornworth*. But before My Lord landed at *Hamborough*, his eldeft Son *Charles*, Lord *Mansfield*, fell fick of the Small-Pox, and not long after his younger Son, *Henry*, now Earl of *Ogle*, fell likewife dangeroufly ill of the Meafels; but it pleafed God that they both happily recovered.

My Lord finding his Company and Charge very great, although he fent feveral of his Servants back again into *England*, and having no means left to maintain him, was forced to feek for Credit; where at laft he got fo much as would in part relieve his neceffities; and whereas heretofore he had been contented, for want of a Coach, to make ufe of a Waggon, when his occafions drew him abroad, he was now able (with the credit he had got) to buy a Coach and nine Horſes of an *Holſatian* breed; for which Horſes he paid £160, and and was afterwards offer'd for one of them an hundred Piſtols at *Paris*, but he refuſed the money, and preſented ſeven of them to Her Majeſty the Queen-Mother of *England*, and kept two for his own uſe.

After my Lord had ſtay'd in *Hamborough* from *July* 1644, till *February* 164$\frac{5}{4}$, he being reſolved to go into *France*, went by Sea from *Hamborough* to *Amſterdam*, and from thence to *Rotterdam*, where he ſent one of his Servants with a Complement and tender of his humble Service to Her Highneſs, the then Princeſs Royal, the Queen of *Bohemia*, the Princeſs Dowager of *Orange*, and the Prince of *Orange*, which was received with much kindneſs and civility.

From *Rotterdam* he directed his Journey to *Antwerp*, and from thence, with one Coach, one Chariot, and two Waggons, he went to *Mechlin* and *Bruſſels*, where he received a Viſit from the Governour, the Marqueſs of *Caſtel Rodrigo*, the Duke of *Lorrain*, and Count *Piccolomini*.

From thence he fet forth for *Valenchin* and *Cambray*, where the Governour of the Town, ufed my Lord with great refpect and civility, and defired him to give the word that night. Thence he went to *Peroon*, a Frontier Town in *France* (where the Vice-Governour, in abfence of the Governour of that place, did likewife entertain my Lord with all refpect, and defired him to give the Word that night), and fo to *Paris* without any further ftay.

My Lord being arrived at *Paris*, which was in *April*, 1645, immediately went to tender his humble duty to Her Majefty, the Queen-Mother of *England*, where it was my Fortune to fee him the firft time, I being then one of the Maids of Honour to Her Majefty; and after he had ftay'd there fome time, he was pleafed to take fome particular notice of me, and exprefs more then an ordinary affection for me; infomuch that he refolved to chufe me for his Second Wife; for he, having but two Sons, purpofed to marry me, a young Woman that might prove fruitful to him and encreafe his Pofterity by a Mafculine Off-fpring. Nay, He was fo defirous of Male-Iffue, that I have heard him fay, He cared not (fo God would be pleafed to give him many Sons), although they came to be perfons of the meaneft Fortunes ; but God (it feems) had ordered it otherwife, and fruftrated his Defigns by making me barren, which yet did never leffen his Love and Affection for me.

After My Lord was married, having no Eftate or Means left him to maintain himfelf and his Family, he was neceffitated to feek for Credit, and live upon the Courtefie of thofe that were pleafed to Truft him ; which although they did for fomewhile, and fhew'd themfelves very civil to My Lord, yet they grew weary at length, infomuch that his Steward was forced one time to tell him, That he was not able to provide a Dinner for him, for his Creditors were refolved to truft him no longer. My Lord being always a great mafter of his Paffions, was, at leaft fhew'd himfelf not in any manner troubled at it, but in a pleafant humour told me, that I muft of neceffity pawn my Cloaths to make fo much Money as would procure a Dinner. I anfwer'd, That my Cloaths would be but of fmall value, and therefore defired my Waiting-

Maid[1] to pawn fome fmall toys, which I had formerly given her, which fhe willingly did. The fame day in the afternoon, My Lord fpake himfelf to his Creditors, and both by his civil Deportment, and perfwafive Arguments, obtained fo much that they did not onely truft him for more neceffaries, but lent him Mony befides to redeem thofe Toys that were pawned. Hereupon I fent my Waiting-Maid into *England* to my Brother, the Lord *Lucas*, for that fmall Portion which was left me, and my Lord alfo immediately after difpatched one of his Servants,[2] who was then Governour to his Sons, to fome of his Friends, to try what means he could procure for his fubfiftance ; but though he ufed all the induftry and endeavour he could, yet he effeded but little, by reafon everybody was fo affraid of the Parliament, that they durft not relieve Him, who was counted a Traitor for his Honeft and Loyal fervice to his King and Country.

Not long after, My Lord had profers made him of fome Rich Matches in *England* for his

---

[1] Mrs. *Chaplain*, now Mrs. *Top.*      [2] Mr. *Benoift.*

two Sons, whom therefore he fent thither with one Mr. *Loving*, hoping by that means to provide both for them and himfelf; but they being arrived there, out of fome reafons beft known to them, declared their unwillingnefs to Marry as yet, continuing neverthelefs in *England*, and living as well as they could.

Some two years after my Lord's Marriage, when he had prevailed fo far with his Creditors, that they began to truft him anew, the firft thing he did was, that he removed out of thofe Lodgings in *Paris*, where he had been neceffitated to live hitherto, to a Houfe which he hired for himfelf and his Family, and furnifhed it as well as his new gotten Credit would permit; and withal, refolving for his own recreation and divertifement in his banifhed condition, to exercife the Art of Mannage, which he is a great lover and Mafter of, bought a Barbary-horfe for that purpofe, which coft him 200 Piftols, and foon after another Barbary-horfe from the Lord *Crofts*, for which he was to pay him 100l. when he returned into *England*.

About this time, there was a Council call'd at St. *Germain*, in which were prefent, befides

My Lord, Her Majesty the now Queen Mother of *England;* His Highness the Prince, our now gracious King, His Cousin Prince *Rupert ;* the Marquess of *Worcester,* the then Marquess, now Duke of *Ormond,* the Lord *Jermyn* now Earl of St. *Albans,* and several others ; where after several debates concerning the then present condition of His Majesty King *Charles* the First, my Lord delivered his sentiment, that he could perceive no other probability of procuring Forces for His Majesty, but an assistance of the *Scots ;* But Her Majesty was pleased to answer my Lord, That he was too quick.

Not long after, When my Lord had begun to settle himsef in his mentioned new house, His gracious Master the Prince, having taken a resolution to go into *Holland* upon some designs, Her Majesty the Queen Mother desired my Lord to follow him, promising to engage for his debts which hitherto he had contracted at *Paris,* and commanding Her Controller[1] and Treasurer[2] to be bound for them in Her behalf ; which they did, although

----

[1] Sir *Henry Wood.*     [2] Sir ——— *Foster.*

the Creditors would not content themfelves, until my Lord had joined his word to theirs ; So great and generous was the bounty and favour of her Majefty to my Lord ! confidering fhe had already given him heretofore near upon 2000l. *Sterling*, even at that time when Her Majefty ftood moft in need of it.

My Lord, after his Highnefs the Prince was gone, being ready to execute Her Majefties Commands in following Him, and preparing for his Journey, wanted the chief thing, which was Money; and having much endeavoured for it, at laft had the good Fortune to obtain upon Credit three or four hundred pounds *fterl.* With which Sum he fet out of *Paris* in the fame Equipage he entred, *viz.* One Coach, which he had newly caufed to be made, (wherein were the Lord *Widdrington*, my Lord's Brother Sir *Charles Cavendifh*, Mr. *Loving*, my Waiting-Maid, and fome others, whereof the two later were then returned out of *England*) one little Chariot, that would onely hold my Lord and my felf; and three Waggons, befides an indifferent number of Servants on Horfe-back.

That day when we left *Paris*, the Creditors

coming to take their Farwell of my Lord, expreffed fo great a love and kindnefs for him,
accompanied with fo many hearty Prayers and
Wifhes, that he could not but profper on his
Journey.

Being come into the King of *Spain's* Dominions, my Lord found a very Noble Reception. At *Cambray* the Governour was fo
civil, that my Lord coming to that place fomewhat late, and when it was dark, he commanded fome Lights and Torches to meet my
Lord, and conduct him to his Lodgings: He
offer'd my Lord the Keys of the City, and
defir'd him to give the Word that night, and
moreover invited him to an Entertainment,
which he had made for him of purpofe ; but
it being late, my Lord (tyred with his Journey)
excufed himfelf as civilly as he could; the
Governour notwithftanding being pleafed to
fend all manner of Provifions to my Lords
Lodgings, and charging our Landlord to take
no pay for any thing we had : Which extraordinary Civilities fhewed that he was a Right
Noble *Spaniard.*

The next morning early, my Lord went on
his Journey, and was very civilly ufed in

every place of His Majefty of *Spain's* Dominions, where he arrived : At laft coming to
*Antwerp*, He took water to *Rotterdam* (which
Town he chofe for his refiding place, during
the time of his ftay in *Holland*) and fent
thither to a Friend of his,[1] a Gentleman of
Quality, to provide him fome Lodgings; which
he did, and procured them at the houfe of
one Mrs. *Beynham*, Widow to an Englifh
Merchant, who had always been very Loyal
to His Majefty the King of *England*, and ferviceable to His Majefties faithful Subjects in
whatfoever lay in his Power.

My Lord being come to *Rotterdam*, was informed that His Highnefs the Prince (now
our Gracious King) was gone to Sea : Wherefore he refolved to follow him, and for that
purpofe hired a Boat, and victual'd it; but
fince nobody knew whither His Highnefs was
gone, and I being unwilling that my Lord
fhould venture upon fo uncertain a Voyage,
and (as the Proverb is) *Seek a Needle in a
Bottle of Hay*, he defifted from that defign :
The Lord *Widdrington* neverthelefs, and Sir

---

[1] Sir *William Throckmorton*, Knight.

*Will. Throckmorton*, being refolved to find out the Prince, but having by a ftorm been driven towards the Coaft of *Scotland*, and endangered their lives, they returned without obtaining their aim.

After fome little time, my Lord having notice that the Prince was arrived at the *Hague*, he went to wait on His Highnefs (which he alfo did afterwards at feveral times, fo long as His Highnefs continued there) expecting fome opportunity where he might be able to fhew his readinefs to ferve His King and Countrey, as certainly there was no little hopes for it; for firft, it was believed that the Englifh fleet would come and render it felf into the obedience of the Prince; next, it was reported that the Duke of *Hamilton* was going out of *Scotland* with a great Army, into *England*, to the affiftance of His Majefty, and that His Majefty had then fome party at *Colchefter*; but it pleafed God that none of thefe proved effectual. For the Fleet did not come in; the Duke of *Hamilton's* Army was deftroyed, and *Colchefter* was taken by the Enemy, where my dear Brother Sir *Charles Lucas*, and his dear Friend Sir *George Lile*, were moſt inhumanly murther'd and ſhot to death, they being both Valiant and Heroick Perſons, good Soldiers, and moſt Loyal Subjeſts to His Majeſty; the one an excellent Commander of Horſe, the other of Foot.

My Lord having now lived in *Rotterdam* almoſt ſix months, at a great charge, keeping an open and noble Table for all comers, and being pleaſed eſpecially to entertain ſuch as were excellent Soldiers, and noted Commanders of War, whoſe kindneſs he took as a great Obligation, ſtill hoping that ſome occaſion would happen to invite thoſe worthy Perſons into *England* to ſerve His Majeſty; but ſeeing no probability of either returning into *England,* or doing His Majeſty any ſervice in that kind, he reſolved to retire to ſome place where he might live privately; and having choſen the City of *Antwerp* for that purpoſe, went to the *Hague* to take his leave of His Highneſs the Prince, our now gracious Soveraign. My Lord had then but a ſmall ſtock of money left; for though the then *Marqueſs* of *Hereford* (after Duke of *Somerſet,* and his Couſin-German, once removed, the now Earl of *Devonſhire* had lent him 2000l. between them; yet all that was spent, and above 1000l. more, which my Lord borrowed during the time he lived in *Rotterdam*, his Expence being the more, by reason (as I mentioned) he lived freely and nobly.

However my Lord, notwithstanding that little provision of Money he had, set forth from *Rotterdam* to *Antwerp*, where for some time he lay in a publick Inne, until one of his Friends that had a great love and respect for my Lord, Mr. *Endymion Porter*, who was Groom of the Bed-chamber to His Majesty King *Charles* the First (a place not onely honourable, but very profitable) being not willing that a Person of such Quality as my Lord, should lie in a publick House, profer'd him Lodgings at the House where he was, and would not let my Lord be at quiet, until he had accepted of them.

My Lord after he had stay'd some while there, endeavouring to find out a House for himself which might fit him and his small Family, (for at that time he had put off most of his Train) and also be for his own content, lighted on one that belonged to the Widow of a famous Picture-drawer, *Van Ruben*,[1] which he took.

About this time my Lord was much necef-fitated for Money, which forced him to try feveral ways for to obtain fo much as would relieve his prefent wants. At laft Mr. *Alef-bury*, the onely Son to Sir *Th. Alefbury*, Knight and Baronet, and Brother to the now Coun-tefs of *Clarendon*, a very worthy Gentleman, and great Friend to my Lord, having fome Moneys that belonged to the now Duke of *Buckingham*, and feeing my Lord in fo great diftrefs, did him the favour to lend him 200l. (which money my Lord fince his return hath honeftly and juftly repai'd). This relief came fo feafonably, that it got my Lord Credit in the City of *Antwerp*, whereas otherwife he would have loft himfelf to his great difadvan-tage; for my Lord having hired the houfe aforementioned, and wanting Furniture for it, was credited by the Citizens for as many Goods as he was pleafed to have, as alfo for Meat and Drink, and all kind of neceffaries

---

[1] This " picture-drawer " was no other than Rubens, the eminent artift. He had a magnificent mufeum, which the duke afterwards purchafed for 1,000l.

and provifions, which certainly was a fpecial Bleffing of God, he being not onely a ftranger in that Nation, but to all appearance, a Ruined man.

After my Lord had been in *Antwerp* some-time, where he lived as retiredly as it was poffible for him to do, he gained much love and refpect of all that knew or had any bufinefs with him: At the beginning of our coming thither, we found but few Englifh (except thofe that were Merchants) but afterwards their number increafed much, efpecially of Perfons of Quality; and whereas at firft there were no more but four Coaches that went the *Tour, viz.* the Governors of the Caftle, my Lords, and two more, they amounted to the number of above a hundred, before we went from thence; for all thofe that had fufficient means, and could go to the price, kept Coaches, and went the *Tour* for their own pleafure. And certainly I cannot in duty and confcience but give this Publick Teftimony to that place. That whereas I have obferv'd, that moft commonly fuch Towns or Cities where the Prince of that Country doth not refide himfelf, or where there is no great refort of the chief Nobility and Gentry, are but little civilifed ; Certainly, the Inhabitants of the faid City of *Antwerp* are the civileft, and beft behaved People that ever I faw ; fo that my Lord lived there with as much content as a man of his condition could do, and his chief paftime and divertifement confifted in the Mannage of the two afore mentioned Horfes ; which he had not enjoyed long, but the *Barbary*-horfe, for which he paid 200 Piftols in *Paris*, died, and foon after the Horfe which he had from the Lord *Crofts* ; and though he wanted prefent means to repair thefe his loffes, yet he endeavoured and obtained fo much Credit at laft that he was able to buy two others, and by degrees fo many as amounted in all to the number of 8. In which he took fo much delight and pleafure, that though he was then in diftrefs for Money, yet he would fooner have tried all other ways, then parted with any of them ; for I have hear'd him fay, that good Horfes are fo rare, as not to be valued for Mony, and that He who would buy him out of his Pleafure (meaning his Horfes), muft pay dear for it. For inftance I fhall mention fome paſſages which happen'd when My Lord was in *Antwerp*.

Firſt; A ſtranger coming thither, and ſeeing my Lords Horſes, had a great mind to buy one of them, which my Lord loved above the reſt, and called him his Favourite, a fine *Spaniſh* Horſe; intreating my Lords Eſcuyer to acquaint him with his deſire, and aſk the price of the ſaid Horſe: My Lord, when he heard of it, commanded his Servant, that if the Chapman returned, he ſhould be brought before him; which being done accordingly, my Lord aſked him, whether he was reſolved to buy his *Spaniſh* Horſe? Yes, anſwered he, my Lord, and I'le give your Lordſhip a good price for him. I make no doubt of it, replied My Lord, or elſe you ſhall not have him: But you muſt know, ſaid he, that the price of that Horſe is 1000*l.* to day, to morrow it will be 2000*l.* next day 3000*l.* and ſo forth. By which the Chapman perceiving that my Lord was unwilling to part with the ſaid Horſe for any Money, took his leave, and ſo went his ways.

The next was, That the Duke *de Guiſe*, who was alſo a great lover of good Horſes, hearing much Commendation of a gray leaping Horfe, which my Lord then had, told the Gentleman that praifed and commended him, That if my Lord was willing to fell the faid Horfe, he would give 600 Piftols for him. The Gentleman knowing my Lords humour, anfwered again, That he was confident, my Lord would never part with him for any mony, and to that purpofe fent a Letter to my Lord from *Paris*; but my Lord was fo far from felling that Horfe, that he was difpleafed to hear that any Price fhould be offer'd for him : So great a Love hath my Lord for good Horfes! And certainly I have obferved, and do verily believe, that fome of them had alfo a particular Love to my Lord; for they feemed to rejoice whenfoever he came into the Stables, by their trampling action, and the noife they made; nay, they would go much better in the Mannage, when my Lord was by, then when he was abfent; and when he rid them himfelf, they feemed to take much pleafure and pride in it. But of all forts of Horfes, my Lord loved *Spanifh* Horfes and *Barbes* beft; faying, That *Spanifh* Horfes were like Princes, and *Barbes* like Gentlemen, in their kind. And this was the chief Recreation and Paſtime my Lord had in *Antwerp*.

I will now return to my former Diſcourſe, and the Relation of ſome Important Affairs and Actions which happen'd about this time: His Majeſty (our now Gracious King, *Charles* the Second) ſome time after he was gone out of *Holland*, and returned into *France*, took his Journey from thence to *Breda* (if I remember well) to treat there with his Subjects of *Scot-land*, who had then made ſome offers of Agree-ment: My Lord, according to his duty, went thither to wait on His Majeſty, and was there in Council with His Majeſty, His Highneſs the then Prince of *Orange*, His Majeſties Brother-in-law, and ſome other Privy-Coun-ſellors; in which, after ſeveral Debates con-cerning that Important Affair, His Highneſs the Prince of *Orange*, and my Lord, agreed in one Opinion, *viz.* That they could perceive no other and better way at that preſent for His Majeſty, but to make an Agreement with His Subjects of *Scotland*, upon any Condition, and to go into *Scotland* in Perſon Himſelf, that he might but be ſure of an Army, there being no probability or appearance then of getting an Army any where elfe. Which Counfel, either out of the then alledged Reafons, or fome others beft known to His Majefty, was embraced; His Majefty agreeing with the *Scots* fo far, (notwithftanding they were fo unreafonable in their Treaty, that His Majefty had hardly Patience to hear them) that he refolved to go into *Scotland* in Perfon; and though my Lord had an earneft defire to wait on His Majefty thither, yet the *Scots* would not fuffer him to come, or be in any part of that Kingdom: Wherefore out of his Loyalty and Duty, he gave His Majefty the beft advice he could, *viz.* that he conceived it moft fafe for His Majefty to adhere to the Earl of *Argyle's* Party, which he fuppofed to be the ftrongeft; but efpecially, to reconcile *Hamilton's* and *Argyle's* Party, and compofe the differences between them; for then His Majefty would be fure of Two Parties, whereas otherwife He would leave an Enemy behind Him, which might caufe His overthrow, and endanger His Majefties Perfon; and if His Majefty could but get the Power into his own hands, he might do hereafter what he pleafed.

His Majefty being arrived in *Scotland*, ordered his affairs fo wifely, that foon after he
got an Army to march with him into *England*; but whether they were all Loyal, is
not for me to difpute : However, *Argyle* was
difcontented, as it appear'd by two complaining Letters he fent to my Lord, which my
Lord gave His Majefty notice of; fo that
onely the Duke of *Hamilton* went with His
Majefty, who fought and died like a Valiant
Man, and a Loyal fubject.  In this fight between the *Englifh* and *Scots*, His Majefty
expreffed an extraordinary Courage ; and
though his Army was in a manner deftroyed,
yet the Glory of an Heroick Prince remained
with our gracious Soveraign.

In the mean time, whileft His Majefty was
yet in *Scotland*, and before he marched with
His Army into *England*, it happen'd that the
Elector of *Brandenburg*, and Duke of *Newburg*,
upon fome differences, having raifed Forces
againft each other, but afterwards concluded
a Peace between them, were pleafed to profer
thofe Forces to my Lord for His Majefties
ufe and fervice, which (as the Lord Chancellour, who was then in *France*, fent word to

my Lord) was the onely Foreign profer that had been made to his Majefty. My Lord immediately gave His Majefty notice of it; but whether it was for want of convenient Tranfportation, or Mony, or that the *Scots* did not like the affiftance, that profer was not accepted.

Concerning the affairs and intrigues that pafs'd in *Scotland*, and *England*, during the time of His Majefties ftay there, I am ignorant of them; neither doth it belong to me now to write, or give an account of any thing elfe but what concerns the Hiftory of my Noble Lord and Hufbands Life, and his own Actions; who fo foon as he had Intelligence that the *Scottifh* Army, which went with His Majefty into *England*, was defeated, and that no body knew what was become of His Majefty, fell into fo violent a Paffion, that I verily believed it would have endanger'd his life; but when afterwards the happy news came of His Majefties fafe arrival in *France*, never any Subject could rejoice more then my Lord did.

About this time it chanced, that my Lords Brother Sir *Charles Cavendifh*, and my felf, took a journey into *England*, occafioned both by my Lord's extream want and neceffity, and his Brothers Eftate; which having been under Sequeftration from the time (or foon after) he went out of *England*, was then, in cafe he did not return and compound for it, to be fold out-right; Sir *Charles* was unwilling to receive his Eftate upon fuch conditions, and would rather have loft it, then compounded for it: But my Lord confidering it was better to recover fomething, then lofe all, intreated the Lord Chancellour, who was then in *Antwerp*, to perfwade his Brother to a compofition, which his Lordfhip did very effectually, and proved himfelf a Noble and true Friend in it. We had fo fmall a Provifion of money when we fet forth our Journey for *England*, that it was hardly able to carry us to *London*, but were forced to ftay at *Southwark*; where Sir *Charles* fent into *London* for one that had formerly been his Steward; and having declared to him his wants and neceffities, defir'd him to try his Credit. He feemed ready to do his Mafter what fervice he could in that kind; but pretending withall, that his Credit was but fmall, Sir *Charles* gave him his

Watch to pawn, and with that money paid thofe fmall fcores we had made in our Lodging there. From thence we went to fome other Lodgings that were prepared for us in *Covent-Garden*; and having refted our felves fome time, I defired my Brother the Lord *Lucas*, to claim, in my behalf, fome fubfiftance for my felf out of my Lords Eftate, (for it was declared by the Parliament, That the Lands of thofe that were banifhed, fhould be fold to any that would buy them, onely their Wives and Children were allowed to put in their Claims:) But he received this Anfwer, That I could not expect the leaft allowance, by reafon my Lord and Hufband had been the greateft Traitor of *England* (that is to fay, the honefteft man, becaufe he had been moft againft them.)

Then Sir *Charles* intrufted fome perfons to compound for his Eftate; but it being a good while before they agreed in their Compofition, and then before the Rents could be received, we having in the mean time nothing to live on, muft of neceffity have been ftarved, had not Sir *Charles* got fome Credit of feveral Perfons, and that not without great difficulty;

for all thofe that had Eftates, were afraid to come near him, much lefs to affift him, until he was fure of his own Eftate.  So much is Mifery and Poverty fhun'd !

But though our Condition was hard, yet my dear Lord and Hufband, whom we left in *Antwerp*, was then in a far greater diftrefs then our felves; for at our departure he had nothing but what his Credit was able to pro-cure him; and having run upon the fcore fo long without paying any the leaft part there-of, his Creditors began to grow impatient, and refolved to truft him no longer : Where-fore he fent me word, That if his Brother did not prefently relieve him, he was forced to ftarve.  Which doleful news caufed great fadnefs and melancholy in us both, and withal made his Brother try his utmoft endeavour to procure what moneys he could for his fubfift-ance, who at laft got 200 l. *fterl.* upon Credit, which he immediately made over to my Lord.

But in the mean time, before the faid money could come to his hands, my Lord had been forced to fend for all his Creditors, and declare to them his great wants and neceffities ; where his Speech was fo effectual, and made fuch an impreffion in them, that they had all a deep fenfe of my Lords Misfortunes; and inftead of urging the payment of his Debts, promifed him, That he fhould not want any thing in whatfoever they were able to affift him; which they alfo very nobly and civilly performed, furnifhing him with all manner of provifions and neceffaries for his further fubfiftance; fo that my Lord was then in a much better condition amongft ftrangers, then we in our Native Countrey.

At laft when Sir *Charles Cavendifh* had compounded for his Eftate, and agreed to pay 4500 l. for it, the Parliament caufed it again to be furveyed, and made him pay 500 l. more, which was more then many others had paid for much greater Eftates; fo that Sir *Charles* to pay this Compofition, and difcharge fome Debts, was neceffitated to fell fome Land of his at an under-rate. My Lords two Sons (who were alfo in *England* at that time) were no lefs in want and neceffity, then we, having nothing but bare Credit to live on; and my Lords Eftate being then to be fold outright, Sir *Charles*, his Brother, endeavoured, if poffible, to fave the two chief Houfes, *viz. Welbeck* and *Bolsover*, being resolved rather to part with some more of his Land, which he had lately compounded for, then to let them fall into the Enemies hands ; but before such time as he could compass the money, some body had bought *Bolsover*, with an intention to pull it down, and make money of the Materials ; of whom Sir *Charles* was forced to buy it again at a far greater Rate then he might have had it at first, notwithstanding a great part of it was pulled down already ; and though my Lords eldest Son *Charles* Lord *Mansfield*, had those mentioned Houses some time in possession, after the death of his Uncle ; yet for want of Means he was not able to repair them.

I having now been in *England* a year and a half, some Intelligence which I received of my Lords being not very well, and the small hopes I had of getting some relief out of his Estate, put me upon design of returning to *Antwerp* to my Lord ; and Sir *Charles*, his Brother, took the same resolution, but was prevented by an Ague that seized upon him. Not long had I been with my Lord, but we received the sad news of his Brothers death, which was an extream affliction both to my Lord, and my felf, for they loved each other entirely : In truth, He was a Perfon of fo great worth, fuch extraordinary civility, fo obliging a Nature, fo full of Generofity, Juftice and Charity, befides all manner of Learning, efpecially in the *Mathematicks*, that not onely his Friends, but even his Enemies, did much lament his lofs.

After my return out of *England*, to my Lord, the Creditors fuppofing I had brought great ftore of money along with me, came all to my Lord to folicite the payment of their Debts; but when my Lord had informed them of the truth of the bufinefs, and defired their patience fomewhat longer, with affurance that fo foon as he received any money, he would honeftly and juftly fatisfie them, they were not onely willing to forbear the payment of thofe Debts he had contracted hitherto, but to credit him for the future, and fupply him with fuch Neceffaries as he fhould defire of them. And this was the onely happinefs which my Lord had in his diftreffed condition, and the chief bleffing of the Eternal and Merciful God, in whofe Power are all things, who ruled the hearts and minds of men, and filled them with Charity and Compaſſion ; for certainly it was a work of Divine Providence, that they ſhewed ſo much love, reſpect and honour to my Lord, a ſtranger to their Nation ; and notwithſtanding his ruined Condition, and the ſmall appearance of recovering his own, credited him whereſoever he lived, both in *France, Hòlland, Brabant* and *Germany;* that although my Lord was baniſhed his Native Countrey, and diſpoſſeſſed from his own Eſtate, could neverthelefs live in ſo much Splendor and Grandure as he did.

In this Condition (and how little ſoever the appearance was) my Lord was never without hopes of ſeeing yet (before his death) a happy iſſue of all his misfortunes and ſuffèrings, eſpecially of the Reſtauration of His moſt Gracious King and Maſter, to His Throne and Kingly Rights, whereof he always had aſſured Hopes, well knowing, that it was impoſſible for the Kingdom to ſubſiſt long under ſo many changes of Government ; and whenſoever I expreſſed how little faith I had in it, he would gently reprove me, ſaying, I believ'd leaſt, what I deſir'd moſt ; and could never be happy if I endeavour'd to exclude all hopes, and entertain'd nothing but doubts and fears.

The City of *Antwerp* in which we lived, being a place of great refort for Strangers and Travellers, His Majefty (our now gracious King, *Charles* the Second) paffed thorough it, when he went his Journey towards *Germany;* and after my Lord had done his humble duty, and waited on His Majefty, He was pleafed to Honour him with his Prefence at his Houfe. The fame did almoft all ftrangers that were Perfons of Quality; if they made any ftay in the Town, they would come and vifit my Lord, and fee the Mannage of his Horfes:[1] And, amongft the reft, the Duke of *Olden-burg*, and the Prince of *Eaft-Friefland*, did my Lord the Honour, and prefented him with Horfes of their own breed.

One time it happen'd, that His Highnefs *Dom John d' Auftria* (who was then Governour of thofe Provinces) came to *Antwerp*, and ftayed there fome few days; and then almoft all his Court waited on my Lord, fo that one day I reckoned about feventeen Coaches, in

---

[1] Another Philip !

which were all Perfons of Quality, who came
in the morning of purpofe to fee my Lord's
Mannage; My Lord receiving fo great an
honour thought it fit to fhew his refpect and
civility to them, and to ride fome of his Horfes
himfelf, which otherwife he never did but for
his own excercife and delight. Amongft the
reft of thofe great and noble Perfons, there
were two of our Nation, *viz.* the then Marquefs, now Duke of *Ormond*, and the Earl of
*Briftol*; but *Dom John* was not there in Perfon, excufing himfelf afterwards to my Lord
(when my Lord waited on him) that the mul-
tiplicity of his weighty affairs had hindred his
coming thither, which my Lord accounted as
a very high honour and favour from fo great
a Prince; and conceiving it his duty to wait
on his Highnefs, but being unknown to him,
the Earl of *Briftol*, who had acquaintance with
him, did my Lord the favour, and upon his
requeft, prefented him to his Highnefs; which
favour of the faid Earl my Lord highly refented.[1]

---

[1] This now obfolete ufe of the word *refented* founds
fingular to modern ears: we now never refent a favour, though we may refent an injury. The French

·*Dom John* received my Lord with all kindnefs and refpect; for although there were
many great and noble Perfons that waited on
him in an out room, yet fo foon as his Highnefs heard of my Lord's, and the Earl of
*Briftol's* being there, he was pleafed to admit
them before all the reft. My Lord, after he
had paffed his Complements, told His Highnefs, That he found himfelf bound in all duty
to make his humble acknowledgments for the
Favour he received from His Catholick Majefty for permitting and fuffering him (a
banifhed man) to live in His Dominions, and
under the Government of His Highnefs;
whereupon *Dom John* afk'd my Lord whether
he wanted any thing, and whether he liv'd
peaceably without any moleftation or difturbance? My Lord anfwer'd, That he lived as
much to his own content as a banifh'd man
could do; and received more refpect and civility
from that City then he could have expected,
for which he returned his moft humble thanks
to his Catholick Majefty, and His Highnefs.

---

*reffentir* means equally, to take well or ill; and in the
feventeenth century to refent implied either an emotion
of gratitude, or a feeling of revenge.

After some short Discourse, my Lord took his leave of *Dom John;* Several of the *Spaniards* advising him to go into *Spain,* and assuring him of His Catholick Majesties Kindness and Favour; but my Lord being engaged in the City of *Antwerp,* and besides in years, and wanting means for so long and chargeable a voyage, was not able to embrace their motions; and surely he was so well pleased with the great Civilities he received from that City, that then he was resolved to chuse no other residing place all the time of his banishment but that; he being not onely credited there for all manner of Provisions and Necessaries for his subsistance, but also free both from ordinary and extraordinary Taxes, and from paying Excise, which was a great favour and obligation to my Lord.

After His Highness *Dom John* had left the Government of those Provinces the Marquess of *Caracena* succeeded in his place, who having a great desire to see my Lord ride in the Mannage, entreated a Gentleman of the City, that was acquainted with my Lord, to beg that favour of him. My Lord having not been at that Exercise six weeks, or two months, by reason of fome ficknefs that made him unfit for it, civilly begg'd his excufe ; but he was fo much importuned by the faid Gentleman that at laft he granted his Requeft, and rid one or two Horfes in prefence of the faid Marquefs of *Caracena*, and the then Marquefs, now Duke of *Ormond*, who often ufed ·to honour my Lord with his Company. The faid Marquefs of *Caracena* feem'd to take much pleafure and fatisfaction in it, and highly complemented my Lord; and certainly I have obferved, That Noble and Meritorious perfons take great delight in honouring each other.

But not onely ftrangers, but His Majefty Himfelf (our now Gracious Soveraign) was pleafed to fee my Lord ride, and one time did ride Himfelf, He being an Excellent Mafter of that Art, and inftructed by my Lord, who had the Honour to fet Him firft on· a Horfe of Mannage, when he was His Governour; where His Majefties Capacity was fuch, that being but Ten years of Age, he would ride leaping Horfes, and fuch as would overthrow others, and mannage them with the greateft Skill and Dexterity, to the admiration of all that beheld Him.

Nor was this the onely Honour my Lord received from His Majesty, but His Majesty and all the Royal Race; that is to say, Her Highness the then Princess Royal, His Highness the Duke of *York*, with His Brother the Duke of *Glocester*, (except the Princesse *Henrietta*, now Duchess of *Orleans*,) being met one time in *Antwerp*, were pleased to honour my Lord with their Presence, and accept of a small Entertainment at his House, such as his present Condition was able to afford them. And some other time His Majesty passing through the City was pleased to accept of a private Dinner at my Lord's House; after which I receiving that gracious Favour from His Majesty, that he was pleased to see me, he did merrily and in jest, tell me, *That he perceived my Lord's Credit could procure better Meat then His own.* Again, some other time, upon a merry Challenge playing a Game at Butts with my Lord (when my Lord had the better of Him), *What* (said He) *my Lord, have you invited me to play the Rook with me?*[1]

---

[1] " To play the Rook," means to play the *sharper*. "Rook" is synonymous with a cheat.  A " rookery "

Although their Stakes were not at all confiderable, but onely for Paftime.

Thefe paffages I mention onely to declare
my Lord's happinefs in his miferies, which he
received by the honour and kindnefs not onely
of foreign Princes, but of his own Mafter and
Gracious Soveraign: I will not fpeak now of
the good efteem and repute he had by his late
Majefty King *Charles* the Firft, and Her
Majefty the now Queen-Mother, who always
held and found him a very loyal and faithful
Subject, although Fortune was pleafed to
oppofe him in the height of his endeavours;
for his onely and chief intention was to hinder
His Majefties Enemies from executing that
cruel defign which they had upon their gracious
and merciful King; In which he tried his
uttermoft power, in fo much that I have heard
him fay out of a paffionate Zeal and Loyalty,
That he would willingly facrifice himfelf and
all his Pofterity, for the fake of his Majefty
and the Royal Race. Nor did he ever repine

---

in many of our old towns is the rendezvous of difhoneft
perfons. That pleafant bird, the rook, was formerly
regarded as a thief—but he does far more good than
harm.

either at his loſſes or ſufferings, but rejoyced rather that he was able to ſuffer for His King and Countrey. His Army was the onely Army that was able to uphold His Majeſties Power; which ſo long as it was Victorious it preſerved both His Majeſties Perſon and Crown; but ſo ſoon as it fell, that fell too: and my Lord was then in a manner forced to ſeek his own preſervation in foreign Countries, where God was pleaſed to make ſtrangers his Friends, who received and protected him when he was baniſhed his native Country, and relieved him when his own Country-men ſought to ſtarve him, by withholding from him what was juſtly his own, onely for his Honeſty and Loyalty; which relief he received more from the Commons of thoſe parts where he lived, then from Princes, he being unwilling to trouble any foreign Prince with his wants and miſeries, well knowing, that Gifts of Great Princes come ſlowly, and not without much difficulty; neither loves he to petition any one but His own Soveraign.

But though my Lord by the civility of Strangers, and the aſſiſtance of ſome few Friends of his native Country, lived in an in-

different Condition, yet (as it hath been declared heretofore) he was put to great plunges
and difficulties, in fo much that his dear Brother Sir *Charles Cavendifh* would often fay,
That though he could not truly complain of
want, yet his meat never did him good by
reafon my Lord, his Brother, was always fo
near wanting, that he was never fure after one
meal to have another: And though I was not
afraid of ftarving or begging, yet my chief
fear was, that my Lord for his debts would
fuffer Imprifonment, where fadnefs of Mind,
and want of Exercife, and Air, would have
wrought his deftruction, which yet by the
Mercy of God he happily avoided.

Some time before the Reftauration of His
Majefty to his Royal Throne, my Lord, partly
with the remainder of his Brothers Eftate,
which was but little, it being wafted by felling
of Land for compounding with the Parliament,
paying of feveral debts, and buying out the
two Houfes aforementioned, *viz. Welbeck* and
*Bolfover;* and the Credit which his Sons had
got, which amounted in all to 2400l. a year,
fprinkled fomething amongft his Creditors,
and borrowed fo much of Mr. *Top* and Mr.

*Smith* (though without affurance) that he could pay fuch fcores as were moft preffing, contracted from the poorer fort of Trades-men, and fend ready mony to Market, to avoid cozenage (for fmall fcores run up moft unreafonably, efpecially if no ftrict accounts be kept, and the rate be left to the Creditors pleafure) by which means there was in a fhort time fo much faved, as it could not have been imagined.

About this time, a report came of a great number of Sectaries, and of feveral difturbances in *England,* which heightned my Lord's former ·hopes into a firm belief of a fudden Change in that Kingdom, and a happy Reftauration of His Majefty, w.hich it alfo pleafed God to fend according to his expectation; for His Majefty was invited by his Subjects, who were not able longer to endure thofe great confufions and encumbrances they had fuftained hitherto, to take poffeffion of His · Hereditary Rights, and the power of all his Dominions : And being then at the *Hague* in *Holland,* to take fhipping in thofe parts for *England,* my Lord went thither to wait on his Majefty, who ufed my Lord very Gracioufly;

and his Highnefs the Duke of *York* was pleafed to offer him one of thofe Ships that were ordered to tranfport His Majefty; for which he returned his moft humble thanks to his Highnefs, and begg'd leave of His Highnefs that he might hire a Veffel for himfelf and his Company.

In the mean time whilft my Lord was at the *Hague*, His Majefty was pleafed to tell him, That General *Monk*, now Duke of *Albemarle*, had defired the Place of being Mafter of the Horfe: To which my Lord anfwer'd, That that gallant Perfon was worthy of any Favour that His Majefty could confer upon him: And having taken his leave of His Majefty, and His Highnefs the Duke of *York*, went towards the Ship that was to tranfport him for *England*, (I might better call it a Boat, then a Ship; for thofe that were intrufted by my Lord to hire a Ship for that purpofe, had hired an old rotten Fregat, that was loft the next Voyage after; infomuch, that when fome of the Company that had promifed to go over with my Lord, faw it, they turn'd back, and would not endanger their lives in it, except the now Lord *Wid-*

*drington,* who was refolved not to forfake my Lord.)

My Lord (who was fo tranfported with the joy of returning into his Native Countrey, that he regarded not the Veffel) having fet Sail from *Rotterdam,* was fo becalmed, that he was fix dayes and fix nights upon the Water, during which time he pleafed himfelf with mirth, and pafs'd his time away as well as he could ; Provifions he wanted not, having them in great ftore and plenty.  At laft being come fo far that he was able to difcern the fmoak of *London,* which he had not feen in a long time, he merrily was pleafed to defire one that was near him, to jogg and awake him out of his dream, for furely, faid he, I have been fixteen years afleep, and am not throughly awake yet.  My Lord lay that night at *Greenwich,* where his Supper feem'd more favoury to him, then any meat he had hitherto tafted ; and the noife of fome fcraping Fidlers, he thought the pleafanteft harmony that ever he had heard.

In the mean time my Lords Son, *Henry* Lord *Mansfield,* now Earl of *Ogle,* was gone to *Dover* with intention to wait on His Majefty, and receive My Lord his Father, with all joy and duty, thinking he had been with His Majesty ; but when he mifs'd of his defign, he was very much troubled, and more, when His Majesty was pleas'd to tell him, That my Lord had fet to Sea, before His Majesty Himself was gone out of *Holland*, fearing my Lord had met with fome Misfortune in his Journey, becaufe he had not heard of his Landing. Wherefore he immediately parted from *Dover*, to feek my Lord, whom at laft he found at *Greenwich ;* with what joy they embraced and faluted each other, my Pen is too weak to exprefs.

But all this while, and after my Lord was gone from *Antwerp*, I was left alone there with fome of my fervants ; for my Lord being in *Holland* with His Majesty, declared in a Letter to me his intention of going for *England*, withal commanding me to ftay in that City, as a Pawn for his debts, until he could compafs money to difcharge them ; and to excufe him to the Magiftrates of the faid City for not taking his leave of them, and paying his due thanks for their great civilities, which he defired me to do in his behalf. And certainly my Lords affection to me was fuch, that it made him very induſtrious in providing thoſe means ; for it being uncertain what or whether he ſhould have any thing of his Eſtate, made it a difficult buſineſs for him to borrow Mony; At laſt he received ſome of one Mr. *Aſh*, now Sir *Joſeph Aſh*, a Merchant of *Antwerp*, which he returned to me ; but what with the expence I had made in the mean while, and what was required for my tranſporting into *England*, beſides the debts formerly contracted, the ſaid money fell too ſhort by 400l. and although I could have upon my own word taken up much more, yet I was unwilling to leave an engagement amongſt ſtrangers : Wherefore I ſent for one Mr. *Shaw*, now Sir *John Shaw*, a near kindſman to the ſaid Mr. *Aſh*, intreating him to lend me 400l. which he did moſt readily, and ſo diſcharged my debts.

My departure being now divulged in *Antwerp*, the Magiſtrates of the City came to take their leaves of me, where I deſired one Mr. *Duart* a very worthy Gentleman, and one of the chief of the City, though he derives his Race from the *Portuguez* (to whom and his Siſters, all very ſkilful in the Art of Muſick, though for their own paſtime and Recreation,

both my Lord and my felf were much bound
for their great civilities) to be my Interpreter.
They were pleafed to exprefs that they were
forry for our departure out of their City, but
withal rejoyced at our happy returning into
our Native Country, and wifhed me foon and
well to the place where I moft defired to be :
Whereupon I having excufed my Lord's hafty
going away without taking his leave of them,
returned them mine and my Lord's hearty
Thanks for their great civilities, declaring how
forry I was that it lay not in my power to
make an acknowledgment anfwerable to them.
But after their departure from me, they were
pleafed to fend their Under-Officers (as the
cuftom there is) with a Prefent of Wine,
which I received with all refpect and thankfulnefs.

I being thus prepar'd for my Voyage, went
with my Servants to *Fluffing*, and finding no
*Englifh* Man of War there, being loth to truft
my felf with a lefs Veffel, was at laft informed
that a *Dutch* man of War lay there ready to
Convoy fome Merchants ; I forthwith fent for
the Captain thereof, whofe name was *Bankert*,
and afked him whether it was poffible to obtain

the favour of having the ufe of his Ship to tranfport me into *England?* To which he anfwered, That he queftion'd not but I might; for the Merchants which he was to convey, were not ready yet, defiring me to fend one of my fervants to the State, to requeft that favour of them; with whom he would go himfelf, and affift him the beft he could; which he alfo did. My fuit being granted, my felf and my chief fervants embarqued in the faid Ship; the reft, together with the Goods, being conveyed in another good ftrong Veffel, hired for that purpofe.

After I was fafely arrived at *London*, I found my Lord in Lodgings; I cannot call them unhandfome; but yet they were not fit for a Perfon of his Rank and Quality, nor of the capacity to contain all his Family: Neither did I find my Lord's Condition fuch as I expected: Wherefore out of fome paffion I defir'd him to leave the Town, and retire into the Countrey; but my Lord gently reproved me for my rafhnefs and impatience, and foon after removed into *Dorfet*-houfe; which, though it was better then the former, yet not altogether to my fatisfaction, we having but a part of the faid Houfe in poffeffion. By this removal I judged my Lord would not haftily depart from *London;* but not long after, he was pleafed to tell me, That he had difpatched his bufinefs, and was now refolved to remove into the Country, having already given order for Waggons to tranfport our goods, which was no unpleafant news to me, who had a great defire for a Countrey-life.

My Lord before he began his Journey, went to his Gracious Soveraign, and begg'd leave that he might retire into the Countrey, to reduce and fettle, if poffible, his confufed, entangled, and almoft ruined Eftate, *Sir*, faid he to His Majefty, *I am not ignorant, that many believe I am difcontented; and 'tis probable they'l fay, I retire through difcontent: But I take God to witnefs, That I am in no kind or ways difpleas'd; for I am fo joyed at your Majefties happy Reftauration, that I cannot be fad or troubled for any Concern to my own particular; but whatfoever Your Majefty is pleafed to command me, were it to facrifice my Life, I fhall moft obediently perform it; for I have no other Will, but Your Majefties Pleafure.*

Thus he kiffed His Majefty's hand, and.

went the next day into *Nottingham-fhire*, to his Mannor-houfe call'd *Welbeck;* but when he came there, and began to examine his Eftate, and how it had been ordered in the time of his Banifhment, he knew not whether he had left any thing of it for himfelf, or not, till by his prudence and wifdom he inform'd himfelf the beft he could, examining thofe that had moft knowledg therein. Some Lands, he found, could be recover'd no further then for his life, and fome not at all : Some had been in the Rebels hands, which he could not recover, but by His Highnefs the Duke of *York*'s favour, to whom His Majefty had given all the Eftates of thofe that were condemned and executed for murdering his Royal Father of bleffed memory, which by the Law were forfeited to His Majefty ; whereof His Highnefs gracioufly reftor'd my Lord fo much of the Land that formerly had been his, as amounted to 730l. a year. And though my Lord's Children had their Claims granted, and bought out the life of my Lord, their Father, which came near upon the third part, yet my Lord received nothing for himfelf out of his own Eftate, for the fpace of eighteen

years, viz. During the time from the firft
entring into Warr, which was *June* 11. 1642,
till his return out of Banifhment, *May* 28.
1660; for though his Son *Henry*, now Earl
of *Ogle*, and his eldeft Daughter, the now
Lady *Cheiny*, did all what lay in their power
to relieve my Lord their Father, and fent
him fome fupplies of moneys at feveral times
when he was in banifhment ; yet that was of
their own, rather then out of my Lord's
Eftate ; for the Lady *Cheiny* fold fome few
Jewels which my Lord, her Father, had left
her, and fome Chamber-Plate which fhe had
from her Grandmother, and fent over the
money to my Lord, befides 1000l. of her Portion : And the now Earl of *Ogle* did at feveral
times fupply my Lord, his Father, with fuch
moneys as he had partly obtained upon Credit,
and partly made by his Marriage.

After my Lord had begun to view thofe
Ruines that were neareft, and tried the Law
to keep or recover what formerly was his,
(which certainly fhew'd no favour to him,
befides that the Act of Oblivion proved a
great hinderance and obftruction to thofe his
defigns, as it did no lefs to all the Royal Party)

and had fetled fo much of his Eftate as poffibly he could, he caft up the Summ of his Debts, and fet out feveral parts of Land for the payment of them, or of fome of them (for fome of his Lands could not be eafily fold, being entailed) and fome he fold in *Derbyſhire* to buy the Caftle of *Nottingham*, which although it is quite ruined and demoliſht, yet, it being a feat which had pleafed his Father very much, he would not leave it fince it was offer'd to be fold.

His two Houfes *Welbeck* and *Bolfover* he found much out of repair, and this later half pull'd down, no furniture or any neceffary Goods were left in them, but fome few Hangings and Pictures, which had been faved by the care and induftry of his Eldeft Daughter the Lady *Cheiny*, and were bought over again after the death of his eldeft Son *Charles*, Lord *Mansfield*; for they being given to him, and he leaving fome debts to be paid after his death, My Lord fent to his other Son *Henry*, now Earl of *Ogle*, to endeavour for fo much Credit, that the faid Hangings and Pictures (which my Lord efteemed very much, the Pictures being drawn by *Van Dyke*) might be saved; which he also did, and My Lord hath paid the debt since his return.

Of eight Parks, which my Lord had before the Wars, there was but one left that was not quite destroyed, *viz. Welbeck*-Park of about four miles compass; for my Lord's Brother Sir *Charles Cavendish*, who bought out the life of my Lord in that Lordship, saved most part of it from being cut down; and in *Blore*-Park there were some few Deer left: The rest of the Parks were totally defaced and destroyed, both Wood, Pales and Deer; amongst which was also *Clipston*-Park of seven miles compass, wherein my Lord had taken much delight formerly, it being rich of Wood, and containing the greatest and tallest Timber-trees of all the Woods he had; in so much, that onely the Pale-row was valued at 2000l. It was water'd by a pleasant River that runs through it, full of fish and Otters; was well stock'd with Deer, full of Hares, and had great store of Partriges, Poots,[1] Pheasants, *&c.*

---

[1] *Poots.* I had a difficulty as to the meaning of this word; but through two able ornithologists I learn that *powt* signifies either the Black-cock or the Red-grouse, but more probably the former, which is a great fre-

befides all forts of Water-fowl; fo that this Park afforded all manner of fports, for Hunting, Hawking, Courfing, Fifhing, &c. for which my Lord efteemed it very much: And although his Patience and Wifdom is fuch, that I never perceived him fad or difcontented for his own Loffes and Misfortunes, yet when he beheld the ruines of that Park, I obferved him troubled, though he did little exprefs it, onely faying, he had been in hopes it would not have been fo much defaced as he found it, there being not one Timber-tree in it left for fhelter. However he patiently bore what could not be helped, and gave prefent order for the cutting down of fome Wood that was left him in a place near adjoining, to repale it, and got from feveral Friends Deer to ftock it.

Thus though his Law-fuits and other unavoidable expences were very chargeable to him, yet he order'd his affairs fo prudently,

---

quenter of woods. Primarily it fignifies a chicken of any kind, efpecially a young game bird. The word is doubtlefs of common etymology with *pullet, poultry*, &c. In fome provincial dialects the word *polt* is applied to a young pigeon.

that by degrees he ftock'd and manur'd thofe
Lands he keeps for his own ufe, and in part
repaired his Mannor-houfes, *Welbeck*, and *Bolfover*, to which latter he made fome additional
building; and though he has not yet built the
Seat at *Nottingham*, yet he hath ftock'd and
paled a little Park belonging to it.

Nor is it poffible for him to repair all the
ruines of the Eftate that is left him, in fo
fhort a time, they being fo great, and his loffes
fo confiderable, that I cannot without grief
and trouble remember them; for before the
Wars my Lord had as great an Eftate as
any fubject in the Kingdom, defcended upon
him moft by Women, *viz.* by his Grandmother of his Father's fide, his own Mother,
and his firft Wife.

What Eftate his Grandfather left to his
Father Sir *Charles Cavendifh*, I know not;
nor can I exactly tell what he had from his
Grandmother, but fhe was very rich; for her
third Hufband Sir *Will.* Saint *Loo*, gave her
a good Eftate in the Weft, which afterwards
defcended upon my Lord, my Lord's Mother
being the younger daughter of the Lord *Ogle*,
and fole Heir, after the death of her eldeft

Sifter *Jane*, Countefs of *Shrewsfbury*, whom King *Charles* the Firft reftored to her Fathers Dignity, *viz.* Baronefs of *Ogle :* This Title defcended upon my Lord and his Heirs General, together with 300l. a year in *Northumberland;* and befides the Eftate left to my Lord, fhe gave him 20000l. in Money, and kept him and his Family at her own charge for feveral years.

My Lord's firft Wife, who was Daughter and Heir to *William Baffet* of *Blore*, Efq; Widow to *Henry Howard*, younger Son to *Thomas* Earl of *Suffolk*, brought my Lord 2400l. a Year Inheritance, between fix and feven thoufand Pounds in Money, and a jointure for her life of 800l. a Year. Befides my Lord increafed his own Eftate before the Wars, to the value of 100000l. and had increafed it more, had not the unhappy Wars prevented him; for though he had fome difadvantages in his Eftate, even before the Wars, yet they are not confiderable to thofe he fuffered afterwards for the fervice of his King and Country: For example, His Father Sir *Charles Cavendifh* had lent his Brother in Law *Gilbert* Earl of *Shrewfbury* 16000l. for which, although afterward before his death he fetled 2000l. a year upon him ; yet he having injoyed the faid Money for many years without paying any ufe for it, it might have been improved to my Lord's better advantage, had it been in his Fathers own hands, he being a Perfon of great prudence in managing his Eftate ; and though the faid Earl of *Shrewf- bury* made my Lord his Executor, yet my Lord was fo far from making any advantage by that Truft, even in what the Law allowed him, that he loft 17000l. by it ; and afterwards delivered up his Truft to *William* Earl of *Pem- brook*, and *Thomas* Earl of *Arundel*, who both married two Daughters of the faid Earl of *Shrewfbury ;* And fince his return into *Eng- land*, upon the defire of *Henry Howard*, Second Son to the late Earl of *Arundel*, and Heir apparent, (by reafon of his Eldeft Brother's Diftemper) he refigned his Truft and Intereft to him, which certainly is a very difficult bufinefs, and yet queftionable whether it may lawfully be done, or not ?   But fuch was my Lord's Love to the Family of the *Shrewfburies*, that he would rather wrong himfelf, then it.

To mention fome lawful advantages which

my Lord might have made by the said Trust, it may be noted in the first place, That the Earl of *Shrewsbury*'s Estate was Let in long Leafes, which, by the Law, fell to the Executor.   Next, that after some Debts and Legacies were paid out of those Lands, which were set out for that purpose, they were setled so, that they fell to my Lord.   Thirdly, Seven hundred pounds a year was left as a Gift to my Lord's Brother, Sir *Charles Cavendish*, in case the Countefs of *Kent*, Second Daughter to the said Earl of *Shrewsbury*, had no Children.   But my Lord never made any advantage for himself, of all these; neither was he inquisitive whether the said Countefs of *Kent* cut off the Entail of that Land, although she never had a Child; for my Lord's Nature is so generous, that he hates to be Mercenary, and never minds his own Profit or Interest in any Trust or Employment, more then the good and benefit of him that intrusts or employs him.

But, as I said heretofore, these are but petty Losses in comparison of those he sustained by the late Civil Warrs, whereof I shall partly give you an account : I say partly; for though it may be computed what the lofs of the Annual Rents of his Lands amounts to, of which he never received the leaft worth for himfelf and his own profit, during the time both of his being employed in the Service of Warr, and his Sufferings in Banifhment; as alfo the lofs of thofe Lands that are alienated from him, both in prefent poffeffion, and in reverfion; and of his Parks and Woods that were cut down; yet it is impoffible to render an exact account of his Perfonal Eftate.

As for his Rents during the time he acted in the Warrs, though he fuffer'd others to gather theirs for their own ufe, yet his own either went for the ufe of the Army, or fell into the hands of the Enemy, or were fup-prefs'd and with-held from him by the Cozenage of his Tenants and Officers, my Lord being then not able to look after them himfelf.

About the time when His late Majefty un-dertook the expedition into *Scotland* for the fuppreffing of fome infurrection that happened there; My Lord, as afore is mentioned, amongft the reft, lent His Majefty 10000l. *fterling;* But having newly married a Daughter to the then Lord *Brackly*, now Earl of *Bridg-water*, whofe portion was 12000l. the moiety whereof was paid in Gold on the day of her marriage, and the reft foon after (although fhe was too young to be bedded.) This, together with fome other expences, caufed him to take up the faid 10000l. at Intereft, the Ufe whereof he paid many years after.

Alfo when after his fixteen years Banifh-ment, he returned into *England*, before he knew what Eftate was left him, and was able to receive any Rents of his own, he was neceffitated to take 5000l. upon Ufe for the maintenance of himfelf and his Family; whereof the now Earl of *Devonfhire*, his Coufin German, once removed, lent him 1000l. for which and the former 1000l. men-tioned heretofore, he never defired nor re-ceived any Ufe from my Lord, which I men-tion, to declare the favour and bounty of that Noble Lord.

But though it is impoffible to render an exact account of all the loffes which My Lord has fuftained by the faid Wars, yet as far as they are accountable, I fhall endeavour to reprefent them in thefe following Particulars :

In the firſt place, I ſhall give you a juſt particular of My Lords Eſtate in Lands, as it was before the Wars, partly according to the value of his own Surveighers, and partly according to the rate it is let, at this preſent.

Next, I ſhall accompt the Woods cut down by the Rebellious Party, in ſeveral places of My Lords Eſtate.

Thirdly, I ſhall compute the Value of thoſe Lands which My Lord hath loſt, both in preſent poſſeſſion, and in reverſion; that is to ſay, thoſe which he has loſt altogether, both for himſelf, and his Poſterity; and thoſe he has recovered onely during the time of his life, and which his onely Son and Heir, the now Earl of *Ogle,* muſt loſe after his Fathers deceaſe.

Fourthly, I ſhall make mention, how much of Land my Lord hath been forced to ſell for the payment of ſome of his Debts, contraᴄted during the time of the late Civil Wars, and when his Eſtate was ſequeſtred; I ſay ſome, for there are a great many to pay yet.

To which I ſhall, Fifthly, add the Compoſition of his Brothers Eſtate; and the loſs of it for Eight years.

*A Particular of My Lords Eſtate in plain
Rents, as it was partly ſurveighed in
the Year* 1641, *and partly is let at
this preſent.*

## Nottingham-ſhire.

|  | l. | s. | d. |
|---|---|---|---|
| THE Mannor of *Welbeck* . | 600 | 0 | 0 |
| The Mannor of *Norton, Carbarton,* and the *Granges* . | 454 | 19 | 1 |
| *Warkſopp* . . . . . . . . | 51 | 6 | 8 |
| The Mannor-houſe of *Soakholm* | 308 | 10 | 3 |
| The Manor of *Clipſton* & *Edwin-ſtow* . . . . . . . . . | 334 | 9 | 8 |
| *Drayton* . . . . . . . . | 8 | 16 | 6 |
| *Dunham* . . . . . . . . | 99 | 17 | 8 |
| *Sutton* . . . . . . . . | 185 | 0 | 5 |
| The Mannor of *Kirby,* &c. . . | 1075 | 7 | 2 |
| The Mannor of *Cotham* . . . | 833 | 18 | 8 |
| The Mannor of *Sitthorp* . . . | 704 | 1 | 0 |
| *Carcholſton* . . . . . . . | 450 | 3 | 0 |
| *Hauksworth,* &c. . . . . . | 139 | 4 | 2 |
| *Flawborough* . . . . . . | 512 | 11 | 8 |
| *Mearing* and *Holm*-Meadow . | 471 | 2 | 0 |
|  | 6229 | 7 | 11 |

### Lincoln-shire.

|  | l. | s. | d. |
|---|---|---|---|
| *Wellinger* and *Ingham* Meales   . | 100 | 0 | 0 |

### Derby-shire.

|  | l. | s. | d. |
|---|---|---|---|
| The Barrony of *Bolsover* and *Woodthorp* . . . . . . . | 846 | 8 | 11 |
| The Mannor of *Chesterfield* . . | 378 | 0 | 0 |
| The Mannor of *Barlow* . . . | 796 | 17 | 6 |
| *Tissington* . . . . . . . . | 159 | 11 | 0 |
| *Dronfield* . . . . . . . | 486 | 15 | 10 |
| The Mannor of *Brampton* . . | 142 | 4 | 8 |
| Little-*Longston* . . . . . . | 87 | 2 | 0 |
| The Mannor of *Stoak* . . . | 212 | 3 | 0 |
| *Birth*-Hall, and *Peak*-Forrest . | 131 | 8 | 0 |
| The Mannor of *Gringlow* . . | 156 | 8 | 0 |
| The Mannor of *Hucklow* . . | 162 | 10 | 8 |
| The Mannor of *Blackwall* . . | 306 | 0 | 4 |
| *Buxton* and *Tids-Hall* . . . | 153 | 2 | 0 |
| *Mansfield*-Park . . . . . | 100 | 0 | 0 |
| *Mappleton* and *Thorp* . . . . | 207 | 5 | 0 |
| The Mannor of *Windly*-Hill . | 238 | 18 | 0 |
| The Mannor of *Litchurch* and *Markworth* . . . . . . . | 713 | 15 | 1 |
| *Church* and *Meynel Langly* Mannor | 850 | 1 | 0 |
|  | 6128 | 11 | 10 |

## Stafford-shire.

|  | l. | s. | d. |
|---|---|---|---|
| The Mannor of *Bloar* with *Caul-ton* . . . . . . . . | 573 | 13 | 4 |
| The Mannor of *Grindon*, *Cauldon*, with *Waterfull* . . . | 822 | 3 | 0 |
| The Mannor of *Cheadle* with *Kinsly* . . . . . . . . | 259 | 18 | 0 |
| The Mannor of *Barleston*, &c. . | 694 | 3 | 0 |
|  | 2349 | 17 | 4 |

## Glocester-shire.

|  | l. | s. | d. |
|---|---|---|---|
| The Manor of *Tormorton* with *Litleton* . . . . . . . | 1193 | 16 | 0 |
| The Mannor of *Acton Turvil* . | 388 | 3 | 2 |
|  | 1581 | 19 | 2 |

## Summerset-shire.

|  | l. | s. | d. |
|---|---|---|---|
| The Mannor of *Chewstoak* . . | 816 | 15 | 6 |
| *Knighton Sutton* . . . . . . | 300 | 14 | 4 |
| *Stroud* and *Kingsham*-Park . . | 186 | 4 | 0 |
|  | 1303 | 13 | 10 |

## York-fhire.

The Manors of *Slingſby*, *Ho-
verngham* and *Friton*, *Nor-
thinges* and *Pomfret* . . . 1700   0   0

## Northumberland.

The Barrony of *Bothal*, *Ogle*
and *Hepple*, &c. . . . . . . 3000   0   0

*Totall* 22393   10   1

That this Particular of My Lords Eſtate
was no leſs then is mentioned, may partly
appear by the rate, as it was furveighed, and
fold by the Rebellious Parliament; for they
raiſed, towards the later end of their power,
which was in the year 1652, out of my Lord's
Eſtate, the fumme of 111593l. 10s. 11d. at
five years and a half Purchaſe, which was at
above the rate of 18000l. a year, befides
Woods; and his Brother Sir *Charles Cavendiſh*'s Eſtate, which Eſtate was 2000l. a year,
which falls not much ſhort of the mentioned
account; and certainly, had they not fold fuch
Lands at eaſie rates, few would have bought
them, by reaſon the Purchaſers were uncer-

tain how long they fhould enjoy their purchafe: Befides, Under-Officers do not ufually refufe Bribes; and it is well known that the Surveighers did under-rate Eftates according as they were feed by the Purchafers.

Again, many of the Eftates of banifhed Perfons were given to Soldiers for the payment of their Arrears, who again fold them to others which would buy them at eafier rates. But chiefly, it appears by the rate as my Lords Eftate is let at prefent, there being feveral of the mentioned Lands that are let at a higher rate now then they were furveighed; nor are they all valued in the mentioned particular according to the furveigh, but many of them which were not furveighed, are accounted according to the rate they are let at at this prefent.

The Lofs of my Lords Eftate, in plain Rents, as alfo upon ordinary Ufe, and Ufe upon Ufe, is as followeth:

The Annual Rent of My Lords Lands, *viz.* 22393l. 10s. 1d. being loft for the fpace of 18 years, which was the time of his acting in the Wars, and of his Banifhment, without any benefit to him, reckoned without any Intereft, amounts to 40308l. But being accounted with the ordinary Ufe at Six in the Hundred, and Ufe upon Ufe for the mentioned fpace of 18 Years, it amounts to 733579l.

But fome perhaps will fay, That if My Lord had enjoyed his Eftate, he would have fpent it, at leaft fo much as to maintain him-felf according to his degree and quality.

I anfwer; That it is very improbable My Lord fhould have fpent all his Eftate, if he had enjoyed it he being a man of great Wifdom and Prudence, knowing well how to fpend, and how to manage; for though he lived nobly before the time of the Wars, yet not beyond the Compafs of his Eftate; nay, fo far he would have been from fpending his Eftate, that no doubt but he would have in-creaft it to a vaft value, as he did before the Wars; where notwithftanding his Hofpitality and noble Houfe-keeping, his charges of Building came to about 31000l; the portion of his fecond Daughter, which was 12000l; the noble entertainments he gave King *Charles* the Firft, one whereof came to almoft 15000l. another to above 4000l, and a third to 1700l. as hereafter fhall be mentioned; and his great expences during the time of his being Governour to his Majefty that now is, he yet encreafed his Eftate to the value of 100000l. which is 5000 *per annum,* when it was by fo much lefs.

But if any one will reckon the charges of his Houfe-keeping during the time of his Exile, and when he had not the enjoyment of his Eftate, he may fubftract the fum accounted for the payment of his debts, contracted in the time of his Banifhment, which went to the maintenance of himfelf and his Family; or in lieu thereof, confidering that I do not account all My Lords loffes, but onely thofe that are certainly known, he may compare it with the lofs of his perfonal Eftate, whereof I fhall make fome mention anon, and he'll find that I do not heighten my Lords Loffes, but rather diminifh them; for furely the loffes of his perfonal Eftate, and thofe I account not, will counterballance the charges of his Houfe-keeping, if not exceed them.

Again, others will fay, That there was much Land fold in the time of My Lords Banifhment by his Sons, and Feoffees in Truft.

I anfwer, Firft, That whatfoever was fold, was firft bought of the Rebellious Power: Next, although they fold fome Lands, yet My Lord knew nothing of it, neither did he receive a penny worth for himfelf, neither of what they purchafed, nor fold, all the time of his Banifhment till his return.

And thus much of the lofs of My Lords Eftate in Rents: Concerning the lofs of his Parks and Woods, as much as is generally known, (for I do not reckon particular Trees cut down in feveral of his Woods yet ftanding) 'tis as follows:

1. *Clipfton*-Park and Woods cut down to the value of 20000 l.

2. *Kirkby*-Woods, for which my Lord was formerly proferr'd 10000 l.

3. Woods cut down in *Derbyfhire* 8000 l.

4. *Red-lodg*-Wood, *Rome*-wood and others near *Welbeck* 4000 l.

5. Woods cut down in *Stafford*-fhire 1000 l.

6. Woods cut down in *York*-fhire 1000 l.

7. Woods cut down in *Northumberland* 1500 l.

The *Total* 45000 l.

The Lands which My Lord hath loft in prefent pofeffion are 2015 l. *per annum*, which at 20 years purchafe come to 40300 l. and thofe which he hath loft in Reverfion, are 3214 l. *per annum*, which at 16 years purchafe amount to the value of 51424 l.

The Lands which my Lord fince his return has fold for the payment of fome of his debts, occafioned by the Wars (for I do not reckon thofe he fold to buy others) come to the value of 56000 l. to which out of his yearly revenue he has added 10000 l. more, which is in all 66000 l.

Laftly, The Compofition of his Brothers Eftate was 5000 l. and the lofs of it for eight years comes to 16000 l.

All which, if fumm'd up together, amounts to 941303 l.

Thefe are the accountable loffes, which My Dear Lord and Hufband has fuffered by the late Civil Wars, and his Loyalty to his King and Country. Concerning the lofs of his perfonal Eftate, fince (as I often mentioned) it cannot be exactly known; I fhall not endeavour to fet down the Particulars thereof, onely in General give you a Note of what partly they are:

1. The pulling down of feveral of his dwelling or Mannor-houfes.

2. The disfurnifhing of them, of which the Furniture at *Bolfover* and *Welbeck* was very noble and rich: Out of his *London*-houfe at *Clarken-well*, there were taken, amongft other

Goods, fuits of Linnen, *viz.* Table-Cloths, Sideboard-cloths, Napkins, *&c.* whereof one fuit coft 160 l. they being bought for an Entertainment which My Lord made for Their Majefties, King *Charles* the Firft, and the Queen, at *Bolfover*-Caftle; And of 150 Suits of Hangings of all forts in all his Houfes, there were not above 10 or 12 faved.

Of Silver-plate, My Lord had fo much as came to the value of 3800 l. befides feveral Curiofities of Cabinets, Cups, and other things, which after My Lord was gone out of *England,* were taken out of his Mannor-houfe, *Welbeck,* by a Garifon of the Kings Party that lay therein, whereof he recovered onely 1100 l. which Money was fent him beyond the Seas, the reft was loft.

As for Pewter, Brafs, Bedding, Linnen, and other Houfhold-ftuff, there was nothing elfe left but fome few old Feather-beds, and thofe all fpoiled, and fit for no ufe.

3. My Lord's Stock of Corn, Cattel, *&c.* was very great before the Warrs, by reafon of the largenefs and capacity of thofe grounds, and the great number of Granges he kept for his own ufe; as for example, *Barlow, Carkholfton, Gleadthorp, Welbeck,* and feveral more,

which were all well manured and ftockt. But all this ftock was loft, befides his Race of Horfes in his Grounds, Grange-Horfes, Hackny-Horfes, Mannage-Horfes, Coach-Horfes, and others he kept for his ufe.

To thefe Loffes I may well and juftly join the charges which my Lord hath been put to fince his return into *England*, by reafon they were caufed by the ruines of the faid Warrs; whereof I reckon,

1. His Law-fuits, which have been very chargeable to him, more than advantagious.

2. The Stocking, Manuring, Paling, Stubbing, Hedging, &c. of his Grounds and Parks; where it is to be noted, That no advantage or benefit can be made of Grounds, under the fpace of three years, and of Cattel not under five or fix.

3. The repairing and furnifhing of fome of his Dwelling-Houfes.

4. The fetting up a Race or Breed of Horfes, as he had before the Warrs; for which purpofe he hath bought the beft Mares he could get for money.

In fhort, I can reckon 12000 l. laid out barely for the repair of fome Ruines, which my Lord could not be without, there being many of them to repair yet; neither is this all that is laid out, but much more which I cannot well remember; nor is there more but one Grange ftock'd, amongft feveral that were kept for furnifhing his Houfe with Provifions: As for other Charges and Loffes, which My Lord hath fuftained fince his return, I will not reckon them, becaufe my defign is onely to account fuch loffes as were caufed by the Wars.

By which, as they have been mentioned, it may eafily be concluded, That although My Lord's Eftate was very great before the Wars, yet now it is fhrunk into a very narrow compafs, that it puts his Prudence and Wifdom to the Proof, to make it ferve his neceffities, he having no other affiftance to bear him up; and yet notwithftanding all this, he hath fince his return paid both for Himfelf and his Son, all manner of Taxes, Lones, Levies, Affeff-ments, &c. equally with the reft of His Majefties Subjects, according to that Eftate that is left him, which he has been forced to take upon Intereft.

The

# Life of the Moſt Illuſtrious Prince, William Duke of Newcaſtle.

### *THE THIRD BOOK.*

HUS having given you a faithful Account of all My Lords Actions, both before, in, and after the Civil Warrs, and of his Loſſes; I ſhall now conclude with ſome particular heads concerning the deſcription of his own Perſon, his Natural Humour, Diſpoſition, Qualities, Vertues; his Pedigree, Habit, Diet, Exerciſes, &c. together with ſome other Remarks and Particulars which I thought requiſite to be inſerted, both to illuſtrate the former Books, and to render the Hiſtory of his Life more perfect and compleat.

### 1. *Of his Power.*

AFTER His Majesty King *Charles* the First, had entrusted my Lord with the Power of raising Forces for His Majesties Service, he effected that which never any Subject did, nor was (in all probability) able to do; for though many Great and Noble Persons did also raise Forces for His Majesty, yet they were Brigades, rather then well-formed Armies, in comparison to my Lord's. The reason was, That my Lord, by his Mother, the Daughter of *Cuthbert* Lord *Ogle*, being allyed to most of the most ancient Families in *Northumberland*, and other the Northern parts, could pretend a greater Interest in them, then a stranger; for they through a natural affection to my Lord as their own Kinsman, would sooner follow him, and under his Conduct sacrifice their Lives for His Majesty's Service, then any body else, well knowing, That by deserting my Lord, they deserted themselves; and by this means my Lord raised first a Troup of Horse consisting of a hundred and twenty, and a Regiment of Foot; and then an Army of Eight thousand

Horſe, Foot and Dragoons, in thoſe parts ;
and afterwards upon this ground, at ſeveral
times, and in ſeveral places, ſo many ſeveral
Troups, Regiments and Armies, that in all
from the firſt to the laſt, they amounted to
above 100000 men, and thoſe moſt upon his
own Intereſt, and without any other conſiderable help or aſſiſtance ; which was much for
a particular Subject, and in ſuch a conjuncture of time ; for ſince Armies are
ſooneſt raiſed by Covetouſneſs, Fear and
Faction ; that is to ſay, upon a conſtant and
ſettled Pay, upon the Ground of Terrour,
and upon the Ground of Rebellion ; but very
ſeldom or never upon uncertainty of Pay ;
and when it is as hazardous to be of ſuch a
Party, as to be in the heat of a Battel ; alſo
when there is no other deſign but honeſt
duty ; it may eaſily be conceived that my
Lord could have no little love and affection
when He raiſed his Army upon ſuch grounds
as could promiſe them but little advantage at
that time.

Amongſt the reſt of his Army, My Lord
had choſen for his own Regiment of Foot,
3000 of ſuch Valiant, ſtout and faithful men,

(whereof many were bred in the Moorish-grounds of the Northern parts) that they were ready to die at my Lord's feet, and never gave over, whenfoever they were engaged in action, until they had either conquer'd the Enemy, or loft their lives.     They were called White-coats, for this following reafon: My Lord being refolved to give them new Liveries, and there being not red Cloth enough to be had, took up fo much of white as would ferve to cloath them, defiring withal, their patience until he had got it dyed; but they impatient of ftay, requefted my Lord, that he would be pleafed to let them have it un-dyed as it was, promifing they themfelves would die it in the Enemies Blood: Which requeft my Lord granted them, and from that time they were called White-Coats.

To give you fome inftances of their Valour and Courage, I muft beg leave to repeat fome paffages mentioned in the firft Book. The Enemy having clofely befieged the City of *York*, and made a paffage into the Mannor-yard, by fpringing a Mine under the Wall thereof, was got into the Mannor-houfe with a great number of their Forces; which My

Lord perceiving, he immediately went and drew 80 of the faid White-coats thither, who with the greateft Courage went clofe up to the Enemy, and having charged them, fell Pell-mell with the But-ends of their Mufquets upon them, and with the affiftance of the reft that renewed their Courage by their example, kill'd and took 1500, and by that means faved the Town.

How valiantly they behaved themfelves in the laft fatal Battel upon *Heffom-moor* near *York*, has been alfo declared heretofore; in fo much, that although moft of the Army were fled, yet they would not ftir, until by the Enemies Power they were overcome, and moft of them flain in rank and file.

Their love and affection to my Lord was fuch, that it lafted even when he was deprived of all his power, and could do them little good; to which purpofe I fhall mention this following paffage:

My Lord being in *Antwerp*, received a Vifit from a Gentleman, who came out of *England*, and rendred My Lord thanks for his fafe Efcape at Sea; My Lord being in amaze, not knowing what the Gentleman meant, he was pleafed to acquaint Him, that in his coming over Sea out of *England*, he was fet upon by Pickaroons,[1] who having examined him, and the reft of his Company, at laft fome afked him, whether he knew the Marquefs of *Newcaftle?* To whom he anfwered, That he knew him very well, and was going over into the fame City where my Lord lived. Where-upon they did not onely take nothing from him, but ufed him with all Civility, and de-fired him to remember their humble duty to their Lord General, for they were fome of his White-Coats that had efcaped death; and if my Lord had any fervice for them, they were ready to affift him upon what Defigns foever, and to obey him in whatfoever he fhould be pleafed to Command them.

This I mention for the Eternal Fame and Memory of thofe Valiant and Faithful Men. But to return to the *Power* my Lord had in the late Warrs: As he was the Head of his own Army, and had raifed it moft upon his own Interèft for the Service of His Majefty; fo he was never Ordered by His Majefty's

---

[1] Rogues, from the Spanifh *Picaro.*

Privy Council, (except that some forces of His were kept by His late Majesty, (which he sent to Him) together with some Arms and Ammunition heretofore mentioned) until His Highness Prince *Rupert* came from His Majesty, to join with him at the Siege of *York*. He had moreover the Power of Coyning, Printing, Knighting, *&c.* which never any Subject had before, when His Soveraign Himself was in the Kingdom; as also the Command of so many Counties, as is mentioned in the First Book, and the Power of placing and displacing what Governours and Commanders he pleased, and of constituting what Garisons he thought fit; of the chief whereof I shall give you this following list.

*A Particular of the Principal Garisons, and the Governors of them, constituted by my Lord.*

*In* Northumberland.

NEWCASTLE upon *Tyne*, Sir *John Marley* Knight.

*Tynmouth Castle* and *Sheilds*, Sir *Thomas Riddal*, Knight.

*In the Bifhoprick of* Durham.

*Hartlepool*, Lieutenant Colonel Henry Lambton.

*Raby-Caftle*, Sir *William Savile*, Knight and
Baronet.

*In* Yorkfhire.

The City of *York*, Sir *Thomas Glenham* Knight
and Baronet; and afterwards when he
took the Field, the Lord *Jo. Bellafyfe.*

*Pomfret-Caftle*, Colonel *Mynn*, and after him
Sir *Jo. Redman.*

*Sheffield-Caftle*, Major *Beamont.*

*Wortly-Hall*, Sir *Francis Wortley.*

*Tickhill-Caftle*, Major *Mountney.*

*Doncafter*, Sir *Francis Fane*, Knight of the
Bath, afterwards Governour of *Lincoln.*

*Sandal-Caftle*, Captain *Bonivant.*

*Skipton-Caftle*, Sir *John Mallary*, Baronet.

*Bolton-Caftle*, Mr. *Scroope.*

*Hemfley-Caftle*, Sir *Jordan Crofland.*

*Scarborough*-Caftle and Town, Sir *Hugh
Chomley.*

*Stamford-Bridg*, Colonel *Galbreth.*

*Hallifax*, Sir *Francis Mackworth.*

*Tadcaster*, Sir *Gamaliel Dudley*.
*Eyrmouth*, Major *Kaughton*.


### *In* Cumberland.

The City of *Carlifle*, Sir *Philip Mufgrave*,
Knight and Baronet.
*Cockermouth*, Colonel *Kirby*.


### *In* Nottinghamſhire.

*Newark* upon *Trent*, Sir *John Henderfon*,
Knight; and afterwards, Sir *Richard Byron*,
Knight, now Lord *Byron*.
*Wyrton-Houſe*, Colonel *Rowland Hacker*.
*Welbeck*, Colonel *Van Peire*; and after,
Colonel *Beeton*.
*Shelford-Houſe*, Col. *Philip Stanhop*.


### *In* Lincolnſhire.

The City of *Lincoln*, firſt Sir *Francis Fane*,
Knight of the Bath; ſecondly, Sir *Peregrine
Bartu*.
*Gainſborough*, Colonel St. *George*.
*Bullingbrook* - Caſtle,    Lieutenant    Colonel
*Cheſter*.
*Beluoir*-Caſtle, Sir *Gervas Lucas*.

*In* Derbyſhire.

*Bolſover*-Caſtle, Colonel *Muſchamp.*
*Wingfield* Mannor, Colonel *Roger Molyneux.*
*Staly*-Houſe, the now Lord *Fretchwile.*


## *A* LIST *of the General* OFFICERS *of the* ARMY.

1. THE Lord General, the now Duke of *Newcaſtle*, the Noble Subject of this Book.

2. The Lieutenant General of the Army; firſt the Earl of *Newport*, afterwards the Lord *Eythin.*

3. The General of the Ordnance, *Charles* Viſcount *Mansfield.*

4. The General of the Horſe, *George* Lord *Goring.*

5. The Colonel General of the Army, Sir *Thomas Glenham.*

6. The Major General of the Army, Sir *Francis Mackworth.*

7. The Lieutenant General of the Horſe, Firſt Mr. *Charles Cavendiſh*, after him Sir *Charles Lucas.*

8. Commiſſary General of Horſe, Firſt Colonel *Windham*, after him Sir *William Throckmorton*, and after him Mr. *George Porter*.

9. Lieutenant General of the Ordnance, Sir *William Davenant*.

10. Treaſurer of the Army, Sir *William Carnaby*.

11. Advocate-General of the Army, Dr. *Liddal*.

12. Quarter-Maſter General of the Army, Mr. *Ralph Errington*.

13. Providore-General of the Army, Mr. *Gervas Nevil*, and after Mr. *Smith*.

14. Scout-Maſter-General of the Army, Mr. *Hudſon*.

15. Waggon-Maſter-General of the Army, *Baptiſt Johnſon*.

*William* Lord *Widdrington* was Preſident of the Council of War, and Commander in chief of the three Counties of *Lincoln*, *Rutland* and *Nottingham*, and the forces there.

When my Lord marched with his Army to *Newcaſtle* againſt the *Scots*, then the Lord *John Bellaſſis* was conſtituted Governour of

*York*, and Commander in Chief, or Lieutenant General of *York-shire*.

As for the reft of the Officers and Commanders of every particular Regiment and
Company, they being too numerous, cannot
well be remembred, and therefore I fhall give
you no particular accompt of them.

2. *Of His Misfortunes and obstructions.*

ALTHOUGH Nature had favour'd My
Lord, and endued him with the beft
Qualities and Perfections fhe could infpire
into his foul; yet Fortune hath ever been
fuch an inveterate Enemy to him, that fhe
invented all the fpight and malice againft him
that lay in her power; and notwithftanding
his prudent Counfels and Defigns, caft fuch
obftructions in his way, that he feldom proved
fuccefsful, but where he acted in Perfon.
And fince I am not ignorant that this unjuft
and partial Age is apt to fupprefs the worth of
meritorious perfons, and that many will endeavour to obfcure my Lords noble Actions
and Fame, by cafting unjuft afperfions upon
him, and laying (either out of ignorance or

malice) Fortunes envy to his charge, I have purposed to reprefent thefe obftructions which confpired to render his good intentions and endeavours ineffectual, and at laft did work his ruine and deftruction, in thefe following particulars.

1. At the time when the Kingdom became fo infatuated, as to oppofe and pull down their Gracious King and Soveraign, the Treafury was exhaufted, and no fufficient means to raife and maintain Armies to reduce His Majefties Rebellious Subjects; fo that My Lord had little to begin withal but what his own Eftate would allow, and his Intereft procure him.

2. When his late Majefty, in the beginning of the unhappy Wars, fent My Lord to *Hull*, the ftrongeft place in the Kingdom, where the Magazine of Arms and Ammunition was kept, and he by his prudence had gained it to his Majefties fervice; My Lord was left to the mercy of the Parliament, where he had furely fuffered for it, (though he acted not without His Majefties Commiffion) if fome of the contrary party had not quitted him, in hopes to gain him on their fide.

3. After His Majesty had sent My Lord to *Newcastle* upon *Tyne*, to take upon him the Government of that place, and he had raised there, of Friends and Tenants, a troup of Horse and Regiment of Foot, which he ordered to conveigh some Arms and Ammunition to His Majesty, sent by the Queen out of *Holland*; His Majesty was pleased to keep the same Convoy with him to encrease his own Forces, which although it was but of a small number, yet at that present time it would have been very serviceable to my Lord, he having then but begun to raise Forces.

4. When Her Majesty the now Queen-Mother, after her arrival out of *Holland* to *York*, had a purpose to conveigh some Armes to His Majesty, My Lord order'd a Party of 1500 to conduct the same, which His Majesty was pleased to keep with him for his own service.

5. After Her Majesty had taken a resolution to go from *York* to *Oxford*, where the King then was; my Lord for Her safer conduct quitted 7000 men of his Army, with a convenient Train of Artillery, which likewise never returned to my Lord.

6. When the Earl of *Montrofs* was going into *Scotland*, he went to my Lord at *Durham*, and defired of him a fupply of fome Forces for His Majefties fervice; where my Lord gave him 200 Horfe and Dragoons, even at fuch a time when he ftood moft in need of a fupply himfelf, and thought every day to encounter the *Scottifh* Army.

7. When my Lord out of the Northern parts went into *Lincoln-* and *Derby-fhires* with his Army, to order and reduce them to their Allegiance and Duty to His Majefty, and from thence refolved to march into the Affociate Counties, (where in all probability he would have made an happy end of the Warr) he was fo importuned by thofe he left behind him, and particularly the Commander in Chief, to return into *York-fhire*, alledging the Enemy grew ftrong, and would ruine them all, if he came not fpeedily to fuccour and affift them; that in honour and duty he could do no otherwife but grant their Requefts; when as yet being returned into thofe parts, he found them fecure and fafe enough from the Enemies Attempts.

8. My Lord (as heretofore mentioned) had

as great private Enemies about His Majefty,
as he had publick Enemies in the Field, who
ufed all the endeavour they could to pull him
down.

9. There was fuch Jugling, Treachery,
and Falfhood in his own Army, and amongft
fome of his own Officers, that it was impoffible for my Lord to be profperous and fuccefsful in his Defigns and Undertakings.

.10. My Lord's Army being the chief and
greateft Army which His Majefty had, and
in which confifted His prime Strength and
Power; the Parliament refolved at laft, to
join all their Forces with the Army of the
*Scots*, (which when it came out of *Scotland*,
was above Twenty thoufand Men) to oppofe,
and if poffible, to ruine it; well knowing,
that if they did pull down my Lord, they
fhould be Mafters of all the Three Kingdoms; fo that there were Three Armies
againft One. But although my Lord fuffered
much by the Negligence (and fometimes
Treachery) of his Officers, and was unfortunately called back into *York-fhire*, from his
March he defigned for the Affociate Counties,
and was forced to part with a great number

of his Forces and Ammunition, as aforementioned; yet he would hardly have been overcome, and his Army ruined by the Enemy,
had he but had fome timely fupply and affiftance at the Siege of *York*, or that his Counfel
had been taken in not fighting the Enemy
then, or that the Battel had been differ'd fome
two or three dayes longer, until thofe Forces
were arrived which he expected, namely three
thoufand men out of *Northumberland*, and Two
thoufand drawn out of feveral Garifons. But
the chief Misfortune was, That the Enemy
fell upon the Kings Forces before they were
all put into a *Battallia*, and took them at their
great difadvantage; which caufed fuch a
Panick fear amongft them, that moft of the
Horfe of the right Wing of His Majefty's
Forces, betook themfelves to their heels; infomuch, that although the left Wing (commanded by the Lord *Goring*, and my Brother
Sir *Charles Lucas*) did their beft endeavour,
and beat back the Enemy three times, and
My Lord's own Regiment of Foot charged
them fo couragioufly, that they never broke,
but died moft of them in their Ranks and
Files; yet the Power of the Enemy being

too ſtrong, put them at laſt to a total rout and confuſion. Which unlucky diſaſter put an end to all future hopes of His Majeſties Party; ſo that my Lord ſeeing he had nothing left in his Power to do His Majeſty any further ſervice in that kind (for had he ſtayed, he would have been forced to ſurrender all thoſe Towns and Gariſons in thoſe parts, that were yet in His Majeſties Devotion, as afterwards it alſo happen'd) reſolved to quit the Kingdom, as formerly is mentioned.

And theſe are chiefly the obſtructions to the good ſucceſs of my Lord's Deſigns in the late Civil Wars; which being rightly conſidered, will ſave him blameleſs from what otherwiſe would be laid to his charge ; for, as according to the old ſaying, *'Tis eaſie for men to ſwim, when they are held up by the chin:* So on the other ſide, it is very dangerous and difficult for them to endeavour it, when they are pulled down by the Heels, and beaten upon their Heads.

### 3. *Of His Loyalty and Sufferings.*

I DARE boldly and juſtly ſay, That there never was, nor is a more Loyal and Faithful

Subject then My Lord: Not to mention the Truſt he diſcharged in all thoſe imployments, which either King *James*, or King *Charles* the Firſt, or His now Gracious Maſter King *Charles* the Second, were pleaſed to beſtow upon him, which he performed with ſuch care and fidelity, that he never diſobeyed their Commands in the leaſt; I will onely note,

1. That he was the Firſt that appear'd in Armes for His Majeſty, and engaged Himſelf and all his Friends he could for His Majeſties Service; and though he had but two Sons which were young, and one onely Brother, yet they all were with him in the Wars: His two Sons had Commands, but His Brother, though he had no Command, by reaſon of the weakneſs of his body, yet he was never from My Lord when he was in action, even to the laſt; for he was the laſt with my Lord in the Field in that fatal Battel upon *Heſſom-moor*, near *York*; and though my Brother, Sir *Charles Lucas*, deſired my Lord to ſend his ſons away, when the ſaid Battel was fought, yet he would not, ſaying, His ſons ſhould ſhew their Loyalty and Duty to His Majeſty, in venturing their lives, as well as Himſelf.

2. My Lord was the chief and onely Perſon, that kept up the Power of His late Majeſty; for when his Army was loſt, all the Kings Party was ruined in all three of his Majeſties Kingdoms; becauſe in his Army lay the chief ſtrength of all the Royal Forces; it being the greateſt and beſt formed Army which His Majeſty had, and the onely ſupport both of his Majeſties Perſon and Power, and of the hopes of all his Loyal Subjects in all his Dominions.

3. My Lord was 16 Years in Baniſhment, and hath loſt and ſuffered moſt of any ſubject, that ſuffer'd either by War, or otherways, except thoſe that loſt their lives, and even that he valued not, but expoſed it to ſo eminent dangers that nothing but Heavens Decree had ordained to ſave it.

4. He never minded his own intereſt more then his Loyaltie and Duty, and upon that account never deſired nor received any thing from the Crown to enrich himſelf, but ſpent great ſums in His Majeſties Service; ſo that after his long baniſhment and return into *England*, I obſerved his ruined Eſtate was like an Earthquake, and his Debts like Thunder-

bolts, by which he was in danger of being utterly undone, had not Patience and Prudence, together with Heavens Bleſſings, ſaved him from that threatening Ruine.

5. He never repined at his Loſſes and Sufferings, becauſe he loſt and ſuffered for his King and Countrey; nay, ſo far was he from that, that I have heard him ſay, If the ſame Warrs ſhould happen again, and he was ſure to loſe both his life, and all he had left him, yet he would moſt willingly ſacrifice it for His Majeſties Service.

6. He never connived or conſpired with the Enemy, neither directly nor indirectly; for though ſome Perſon of Quality being ſent in the late Wars to him into the North, from His late Majeſty, who was then at *Oxford*, with ſome Meſſage, did withal in private acquaint him, that ſome of the Nobility that were with the King, deſired him to ſide with them againſt His Majeſty, alledging that if His Majeſty ſhould become an abſolute Conqueror, both himſelf and the reſt of the Nobility would loſe all their Rights and Priviledges; yet he was ſo far from conſenting to it, that he returned him this anſwer, namely,

That he entred into actions of War, for no other end, but for the fervice of His King and Mafter, and to keep up His Majefties Rights and Prerogatives, for which he was refolved to venture both his Life, Pofterity and Eftate; for certainly, faid he, the Nobility cannot fall if the King be Victorious, nor can they keep up their Dignities, if the King be overcome.

This Meffage was delivered by word of mouth, but none of their names mentioned; fo that it is not certainly known whether it was a real truth or not; more probable it was, that they intended to found my Lord, or to make, if poffible, more divifion; for certainly not all that pretended to be for the King, were His Friends; and I my felf remember very well, when I was with Her Majefty, the now Queen-Mother, in *Oxford*, (although I was too young to perceive their intrigues, yet I was old enough to obferve) that there were great Factions both amongft the Courtiers and Soldiers.. But my Lords Loyalty was fuch, that he kept always faithful and true to His Majefty, and could by no means be brought to fide with the Rebellious Party, or to juggle and mind his own Intereſt more then his Majeſties Service ; and this was the cauſe that he had as great private Enemies at Court, as he had publick Enemies in the Field, who ſought as much his ruine and deſtruction privately, and would caſt aſperſions upon his Loyalty and Duty, as theſe did publickly oppoſe him.

In ſhort, that it may appear the better what loyal and faithful ſervices my Lord has done both for His late Majeſty King *Charles* the Firſt, and His now Gracious Maſter King *Charles* the Second, I have thought fit to ſubjoin both Their Majeſties Commendations which they were pleaſed to give him, when for his Great and Loyal Services they confer'd upon him the Titles and Dignities of *Marqueſs*, and *Duke of Newcaſtle.*

A Copy of the Preamble of My Lord's Patent for *Marqueſs*, Engliſhed.

Rex &c. Salutem.

WHEREAS *it appears to Us, That* William *Earl of* Newcaſtle *upon* Tyne, *beſides his moſt Eminent Birth and ſplendid Alliances, hath equalled all thoſe Titles with which he is adorned by Defert, and hath alfo wonne them by Virtue, Induftry, Prudence, and a ftedfaft Faith: Whileft with dangers and expences gathering together Soldiers, Armes, and all other War-like Habiliments; and applying them as well in Our Affairs, as moft plentifully fending them to Us, (having fore-thought of Our Dignity and fecurity) he was ready with Us in all Actions in* York-fhire, *and governed the Town of* Newcaftle, *and Caftle in the mouth of* Tyne, *at the time of that fatal Revolt of the People who were got together; and with a Bond of his Friends did opportunely feize that Port, and fettled it a Garifon; bringing Armes to Us (then Our onely relief:) In which Service fo ftrongly going on, (which was of grand moment to our affairs) We do gratefully remember him ftill to have ftood to: Afterwards, having Muftered together a good Army, (Our felf being gone elfe-where) the Rebels now enjoying almoft all* York-fhire, *and the chiefeft Fortrefs of all the Country now appearing to have fcarce refuge or fafety for him againft the fwelling Rebels, (the whole Country then defiring and praying for his coming, that he might timely relieve them in their defperate condition) And leading his faid*

M

*Army in the midst of Winter, gave the Rebels Battel in his passage, vanquish'd them, and put them to flight, and took from them several Garisons, and places of Refuge, and restored Health to the Subjects, and by his many Victories, Peace and Security to the Countryes:  Witness those places, made Noble by the death and flight of the Rebels: in *Lincoln-shire*, Gainsborough *and* Lincoln; *in* Derby-shire*, Chesterfield; *but in* York-shire*, Peirce-bridge, Seacroft, Tankerly, Tadcaster, Sheffield, Rotheram, Yarum, Beverly, Cawood, Selby, Halifax, Leeds, *and* above all, *Bradford; *where when the* York-shire-*and* Lancashire-Rebels *were united, and Battel joined with them; when Our Army as well by the great numbers of the Rebels, as much more the badness of Our ground, was so prest upon, that the Soldiers now seemed to think of flying; He, their General, with a full Carier, commanding two Troops to follow him, broke into the very rage of the Battel, and with so much violence fell upon the right Wing of those Rebels, That those who were but now certain of Victory, turn'd their backs, and fled from the Conqueror, who by his Wisdom, Virtue and his own Hand, brought death and flight to the Rebels, Victory* *and Glory to Himself, Plunder to the Soldiery, and 22 great Guns, and many Ensigns to Us. Nor was there before this, wanting to so much Virtue, equal Felicity, for Our most beloved Consort, after a dismal Tempest coming from* Holland, *being drove ashore at* Burlington, *and undergoing a more grievous danger, by the excursions of the Rebels, then the tossing and tumbling of the Sea; He having heard of it, speedily goes to Her with his Army, and dutifully receiveth Her, in safety brings her, and with all security conducts her to Us at* Oxford. *Whereas therefore the aforesaid Earl hath raised so many Monuments of His Virtue and Fidelity towards Us, Our Queen, Children, and Our Kingdom; when also he doth at this time establish with safety, and with His Power defend the Northern parts of Our Kingdom against the Rebels; when lastly, nothing more concerns Mankind and Princes, and nothing can be more just, then that he may receive for his Deeds, a Reward suitable to his name, which requires that he who defends the Borders, should be created by Us,* Governour or Marquess of the Borderers. *Know therefore, &c.*

A Copy of the Preamble of My Lord's
Patent for *DUKE*, Englifhed.

Rex *&c.* Salutem.

*WHEREAS Our moft beloved and faith-
ful Coufin and Counfellor, William
Earl and Marquefs of Newcaftle upon Tyne,
&c. worthy by his famous Name, Blood and
Office, of large Honours, has been eminent in fo
many, and fo great Services performed to Us and
Our Father (of ever bleffed memory) that his
Merits are ftill producing new effects, We have
decreed likewife to add more Honour to his former.
And though thefe his fuch eminent Actions, which
he hath faithfully and valiantly performed to
Us, Our Father, and Our Kingdom, fpeak loud
enough in themfelves; yet fince the valiant Services of a good Subject are always pleafant to
remember, We have thought fit to have them in
part related for a good Example and Encouragement to Virtue.*

*The great proofs of his Wifdom and Piety are
fufficiently known to Us from Our younger years,
and We fhall alwayes retain a fenfe of thofe good
Principles he inftilled into Us; the Care of Our
Youth which he happily undertook for Our good,*

*he as faithfully and well difcharged. Our years growing up amidft bad Times, and the harfh Neceffities of Warr, a new Charge and Care of Loyaltie, the Kingdom and Religion call'd him off to make ufe of his further Diligence and Valour. Rebellion fpread abroad, he levied Loyal Forces in great numbers, oppofed the Enemy, won fo many and fo great Victories in the Field, took in fo many Towns, Caftles and Garifons, as well in Our Northern parts, as elfewhere; and behaved himfelf with fo great Courage and Valour in the defending alfo what he had got, efpecially at the Siege of* York, *which he maintain'd againft three Potent Armies of* Scots *and* Englifh, *clofely beleaguering, and with emulation affaulting it for three Months (till Relief was brought) to the wonder and envy of the Enemy; that, if Loyal and Humane Force could have prevailed, he had foon reftored Fidelity, Peace and his KING to the Nation, which was then hurrying to Ruine by an unhappy Fate; So that Rebellion getting the upper hand, and no place being left for him to act further valiantly in, for his King and Countrey, he ftill retain'd the fame Loyalty and Valour in fuffering, being an infeparable Follower of Our Exile; during which sad Cataſtrophe, his whole Eſtate was ſequeſtred and ſold from him, and his Perſon alwayes one of the firſt of thoſe few who were excepted both for Life and Eſtate (which was offer'd to all others.)  Beſides, his Virtues are accompanied with a Noble Blood, being of a Family by each Stock equally adorn'd and endow'd with great Honours and Riches.   For which Reaſons We have reſolv'd to grace the ſaid Marqueſs with a new Mark of our Favour, he being every way deſerving of it, as one who lov'd vertue equal to his Noble Birth, and poſſeſs'd Patrimonies ſuitable to both, as long as loyalty had any place to ſhew it ſelf in our Realm; which poſſeſſions he ſo well employ'd, and at laſt for Us and Our Fathers ſervice loſt, till he was with Us reſtor'd.   Know therefore, &c.*

### 4. *Of his Prudence and Wiſdom.*

MY Lord's Prudence and Wiſdom hath been ſufficiently apparent both in his Publick and Private Actions and Imployments; for he hath ſuch a Natural Inſpection, and Judicious Obſervation of things, that he ſees beforehand what will come to

paſs, and orders his affairs accordingly. To
which purpoſe I cannot but mention, that
*Laud,* the then Archbiſhop of *Canterbury,* between whom and my Lord, interceded a great
and intire Friendſhip, which he confirmed by
a Legacy of a Diamond, to the value of 200 l.
left to my Lord when he died, which was
much for him to bequeath; for though he
was a great Stateſman, and in favour with his
late Majeſty, yet he was not covetous to hoard
up wealth, but beſtowed it rather upon the
Publick, repairing the Cathedral of St. *Pauls*
in *London,* which, had God granted him life,
he would certainly have beautified, and rendred as famous and glorious as any in Chriſ-
tendom : This ſaid Arch-Biſhop was pleaſed
to tell His late Majeſty, that my Lord was
one of the Wiſeſt and Prudenteſt Perſons that
ever he was acquainted with.

For further proof, I cannot paſs by that
my Lord told His late Majeſty King *Charles*
the Firſt, and Her Majeſty the now Queen-
Mother, ſome time before the Wars, That
he obſerved by the humours of the People,
the approaching of a Civil War, and that His
Majeſties Perſon would be in danger of being

depoſed, if timely care was not taken to prevent it.

Alſo when my Lord was at *Antwerp*, the Marqueſs of *Montroſs*, before he went into *Scotland*, gave my Lord a Viſit, and acquainted him with his intended Journey, aſking my Lord whether he was not alſo going for *England?* My Lord anſwer'd, He was ready to do His Majeſty what ſervice he could, and would ſhun no opportunity, where he perceived he could effect ſomething to His Majeſties advantage; Nay, ſaid he, if His Majeſty ſhould be pleaſed to Command my ſingle Perſon to go againſt the whole Army of the Enemy, although I was ſure to loſe my life, yet out of a Loyal Duty to His Majeſty, and in Obedience to his Commands, I ſhould never refuſe it. But to venture (ſaid he) the life of my Friends, and to betray them in a deſperate action, without any probability of doing the leaſt good to His Majeſty, would be a very unjuſt and unconſcionable act; for my Friends might perhaps venture with me upon an implicite Faith, that I was ſo honeſt as not to engage them without a firm and ſolid foundation; but I wanting that, as having no Ships,

Armes, Ammunition, Provifion, Forts, and places of Rendezvous, and what is the chief thing, Money; To what purpofe would it be to draw them into fo hazardous an Action, but to feek their ruine and deftruction, without the leaft benefit to His Majefty? Then the Marquefs of *Montrofs* afked my Lord's Advice, and what he fhould do in fuch a cafe? My Lord anfwer'd, That he knowing beft his own Countrey, Power and Strength, and what probability he had of Forces, and other Neceffaries for Warr, when he came into *Scotland*, could give himfelf the beft advice; but withall told him, That if he had no Provifion nor Ammunition, Armes and places of Rendezvous for his men to meet and join, he would likely be forced to hide his head, and fuffer for his rafh undertaking: Which unlucky Fate did alfo accordingly befall that worthy Perfon.

Thefe paffages I mention to no other end, but to declare my Lord's Judgment and Prudence in worldly Affairs; whereof there are fo many, that if I fhould fet them all down, it would fwell this Hiftory to a big Volume. They may in fome fort be gather'd from his actions mentioned heretofore, especially the ordering of his affairs in the time of Warr, with such Conduct, Prudence and Wisdom, that notwithstanding at the beginning of his Undertaking that great Trust and honourable Employment which His late Majesty was pleased to confer upon him, he saw so little appearance of performing his Designs with good success, His Majesty's Revenues being then much weakned, and the Magazines and publick Purse, in the Enemies Power, besides several other obstructions and hindrances; yet as he undertook it chearfully, and out of pure Loyalty and Obedience to His Majesty; so he ordered it so wisely, that so long as he acted by his own Counsels, and was personally present at the execution of his Designs, he was always prosperous in his Success. And although he had so great an Army, as aforementioned, yet by his wise and prudent Conduct, there appear'd no visible sign of devastation in any of the Countreys where he marched; for first, he setled a constant Rule for the Regular levy of money for the convenient Maintenance of the Soldiery. Next, he constituted such Officers of his Army, that most of them were known to be Gentlemen of large and fair Eſtates, which drew a good part of their private Revenues, to ſerve and ſupport them in their publick Employments; wherein my Lord did lead them the way by his own good Example.

To which may be added his wiſdom in ordering the Government of the Church, for the advancement of the Orthodox Religion, and ſuppreſſion of Faĉlions; as alſo in Coyning, Printing, Knighting, and the like, which he uſed with great diſcretion and prudence, onely for the Intereſt of His Majeſty, and the benefit of the Kingdom, as formerly has been mentioned.

The Prudent mannage of his private and domeſtick affairs, appears ſufficiently: 1. In his Marriage. 2. In the ordering and increaſing his Eſtate before the Wars, which notwithſtanding his Noble Houſekeeping and Hoſpitality, and his Generous Bounty and Charity, he increaſed to the value of 100000 l. 3. In the ordering his Affairs in the time of Baniſhment, where although he received not the leaſt of his own eſtate, during all the time of his exile, until his return; yet maintained himſelf handſomely and nobly, according to his Quality, as much as his Condition at that time would permit. 4. In reducing his torn and ruined Eſtate after his return, which beyond all probability, himſelf hath ſetled and order'd ſo, that his Poſterity will have reaſon gratefully to remember it.

In ſhort; Although my Lord naturally loves not buſineſs, eſpecially thoſe of State, (though he underſtands them as well as any body) yet what buſineſs or affairs he cannot avoid, none will do them better then himſelf. His private affairs he orders without any noiſe or trouble, not over-haſtily, but wiſely: Neither is he paſſionate in acting of buſineſs, but hears patiently, and orders ſoberly, and pierces into the heart or bottom of a buſineſs at the firſt encounter; but before all things, he conſiders well before he undertakes a buſineſs, whether he be able to go through it or no, for he never ventures upon either publick or private buſineſs, beyond his ſtrength.

And here I cannot forbear to mention, that my Noble Lord, when he was in baniſhment, preſumed out of his Duty and Love to his Gracious Maſter our now Soveraign King

*Charles* the Second, to write and send him a little Book, or rather a Letter, wherein he delivered his Opinion concerning the Government of his Dominions, whenſoever God ſhould be pleaſed to reſtore him to his Throne, together with ſome other Notes and Obſervations of Foreign States and Kingdoms; but it being a private offer to His ſacred Majeſty, I dare not preſume to publiſh it.

### 5. *Of his Bleſſings.*

ALTHOUGH my Lord hath been one of the moſt Unfortunate Perſons of his Rank and Quality, which this later age did produce; yet Heaven hath been ſo propitious to him, that it beſtowed ſome bleſſings upon him even in the midſt of his Misfortunes, and ſupported him againſt Fortunes Malice, which otherwiſe, as it ſeems, had deſigned his total ruine and deſtruction: Of theſe Bleſſings I may name in the firſt place,

1. The Royal Favours of His Gracious Soveraign's, and the good eſteem they had of his Fidelity and Loyalty; which as it was the chief of his endeavours, ſo he eſteemed it

above all the reft: To repeat them particularly would be too tedious, and they are fufficiently apparent out of the precedent Hiftory; onely this I may add, that King *Charles* the Firft, out of a fingular Favour to my Lord, was pleafed upon his moft humble requeft, to create feveral Noble-men; the Names of them, left I commit an offence, I fhall not mention, by reafon moft men ufually pretend fuch claimes upon the Ground of their own Merit.

2. That God was pleafed to blefs him with Wealth and Power, to enable him the better for the fervice of his King and Country.

3. That he made him happy in his Marriage; (for his firft Wife was a very kind, loving and Virtuous Lady) and blefs'd him with Dutiful and Obedient Children, free from Vices, Noble and Generous both in ther Natures and Actions; who did all that lay in their power to fupport and relieve my Lord their Father in his Banifhment, as before is mentioned.

4. The Kindnefs and Civility which my Lord received from Strangers, and the Inhabitants of thofe places, where he lived

during the time of his Banifhment; for had it not been for them, he would have perifhed in his extream wants; but it pleafed God fo to provide for him, that although he wanted an Eftate, yet he wanted not Credit; and although he was banifhed and forfaken by his own Friends and Countrymen, yet he was civilly received and relieved by ftrangers, until God blefs'd him.

Laftly, With a happy return to his Native Country, his dear Children, and his own Eftate; which although he found much ruined and broke, yet by his Prudence and Wifdom, hath order'd as well as he could; and I hope, and pray God to add this bleffing to all the reft, That he may live long to encreafe it for the benefit of his Pofterity.

### 6. *Of his Honours and Dignities.*

THE Honours, Titles and Dignities which were conferr'd upon my Lord, by King *James*, King *Charles* the Firft, and King *Charles* the Second, partly as an encouragement for future Service, and a reward for paft, are following.

1. He was made Knight of the *Bath*, when

he was but 15 or 16 years of Age, at the Creation of *Henry*, Prince of *Wales*, King *James's* Eldeſt Son.[1]

2. King *James* Created him Viſcount *Mansfield*, and Baron of *Bolſover*.

3. King *Charles* the Firſt conſtituted him Lord Lieutenant of *Nottinghamſhire*, and

4. Lord Warden of the Forreſt of *Sherwood*; as alſo,

5. Lord Lieutenant of *Derby-ſhire*.

6. He choſe him Governour to His Son *Charles*, our now gracious King; and

7. Made him one of his Honourable Privy Council.

8. He conſtituted him Governour of the Town and County of *Newcaſtle*, and General of all His Majeſties Forces raiſed, and to be raiſed in the Northern parts of *England*; as alſo of the ſeveral Counties of *Nottingham, Lincoln, Rutland, Derby, Stafford, Leiceſter, Warwick, Northampton, Huntington, Cambridg, Norfolk, Suſſex, Eſſex* and *Hereford*, together with all the Appurtenances belong-

---

[1] This is probably the only inſtance of a knighthood conferred upon ſo young a boy.

ing to fo great a Power, as is formerly de-clared.

9. He conferr'd upon him the Honour and Title of Earl of *Newcaſtle*, and Baron of *Bothal* and *Hepple*.

10. He created him Marquefs of *Newcaſtle*.

11. His Majeſty King *CHARLES* the Second, was pleafed, when my Lord was in baniſhment, to make him Knight of the moſt Noble Order of the Garter ; And

12. After his Return into *England*, Chief Juſtice in *Eyre Trent-North*.

13. He created him Duke of *Newcaſtle*, and Earl of *Ogle*.


7. *Of the Entertainments He made for King* CHARLES *the Firſt*.

THOUGH my Lord hath alwayes been free and noble in his Entertainments and Feaſtings, yet he was pleafed to ſhew his great Affection and Duty to his Gracious King, *Charles* the Firſt, and Her Majeſty the Queen, in fome particular Entertainments which he made of purpofe for them before the late Warrs.

When his Majesty was going into *Scotland* to be Crowned, he took His way through *Nottinghamshire*; and lying at *Worksop-Mannor*, hardly two miles distant from *Welbeck*, where my Lord then was, my Lord invited His Majesty thither to a Dinner, which he was graciously pleased to accept of: This Entertainment cost my Lord between Four and Five thousand pounds; which His Majesty liked so well, that a year after His Return out of *Scotland*, He was pleased to send my Lord word, That Her Majesty the Queen was resolved to make a Progress into the Northern parts, desiring him to prepare the like Entertainment for Her, as he had formerly done for Him: Which My Lord did, and endeavour'd for it with all possible Care and Industry, sparing nothing that might add splendor to that Feast, which both Their Majesties were pleased to honour with their Presence: *Ben Johnson* he employed in fitting such Scenes and Speeches as he could best devise; and sent for all the Gentry of the Country to come and wait on their Majesties; and in short, did all that ever he could imagine, to render it Great, and worthy Their Royal Acceptance.

This Entertainment he made at *Bolfover-*Caftle in *Derbyfhire*, fome five miles diftant from *Welbeck*, and refigned *Welbeck* for Their Majefties Lodging; it coft him in all between Fourteen and Fifteen thoufand pounds.

Befides thefe two, there was another fmall Entertainment which my Lord prepared for His late Majefty, in his own Park at *Welbeck*, when His Majefty came down, with his two Nephews, the now Prince Elector Palatine, and His Brother Prince *Rupert*, into the Forreft of *Sherwood*; which coft him Fifteen hundred pounds.

And this I mention not out of a vain-glory, but to declare the great love and Duty, my Lord had for His Gracious King and Queen, and to correct the miftakes committed by fome Hiftorians, who not being rightly in-formed of thofe Entertainments, make the World believe Falfhood for Truth. But as I faid, they were made before the Warrs, when my Lord had the poffeffion of a great Eftate; and wanted nothing to exprefs his Love and Duty to his Soveraign in that manner; whereas now he fhould be much to feek to do the like, his Eftate being fo much ruined.

by the late Civil Wars, that neither himſelf nor his Poſterity will be able ſo ſoon to recover it.

### 8. *His Education.*

HIS Education was according to his Birth; for as he was born a Gentleman, ſo he was bred like a Gentleman. To School-Learning he never ſhew'd a great inclination; for though he was ſent to the Univerſity, and was a Student of St. *John's* Colledg in *Cambridg,* and had his Tutors to inſtruct him; yet they could not perſwade him to read or ſtudy much, he taking more delight in ſports, then in learning; ſo that his Father being a wiſe man, and ſeeing that his Son had a good natural Wit, and was of a very good Diſpoſition, ſuffer'd him to follow his own Genius; whereas his other Son *Charles,* in whom he found a greater love and inclination to Learning, he encouraged as much that way, as poſſibly he could.

One time it hapned that a young Gentleman, one of my Lord's Relations, had bought ſome Land, at the ſame time when my Lord had bought a Singing-Boy for 50 l. a Horfe for 50 l. and a Dog for 2 l.[1] which humour his Father Sir *Charles* liked fo well, that he was pleafed to fay, That if he fhould find his Son to be fo covetous, that he would buy Land before he was 20 years of Age, he would disinherit him. But above all the reft, my Lord had a great inclination to the Art of Horfemanfhip and Weapons, in which later, his Father Sir *Charles*, being a moft ingenuous and un-parallell'd Mafter of that Age, was his onely Tutor, and kept him alfo feveral Mafters in the Art of Horfemanfhip, and fent him to the *Mewfe* to *Mons. Antoine*, who was then ac-counted the beft Mafter in that Art. But my Lord's delight in thofe Heroick Exercifes was fuch, that he foon became Mafter thereof Himfelf, which encreafed much his Father's hopes of his future perfections, who being himfelf a perfon of a Noble and Heroick

---

[1] What a curious collocation ;—a Horfe for £50, a Dog for £2, and a "Singing-Boy" for £50! As the days of feudalifm, fo far as poffeffing one's fellow-creature was concerned, had paffed, we muft conclude that "My Lord" had engaged the boy for his amufement at the coft of £50, and not purchafed him as a chattel.

nature, was extreamly well pleafed to obferve his Son take delight in fuch Arts and Exercifes as were proper and fit for a perfon of Quality.

### 9. *His Natural Wit and Underftanding.*

ALTHOUGH my Lord has not fo much of Scholarfhip and Learning as his Brother Sir *Charles Cavendifh* had, yet he hath an excellent Natural Wit and Judgment, and dives into the bottom of every thing; as it is evidently apparent in the forementioned Art of Horfemanfhip and Weapons, which by his own ingenuity he has reformed and brought to fuch perfection, as never any one has done heretofore: And though he is no Mathematician by Art, yet he hath a very good Mathematical brain, to demonftrate Truth by natural reafon, and is both a good Natural and Moral Philofopher, not by reading Philofophical Books, but by his own Natural Underftanding and Obfervation, by which he hath found out many Truths.

To pafs by feveral other inftances, I'le but mention, that when my Lord was at *Paris*, in

his Exile, it happen'd one time, that he difcourfing with fome of his Friends, amongft
whom was alfo that Learned Philofopher
*Hobbes*, they began amongft the reft, to argue
upon this fubje&, namely, *Whether it were
poffible to make Man by Art fly as Birds do;* and
when fome of the Company had delivered
their Opinion, *viz.* That they thought it
probable to be done by the help of Artificial
Wings : My Lord declared, that he deemed
it altogether impoffible, and demonftrated it
by this following Reafon : Man's Armes, faid
he, are not fet on his fhoulders in the fame
manner as Bird's wings are ; for that part of
the Arm which joins to the Shoulder, is in
Man placed inward, as towards the breaft,
but in Birds outward, as toward the back ;
which difference and contrary pofition or
fhape, hinders that man cannot have the fame
flying-a&ion with his Armes, as Birds have
with their Wings ; Which Argument Mr.
*Hobbes* liked fo well, that he was pleafed to
make ufe of it in one of his Books called
*Leviathan,* if I remember well.

Some other time they falling into a Difcourfe concerning Witches, Mr. *Hobbes* faid,

That though he could not rationally believe there were Witches, yet he could not be fully fatisfied to believe there were none, by reafon they would themfelves confefs it, if ftrictly examined.

To which my Lord anfwer'd, That though for his part he cared not whether there were Witches or no; yet his Opinion was, That the Confeffion of Witches, and their fuffering for it, proceeded from an Erroneous Belief, *viz.* That they had made a Contract with the Devil to ferve him for fuch Rewards as were in his Power to give them; and that it was their Religion to worfhip and adore him; in which Religion they had fuch a firm and conftant belief, that if any thing came to pafs according to their defire, they believed the Devil had heard their prayers, and granted their requefts, for which they gave him thanks; but if things fell out contrary to their prayers and defires, then they were troubled at it, fearing they had offended him, or not ferved him as they ought, and afked him forgivenefs for their offences. Alfo (faid my Lord) they imagine that their Dreams are real exterior actions; for example, if they dream they flye in the Air, or out of the Chimney top, or that they are turned into feveral fhapes, they be-lieve no otherwife, but that it is really fo: And this wicked Opinion makes them induf-trious to perform fuch Ceremonies to the Devil, that they adore and worfhip him as their God, and chufe to live and dye for him.

Thus my Lord declared himfelf concerning Witches, which Mr. *Hobbes* was alfo pleafed to infert in his fore-mentioned Book: But yet my Lord doth not count this Opinion of his fo univerfal, as if there were none but imaginary Witches; for he doth not fpeak but of fuch a fort of Witches as make it their Religion to worfhip the Devil in the manner aforefaid. Nor doth he think it a Crime to entertain what Opinion feems moft probable to him, in things indifferent; for in fuch cafes men may difcourfe and argue as they pleafe, to exercife their Wit, and may change and alter their Opinions upon more probable Grounds and Reafons; whereas in Funda-mental matters both of Church and State, he is fo ftrict an Adherent to them, that he will never maintain or defend fuch Opinions which are in the leaft prejudicial to either.[1]

One proof more I'le add to confirm his Natural Underftanding and Judgment, which was upon fome Difcourfe I held with him one time, concerning that famous Chymift *Van Helmont*, who in his Writings is very invective againft the School-men, and amongft the reft, accufes them for taking the Radical moifture for the fat of Animal Bodies. Whereupon my Lord anfwer'd, That furely the School-men were too wife to commit fuch an Error; for, faid he, the Radical moifture is not the fat or tallow of an Animal, but an Oily and Balfamous Subftance; for the fat and tallow, as alfo the watery parts, are cold; whereas the Oily and Balfamous parts, have at all times a lively heat; which makes that thofe Creatures which have much of that Oyle or Balfom, are long-liv'd, and appear young; and not onely Animals, but alfo Vegetables, which have much of that Oyle or Balfom, as Ivy, Bayes, Laurel, Holly, and the like, live

---

[1] It is not neceffary here to comment upon witchcraft; but it is pretty clear that the Duke was in advance of popular opinions and notions on that fubject.

long, and appear fresh and green, not onely
in Winter, but when they are old.  Then I
ask'd my Lord's Opinion concerning the
Radical heat: To which he answer'd, That
the Radical heat lived in the Radical moisture;
and when the one decayed, the other decayed
also; and then was produced either an unnatural heat, which caused an unnatural dry-
ness; or an unnatural moisture, which caused
Dropsies, and these, an unnatural coldness.

Lastly; His Natural Wit appears by his
delight in Poetry; for I may justly call him
the best *Lyrick* and *Dramatick* Poet of this
Age:  His Comedies do sufficiently shew his
great Observation and Judgment, for they are
composed of these three Ingredients, *viz. Wit,
Humour* and *Satyre;* and his chief Design in
them, is to divulge and laugh at the follies of
Mankind; to persecute Vice, and to encourage Virtue.

10. *Of his Natural Humour and Disposition.*

MY Lord may justly be compared to *Titus*
the *Deliciæ* of Mankind, by reason of
his sweet, gentle and obliging Nature; for

though his Wifdom and Experience found it impoffible to pleafe all men, becaufe of their different humours and difpofitions; yet his Nature is fuch, that he will be forry when he feeth that men are difpleafed with him out of their own ill Natures, without any caufe; for he loves all that are his Friends, and hates none that are his Enemies: He is a Loyal Subject, a kind Hufband, a Loving Father, a Generous Mafter, and a Conftant Friend.

His natural Love to his Parents has been fo great, that I have heard him fay, he would moft willingly, and without the left repining, have begg'd for his daily relief, fo God would but have let his Parents live.

He is true and juft both in his words and actions, and has no mean or petty Defigns, but they are all juft and honeft.

He condemns not upon Report, but upon Proof; nor judges by Words, but Actions; he forgets not paft Service, for prefent Advantage; but gives a prefent Reward to a prefent Defert.

He hath a great Power over his Paffions, and hath had the greateft tryals thereof; for certainly He muft of neceffity have a great share of Patience, that can forgive so many false, treacherous, malicious and ungrateful Persons as he hath done; but he is so wise, that his Passion never out-runs his Patience, nor his Extravagancies his Prudence; and although his Private Enemies have been numerous, yet I verily believe, there is never a subject more generally beloved then He is.

He hates Pride and loves Humility; is civil to Strangers, kind to his Acquaintance, and respectful to all persons, according to their Quality; He never regards Place, except it be for Ceremony: To the meanest person he'll put off his Hat, and suffer every body to speak to him.

He never refuses any Petition, but accepts them; and being informed of the business, will give a just, and as much as lies in him, a favourable answer to the Petitioning Party.

He easily Pardons, and bountifully Rewards; and always praises particular mens Virtues, but covers their Faults with silence.

He is full of Charity and Compassion to persons that are in misery, and full of Clemency and Mercy; in so much, that when he was General of a great Army, he would never sit in

Council himfelf upon Caufes of Life and Death, but granted Pardon to many Delinquents that were condemned by his Council of War; fo that fome were forced to Petition him not to do it, by reafon it was an ill prefident for others. To which my Lord merrily anfwer'd, That if they did hang all, they would leave him none to fight.

His Courage he always fhew'd in Action, more then in Words, for he would Fight, but not Rant.

He is not Vain-glorious to heighten or brag of his Heroick Actions; Witnefs that great Victory upon *Atherton-moor*, after which he would not fuffer his Trumpets to found, but came quietly and filently into the City of *York*, for which he would certainly have been blamed by thofe that make a great noife upon fmall caufes; and love to be applauded, though their actions little deferve it.

His noble Bounty and Generofity is fo manifeft to all the World, that I fhould light a Candle to the Sun, if I fhould ftrive to illuftrate it; for he has no felf-defigns or felf-intereft, but will rather wrong and injure himfelf then others. To give you but one proof of this noble Vertue, it is known, that where he hath a legal right to Felons Goods, as he hath in a great part of his Eftate, yet he never took or exacted more then fome inconfiderable fhare for acknowledgment of his Right; faying, That he was refolved never to grow rich by other mens misfortunes.

In fhort, I know him not addicted to any manner of Vice, except that he has been a great lover and admirer of the Female Sex; which whether it be fo great a crime as to condemn him for it; I'le leave to the judgment of young Gallants and beautiful Ladies.

11. *Of His outward Shape and Behaviour.*

HIS Shape is neat, and exactly proportioned; his Stature of a middle fize, and his Complexion fanguine.[1]

---

[1] There is an excellent portrait of the Duke in "Lodge's Portraits." It was painted by Vandyke. It reprefents him as a man under forty years of age, with clear, bright, eyes, flowing hair, a mouftache and a *barbe de bouc.* He wears the elaborate lace collar of the period. The expreffion of the countenance is extremely pleafing, amiable, and agreeable. No wonder that the Duchefs could dote on fuch a hufband!

His Behaviour is such, that it might be a Pattern for all Gentlemen; for it is Courtly, Civil, easie and free, without Formality or Constraint; and yet hath something in it of grandure, that causes an awful respect towards him.

## 12. *Of His Discourse.*

HIS Discourse is as free and unconcerned, as his Behaviour, Pleasant, Witty, and Instructive; He is quick in Reparties or sudden answers, and hates dubious disputes, and premeditated Speeches. He loves also to intermingle his Discourse with some short pleasant stories, and witty sayings, and always names the Author from whom he hath them; for he hates to make another man's Wit his own.

## 13. *Of His Habit.*

HE accouters his Person according to the Fashion, if it be one that is not troublesome and uneasie for men of Heroick Exercises and Actions. He is neat and cleanly; which makes him to be somewhat long in

dreffing, though not fo long as many effeminate perfons are. He fhifts ordinarily once a
day, and every time when he ufes Exercife, or
his temper is more hot then ordinary.

## 14. *Of his DIET.*

IN his Diet he is fo fparing and temperate,
that he never eats nor drinks beyond his
fet proportion, fo as to fatisfie onely his natural
appetite : He makes but one Meal a day, at
which he drinks two good Glaffes of Small-
Beer, one about the beginning, the other at
the end thereof, and a little Glafs of Sack in
the middle of his Dinner; which Glafs of
Sack he alfo ufes in the morning for his
Breakfaft, with a Morfel of Bread. His
Supper confifts of an Egg, and a draught of
Small-beer. And by this Temperance he
finds himfelf very healthful, and may yet live
many years, he being now of the Age of
Seventy three, which I pray God from my
foul, to grant him.

## 15. *His Recreation and Exercife.*

HIS prime Paftime and Recreation hath
always been the Exercife of Mannage

and Weapons; which Heroick Arts he ufed to practife every day; but I obferving that when he had over-heated himfelf, he would be apt to take cold, prevail'd fo far, that at laft he left the frequent ufe of the Mannage, ufing neverthelefs ftill the Exercife of Weapons; and though he doth not ride himfelf fo frequently as he hath done; yet he takes delight in feeing his Horfes of Mannage rid by his Efcuyers, whom he inftructs in that Art for his own pleafure. But in the Art of Weapons (in which he has a method beyond all that ever were famous in it, found out by his own Ingenuity and Practice) he never taught any body, but the now Duke of *Buckingham*, whofe Guardian He hath been, and his own two fons.

The reft of his time he fpends in Mufick, Poetry, Architecture and the like.

## 16. *Of His Pedigree.*

HAVING made promife in the beginning of the firft Book, that I would join a more large Defcription of the Pedigree of my Noble Lord and Hufband, to the end of the

Hiftory of his life: I fhall now difcharge my felf; and though I could derive it from a longer time, and reckon up a great many of his Anceftors, even from the time of *William* the Conqueror, He being defcended from the moft ancient family of the *Gernouns*, as *Cambden* relates in his *Britannia*, in the Defcription of *Derbyfhire*; yet it being a work fitter for Heralds, I fhall proceed no further then his Grandfather, and fhew you onely thofe noble Families which my Lord is allied to by his Birth.

My Lord's Grandfather, by his Father, (as is formerly mentioned) was Sir *William Cavendifh*, Privy-Counfellor and Treafurer of the Chamber to King *Henry* the Eighth, *Edward* the Sixth, and Queen *Mary*; who married two Wives; by the firft he had onely two Daughters; but by the fecond, *Elizabeth*, who was my Lords Grandmother, he had three Sons and four Daughters, whereof one Daughter died young. She was Daughter to *John Hardwick* of *Hardwick*, in the County of *Derby*, Efq.; and had four Hufbands: The firft was — *Barlow*, Efq.; who died before they were bedded together, they being both very young. The fecond was Sir *William Cavendish*, my Lord's Grandfather, who being fomewhat in years, married her chiefly for her beauty; fhe had fo much power in his affection, that fhe perfwaded him to fell his Eftate which he had in the Southern parts of *England* (for he was very rich) and buy an Eftate in the Northern parts, *viz.* in *Derby-fhire*, and thereabout, where her own friends and kindred liv'd, which he did; and having there fetled himfelf, upon her further perfwafion, built a Mannor-houfe in the fame County, call'd *Chattefworth*, which, as I have heard, coft firft and laft above 80,000 l. *fterling*. But before this Houfe was finifh'd, he died, and left fix Children, viz. three Sons and three Daughters, which before they came to be marriageable, fhe married a third Hufband, Sir William S$^t$ *Loo* Captain of the Guard to Queen *Elizabeth*, and Grand Butler of *England*; who dying without Iffue, fhe married a fourth Hufband, *George*, Earl of *Shrewfbury*, by whom fhe left no iffue.

The Children which fhe had by her fecond Hufband, Sir *William Cavendifh*, being grown marriageable; the eldeft Son *Henry*, married

*Grace* the youngeſt Daughter of his Father in Law, the ſaid *George* Earl of *Shrewſbury*, which he had by his former Wife *Gertrude*, Daughter of *Thomas Manners*, Earl of *Rutland*, but died without Iſſue.

The ſecond Son *William*, after Earl of *Devonſhire*, had two Wives; the firſt was an Heireſs, by whom he had Children, but all died ſave one Son, whoſe name was alſo *Wiliam*, Earl of *Devonſhire* : His ſecond Wife was Widdow to Sir *Edward Wortly*, who had ſeveral Children by her firſt Huſband, and but one Son by the ſaid *Will. Cavendiſh*, after Earl of *Devonſhire*, who dyed young.

His Son by his firſt Wife, (*William* Earl of *Devonſhire*) married *Chriſtian*, Daughter of *Edward* Lord *Bruce*, a *Scots*-man, by whom he had two Sons, and one Daughter; the Eldeſt Son *William*, now Earl of *Devonſhire*, married *Elizabeth*, the ſecond Daughter of *William* Earl of *Saliſbury*, by whom he has three children, *viz.* Two Sons and one Daughter, whereof the Eldeſt Son *William* is married to the ſecond Daughter of *James* now Duke of *Ormond;* the ſecond Son *Charles* is yet a youth : The Daughter *Anne* married the

Lord *Rich*, the onely Son and Child to *Charles* now Earl of *Warwick*; but he dyed without Iſſue.

The ſecond Son of *William* Earl of *Devonſhire*, and Brother to the now Earl of *Devonſhire*, was unfortunately ſlain in the late Civil Warrs, as is before mentioned.

The Daughter of the ſaid *William* Earl of *Devonſhire*, Siſter to the now Earl of *Devonſhire*, married *Robert* Lord *Rich*, Eldeſt Son to *Robert* Earl of *Warwick*, by whom ſhe had but one Son, who married, but dyed without Iſſue.

The third and youngeſt Son of Sir *William Cavendiſh*, *Charles Cavendiſh*, (my Lord's Father) had two Wives; the firſt was Daughter and Coheir to Sir *Thomas Kidſon*, who dyed a year after her Marriage, without iſſue: The ſecond was the younger Daughter of *Cuthbert* Lord *Ogle*, and after her Elder and onely Siſter *Jane*, Wife to *Edward* Earl of *Shrewſbury*, who dyed without Iſſue, became Heir to her Father's Eſtate and Title; by whom he had three Sons; whereof the eldeſt dyed in his Infancy; the ſecond was *William*, my dear Lord and Huſband; the third, *Charles*, who dyed a Batchelour about the age of Sixty three.

My Lord hath had two Wives; the firſt was *Elizabeth*, Daughter and Heir to *William Baſſet* of *Bloore*, in the County of *Stafford*, Eſq.; and Widow to *Henry Howard*, younger Son to *Thomas* Earl of *Suffolk*; by whom he had ten Children, *viz.* Six Sons, and four Daughters;[1] whereof ·five, *viz.* four Sons, and one Daughter, dyed young; the reſt, *viz.* Two Sons and three Daughters, came to be married.

His Elder Son, *Charles*, Viſcount of *Manſ-field*, married the Eldeſt Daughter and Heir of Mr. *Richard Rogers*, by whom he had but one Daughter, who dyed ſoon after her birth; and he dyed alſo without any other Iſſue.

His ſecond Son *Henry*, now Earl of *Ogle*, married *Francis* the eldeſt Daughter of Mr. *William Pierrepont*, by whom he hath had three Sons, and four Daughters; two Sons

---

[1] In the copy of the " Life " before me this ſeems to be a misſtatement, and from ſome obliterations and correſtions (made, I think, by the Ducheſs herſelf), the number of children appears to have been ſix ſons and four daughters.

were born before their natural time ; the third, *Henry* Lord *Mansfield* is alive : The four Daughters are, the Lady *Elizabeth*, Lady *Frances*, Lady *Margaret*, and Lady *Catherine*.

My Lords three Daughters were thus married ; The eldeſt, Lady *Jane*, married *Charles Cheiney*, Eſq. ; deſcended of a very noble and ancient family ; by whom ſhe hath one Son and two Daughters. The ſecond, Lady *Elizabeth*, married *John* now Earl of *Bridgwater*, then Lord *Brackly*, and eldeſt Son to *John* then Earl of *Bridgwater ;* who died in Childbed, and left five Sons, and one Daughter, whereof the eldeſt Son *John* Lord *Brackly*, married the Lady *Elizabeth*, onely Daughter and Child to *James* then Earl of *Middleſex*.

My Lords third Daughter, the Lady *Frances*, married *Oliver* Earl of *Bullingbrook*, and hath had no Child yet.

After the death of my Lords firſt Wife, who died the 17*th* of *April*, in the Year 1643, he married me, *Margaret*, Daughter to *Thomas Lucas* of St. *Johns* near *Colcheſter*, in *Eſſex*, Eſquire ; but hath no Iſſue by me.

And this is the Posterity of the three Sons of Sir *William Cavendish*, my Lords Grandfather by his Fathers side; The three Daughters were disposed of as followeth :

The eldest, *Frances Cavendish*, married Sir *Henry Pierrepont* of *Holm Pierrepont*, in the County of *Nottingham*, by whom she had two Sons, whereof the first died young; The second, *Robert*, after Earl of *Kingston* upon *Hull*, married *Gertrude*, the eldest Daughter, and Co-heir to *Henry Talbot*, fourth Son to *George* Earl of *Shrewsbury*, by whom he had five Sons and three Daughters, whereof the eldest Son, *Henry*, now Marquess of *Dorchester*, hath had two Wives; the first *Cecilia*, Eldest Daughter to the Lord Viscount *Bayning*, by whom he had several Children, of which there are living onely two Daughters; the eldest *Anne*, who married *John Rosse*, onely Son to *John* now Earl of *Rutland*; the second, *Grace*, who is unmarried. His second Wife was *Catharine*, second Daughter to *James* Earl of *Derby*, by whom he has no Issue living.

The second Son of the Earl of *Kingston*, *William*, married the sole Daughter and Heir of Sir *Thomas Harries*, by whom he had Issue five Sons, and five Daugters, whereof two Sons and two Daughters died unmarried: The other fix are,

*Robert* the Eldeft, who married *Elizabeth*, Daughter and Co-heir to Sir *John Evelyne*, by whom he has three Sons, and one Daughter. The fecond Son *George*, and the third *Gervas*, are yet unmarried.

The eldeft Daughter of *William Pierrepont*, *Frances*, is married to my Lords now onely Son and Heir, *Henry* Earl of *Ogle*, as before is mentioned.

The fecond, *Grace*, is married to *Gilbert* now Earl of *Clare*, by whom he hath Iffue, Two fons, and three daughters.

The third, *Gertrude*, is unmarried.

The third fon of the Earl of *Kingfton*, *Francis Pierrepont*, married *Elizabeth* the eldeft daughter of Mr. *Bray*, by whom he had Iffue, one fon, and one daughter; the fon, *Robert*, married *Anne* the daughter of *Henry Murray*. The daughter, *Frances*, married *William Pagatt*, eldeft fon to *William* Lord *Pagatt*. (Paget.)

The fourth fon of the Earl of *Kingfton*, *Gervafe*, is unmarried.

The fifth fon, *George Pierrepont*, married the daughter of Mr. *Jonas*, by whom he had two fons unmarried, *Henry* and *Samuel.*

The three daughters of the faid Earl of *Kingfton*, are, *Frances* the eldeft, who was married to *Philip Rowlefton;* the fecond, *Mary*, dyed young; the third, *Elizabeth*, is unmarried.

The fecond daughter of Sir *William Cavendifh*, *Elizabeth*, married the Earl of *Lennox*, Unkle to King *James;* by whom fhe had onely one daughter, the Lady *Arabella*, who againft King *Jame's* Commands (fhe being after Him and His Children, the next Heir to the Crown) married *William*, the fecond fon to the Earl of *Hereford;* for which fhe was put into the Tower, where not long after fhe dyed.

The youngeft daughter *Mary Cavendifh*, married *Gilbert Talbot*, fecond fon to *George* Earl of *Shreufbury;* who after the deceafe of his Father, and his elder Brother *Francis*, who dyed without Iffue, became Earl of *Shrewfbury;* by whom fhe had Iffue, four fons, and three daughters; the fons all dyed in their Infancy, but the daughters were married.

The eldeſt, *Mary Talbot*, married *William Herbert*, Earl of *Pembroke*, by whom (ſome eighteen years after her Marriage) ſhe had one ſon, who dyed young.

The ſecond daughter, *Elizabeth*, married Sir *Henry Gray*, after *Earl* of *Kent*, (the fourth Earl of *England*) by whom ſhe had no Iſſue.

The third and youngeſt daughter *Aletheia*, married *Thomas Howard*, Earl of *Arundel*, the firſt Earl, and Earl-Marſhal of *England*; by whom ſhe left two ſons, *James*, who died beyond the ſeas without Iſſue; and *Henry*, who married *Elizabeth*, daughter of *Eſme Stuart*, Duke of *Lennox*; by whom he had Iſſue, ſeveral ſons, and one daughter; whereof the eldeſt ſon, *Thomas*, (ſince the Reſtauration of King *Charles* the Second) was reſtored to the Dignity of his Anceſtors, *viz.* Duke of *Norfolk*, next to the Royal Family, the firſt Duke of *England*.

And this is briefly the Pedigree of my dear Lord and Huſband, from his Grandfather by his Fathers ſide; concerning his Kindred and alliances by his Mother, who was *Katherine*,

Daughter to *Cuthbert* Lord *Ogle*, they are so many, that it is impossible for me to enumerate them all, My Lord being by his Mother related to the chief of the most ancient Families of *Northumberland*, and other the Northern parts; onely this I may mention, that My Lord is a Peer of the Realm, from the first year of King *Edward* the Fourth his Reign.

The
# Life of the Moſt Illuſtrious
Prince, William Duke of
Newcaſtle.

## THE FOURTH BOOK:
CONTAINING SEVERAL ESSAYS AND DISCOURSES
GATHER'D FROM THE MOUTH OF MY
NOBLE LORD AND HVSBAND.

*With ſome few Notes of mine own.*

*I have heard My Lord ſay,*

**I.**

HAT thoſe which command the Wealth of a Kingdom, command the hearts and hands of the People.

**II.**

That He is a great Monarch, who hath a Soveraign Command over Church, Laws and

Armes; and He a wife Monarch, that im-
ploys his fubjects for their own profit, (for
their profit is his) encourages Tradefmen,
and affifts and defends Merchants.

### III.

That it is a part of Prudence in a Commonwealth or Kingdom to encourage dray-
ners; for drowned Lands are onely fit to
maintain and encreafe fome wild Ducks,
whereas being drained, they are able to afford
nourifhment and food to Cattel, befides the
producing of feveral forts of Fruit and Corn.

### IV.

That without a well order'd force, a Prince
doth but reign upon the courtefie of others.

### V.

That great Princes fhould not fuffer their
chief Cities to be ftronger then themfelves.

### VI.

That great Princes are half-armed, when
their fubjects are unarmed, unlefs it be in time
of Foreign Wars.

### VII.

That the Prince is richeft, who is Mafter
of the Purfe; and he ftrongeft that is Mafter

of the Armes; and he wifeſt that can tell how to ſave the one, and uſe the other.

### VIII.

The Great Princes ſhould be the onely Pay-Maſters of their Soldiers, and pay them out of their own Treaſuries; for all men follow the Purſe; and ſo they'l have both the Civil and Martial Power in their hands.

### IX.

That Great Monarchs ſhould rather ſtudy men, then Books; for all affairs or buſineſs are amongſt Men.

### X.

That a Prince ſhould advance Foreign Trade or Traffik to the utmoſt of his Power, becauſe no State or Kingdom can be Rich without it; and where Subjects are poor, the Soveraign can have but little.

### XI.

That Trade and Traffick brings Honey to the Hive; that is to ſay, Riches to the Commonwealth; whereas other Profeſſions are ſo far from that, that they rather rob the Commonwealth, inſtead of enriching it.

### XII.

That it is not fo much unfeafonable Weather that makes the Countrey complain of Scarcity, but want of Commerce; for whenfoever Commodities are cheap, it is a fign that Commerce is decayed; becaufe the cheapnefs of them, fhews a fcarcity of money; for example, put the cafe five men came to Market to buy a Horfe, and each of them had no more but ten pounds, the Seller can receive no more then what the Buyer has, but muft content himfelf with thofe ten pounds, if he be neceffitated to fell his Horfe : But if each one of the Buyers had an hundred pounds to lay out for a Horfe, the Seller might receive as much. Thus Commodities are cheap or dear, according to the plenty or fcarcity of money ; and though we had Mynes of Gold and Silver at home, and no Traffick into Foreign parts, yet we fhould want neceffaries from other Nations, which proves that no Nation can live or fubfift well, without Foreign Trade and Commerce ; for God and Nature have order'd it fo, That no particular Nation is provided with all things.

### XIII.

That Merchants by carrying out more Commodities then they bring in; that is to fay, by felling more then they buy, do enrich a State or Kingdom with money, that hath none in its own bowels; but what Kingdom or State foever hath Mynes of Gold and Silver, there Merchants buy more then they fell, to furnifh and accommodate it with neceffary provifions.

### XIV.

That debafing, and fetting a higher value 'upon money, is but a prefent fhift of poor and needy Princes; and doth more hurt for the future, then good for the prefent.

### XV.

That Foraign Commerce caufes frequent Voyages; and frequent Voyages make fkilful and experienced Seamen, and Skilful Sea men are a Brazen Wall to an Ifland.

### XVI.

That he is the Powerfulleft Monarch that hath the beft fhipping; and that a Prince fhould hinder his Neighbours as much as he can, from being ftrong at Sea.

### XVII.

That wife States-men ought to underftand the Laws, Cuftomes and Trade of the Commonwealth, and have good intelligence both of Foraign Tranfactions and Defigns, and of Domeftick Factions; alfo they ought to have a Treafury, and well-furnifhed Magazine.

### XVIII.

That it is a great matter in a State or Kingdom, to take care of the Education of Youth, to breed them fo, that they may know firft how to obey, and then how to command and order affairs wifely.

### XIX.

That it is great Wifdom in a State, to breed and train up good States-men: As, firft, To let them be fome time at the Univerfities: Next, To put them to the Innes of Court, that they may have fome knowledg of the Laws of the Land; then to fend them to travel with fome Ambaffador, in the quality of Secretary; and let them be Agents or Refidents in Foraign Countreys. Fourthly, To make them Clerks of the Signet, or Council:

And laſtly, To make them Secretaries of State, or give them ſome other Employment in State-Affairs.

### XX.

That there ſhould be more Praying, and leſs Preaching; for much Preaching breeds Faction; but much Praying cauſes Devotion.

### XXI.

That young people ſhould be frequently Catechiſed, and that Wiſe Men rather then Learned, ſhould be choſen heads of Schools and Colledges.

### XXII.

That the more diviſions there are in Church and State, the more trouble and con-fuſion is apt to enſue: Wherefore too many Controverſies and Diſputes in the one, and too many Law-Caſes and Pleadings in the other ought to be avoided and ſuppreſſed.

### XXIII.

That Diſputes and Factions amongſt Stateſ-men, are fore-runners of future diſorders, if not total ruines.

### XXIV.

That all Books of Controverfies fhould be writ in Latin, that none but the Learned may read them, and that there fhould be no Difputations but in Schools, left it breed Factions amongft the Vulgar; for Difputations and Controverfies are a kind of Civil War, maintained by the Pen, and often draw out the fword foon after : Alfo that all Prayer-Books fhould be writ in the native Language; that Excommunications fhould not be too frequent for every little and petty trefpafs ; that every Clergy-man fhould be kind and loving to his Parifhioners, not proud and quarrelfome.

### XXV.

That Ceremony is nothing in it felf, and yet doth every thing ; for without Ceremony there would be no diftinction neither in Church nor State.

### XXVI.

That Orders and Profeffions ought not to entrench upon each other, left in time they make a confufion amongft themfelves.

### XXVII.

That in a Well-ordered State or Government, care fhould be taken left any degree or profeffion whatfoever fwell too big, or grow too numerous, it being not onely a hinderance to thofe of the fame profeffion, but a burden to the Commonwealth, which cannot be well if it exceeds in extreams.

### XXVIII.

That the Taxes fhould not be above the riches of the Commonwealth, for that muft upon neceffity breed Factions and Civil Wars, by reafon a general poverty united, is far more dangerous then a private Purfe; for though their Wealth be fmall, yet their Unity and Combination makes them ftrong; fo that being armed with neceffity, they become outragious with defpair.

### XXIX.

That Heavy Taxes upon Farmes, ruine the Nobility and Gentry; for if the Tenant be poor, the Landlord cannot be rich, he having nothing but his Rents to live on.

### XXX.

That it is not fo much Laws and Religion, nor Rhetorick, that keeps a State or Kingdom in order, but Armes; which if they be not imploy'd to an evil ufe, keep up the right and priviledges both of Crown, Church and State.

### XXXI.

That no equivocations fhould be ufed either in Church or Law; for the one caufes feveral Opinions to the difturbance of mens Confciences; the other long and tedious Suits, to the difturbance of mens private Affairs; and both do oftentimes ruine and impoverifh the State.

### XXXII.

That in Cafes of Robberies and Murthers, it is better to be fevere, then merciful; for the hanging of a few, will fave the lives and Purfes of many.

### XXXIII.

That many Laws do rather entrap, then help the fubject.

### XXXIV.

That no Martial Law fhould be executed, but in an Army.

## XXXV.

That the Sheriffs in this Kingdom of *England* have been fo expenfive in Liveries and Entertainments in the time of their Sherifalty, as it hath ruined many Families that had but indifferent Eftates.

## XXXVI.

That the cutting down of Timber in the time of Rebellion, has been an ineftimable lofs to this Kingdom, by reafon of Shipping; for though Timber might be had out of Foreign Countries that would ferve for the building of Ships, yet there is none of fuch a temper as our *Englifh* Oak; it being not onely ftrong and large, but not apt to fplint, which renders the Ships of other Nations much inferior to ours; and that therefore it would be very beneficial for the Kingdom, to fet out fome Lands for the bearing of fuch Oaks, by fowing of Acorns, and then tranfplanting them; which would be like a Storehoufe for fhipping, and bring an incomparable benefit to the Kingdom, fince in Shipping confifts our greateft ftrength, they being the onely Walls that defend an Ifland.[1]

## XXXVII.

That the Nobility and Gentry in this Kingdom, have done themfelves a great injury, by giving away (out of a petty pride) to the Commonalty, the power of being Juries and Juftices of Peace; for certainly they cannot but underftand, that that muft of neceffity be an act of great Confequence and Power, which concerns mens Lives, Lands and Eftates.

## XXXVIII.

That it is no act of Prudence to make poor and mean perfons Governours or Commanders, either by Land or Sea ; by reafon their poverty

---

[1] This is the firft allufion I have met with to the "Wooden Walls of Old England." Of all the oak grown in this country, the Suffex oak was accounted the tougheft and beft. For ftatements refpecting the almoft wanton deftruction of the forefts and woods of that county, fee my "Contributions to Literature," pp. 115-119. I wifh the Duke's fuggeftion of fowing acorns would be acted upon by our great landed proprietors; for if they did not perfonally derive benefit, their fucceffors would furely do fo.

caufes them to take Bribes, and fo betray their
Truft; at beft, they are apt to extort, which
is a great grievance to the people; befides, it
breeds envy in the Nobility and Gentry, who
by that means rife into Factions, and caufe
difturbances in a State or Commonwealth:
Wherefore the beft way is to chufe Rich and
Honourable Perfons, (or at leaft, Gentlemen)
for fuch Employments, who efteem Fame and
Honourable Actions, above their Lives; and
if they want fkill, they muft get fuch under-
Officers as have more then themfelves, to inftruct them.

### XXXIX.

That great Princes fhould confider, before
they make War againft Foreign Nations,
whether they be able to maintain it; for if
they be not able, then it is better to fubmit
to an honourable Peace, then to make Warr
to their great difadvantage; but if they be
able to maintain Warr, then they'l force (in
time) their Enemies to fubmit and yeild to
what Tearms and Conditions they pleafe.

### XL.

That, when a State or Government is en-

fnarled and troubled, it is more eafie to raife
the common people to a Factious Mutiny,
then to draw them to a Loyal Duty.

### . XLI.

That in a Kingdom where Subjects are
apt to rebel, no Offices or Commands fhould
be fold ; for thofe that buy, will not onely ufe
extortion, and practice unjuft wayes to make
out their purchafe, but be ableft to rebel, by
reafon they are more for private gain, then
the publick good; for it is probable their
Principles are like their Purchafes.

But, that all Magiftrates, Officers, Commanders, Heads and Rulers, in what Profeffion foever, both in Church and State, fhould
be chofen according to their Abilities, Wifdom, Courage, Piety, Juftice, Honefty and
·Loyalty ; and then they'l mind the public
Good, more then their particular Intereft.

### XLII.

That thofe which have Politick Defigns,
are for the moft part difhoneft, by reafon
their Defigns tend more to Intereft, then
Juftice.

### XLIII.

That Great Princes fhould onely have Great, Noble and Rich Perfons to attend them, whofe Purfes and Power may alwayes be ready to affift them.

### XLIV.

That a Poor Nobility is apt to be Factious; and a Numerous Nobility is a burden to a Commonwealth.

### XLV.

That in a Monarchical Government, to be for the King, is to be for the Commonwealth; for when Head and Body are divided, the Life of Happinefs dies, and the Soul of Peace is departed.

### XLVI.

That, as it is a great Error in a State to have all Affairs put into *Gazettes*, (for it over-heats the peoples brains, and makes them neglect their private Affairs, by over-bufying themfelves with State-bufinefs;) fo it is great Wifdom for a Council of State to have good Intelligences (although they be bought with great Coft and Charges) as well of Domeftick, as Foreign Affairs and Tranfactions, and to keep them in private for the benefit of the Commonwealth.

### XLVII.

That there is no better Policy for a Prince to pleafe his People, then to have many Holy-dayes for their eafe, and order feveral Sports and Paftimes for their Recreation, and to be himfelf fometime Spectator thereof; by which means he'l not onely gain love and refpect from the people, but bufie their minds in harmlefs actions, fweeten their Natures, and hinder them from Factious Defigns.

### XLVIII.

That it is more difficult and dangerous for a Prince or Commander to raife an Army in fuch a time when the Countrey is embroiled in a Civil Warr, then to lead out an Army to fight a Battel; for when an Army is raifed, he hath ftrength; but in raifing it, he hath none.

### XLIX.

That good Commanders, and experienced Soldiers, are like fkilfull Fencers, who defend

with Prudence, and affault with Courage, and
kill their Enemies by Art, not trufting their
Lives to Chance or Fortune; for as a little
man with fkill, may eafily kill an ignorant
Giant; fo a fmall Army that hath experienced
Commanders, may eafily overcome a great
Army that hath none.

### L.

That Gallant men having no employment
for Heroick Actions, become lazy, as hating
any other bufinefs; whereas Cowards and
bafe perfons are onely active and ftirring in
times of Peace, working ill defigns to breed
Factions, and caufe difturbances in a Com-
mon-wealth.

### LI.

That there have been many Queftions and
Difputes concerning the Governments of
Princes; as, Whether they ought to govern
by Love, or Fear? But the beft way of
Government is, and has alwayes been by juft
Rewards and Punifhments; for that State
which cannot tell how and when to punifh
and reward, does not know how to govern,
by reafon all the World is governed that way.

### LII.

That if the ancient *Britains* had had skill, according to their Courage, they might have conquer'd all the World, as the *Romans* did.

### LIII.

That it would be very beneficial for great Princes to be sometimes present in Courts of Judicature, to examine the Causes of their poor Subjects, and find out the Extortions and Corruptions of Magistrates and Officers; by which glorious Act they would gain much Love and Fame from the People.

### LIV.

That it would be very advantagious for Subjects, and not in the least prejudicial to the Soveraign, to have a general Register in every County, for the Entry of all manner of Deeds, and Conveyance of Land between party and party, and Offices of Record; for by this means, whosoever buyes, would see clearly what Interest and Title there is in any Land he intends to purchase, whereby he shall be assur'd that the Sale made to him is good and firm, and prevent many Law-suits touching the Title of his Purchase.

### LV.

That there fhould be a Limitation for Law-Suits; and that the longeft Suit fhould not laft above two Tearms, at length not above a Year; which would certainly be a great benefit to the Subjects in general, though not to Lawyers; and though fome Polititians object, That the more the people is bufie about their private Affairs, the lefs time have they to make difturbance in the publick; yet this is but a weak Argument, fince Law-fuits are as apt to breed Factions, as any thing elfe; for they bring people into poverty, that they know not how to live, which muft of neceffity breed difcontent, and put them upon ill defigns.

### LVI.

That Power, for the moft part, does more then Wifdom; for Fools with Power, feem wife; whereas wife men, without Power, feem Fools; and this is the reafon that the World takes Power for Wifdom; and the want of Power for Foolifhnefs.

### LVII.

That a valiant man will not refuse an honourable Duel; nor a wise man fight upon a Fools Quarrel.

### LVIII.

. That men are apt to find fault with each other's actions; believing they prove themselves wise in finding fault with their Neighbours.

### LIX.

That a wise man will draw several occasions to the point of his design, as a Burning-Glass doth the several beams of the Sun.

### LX.

That although actions may be prudently designed, and valiantly performed; yet none can warrant the issue; for Fortune is more powerful then Prudence, and had *Cæsar* not been fortunate, his Valour and Prudence would never have gained him so much applause.

### LXI.

That ill Fortune, makes wise and honest men seem Fools and Knaves; but good

Fortune makes Fools and Knaves ſeem wiſe and honeſt men.

### LXII.

That ill Fortune doth oftner ſucceed good; then good Fortune ſucceeds ill ; for thoſe that have ill Fortune, do not ſo eaſily recover it, as thoſe that have good Fortune are apt to loſe it.

### LXIII.

That he had obſerved, That ſeldom any perſon did laugh, but it was at the follies or misfortunes of other men ; by which we may judg of their good natures.

### LXIV.

I have heard my Lord ſay, That when he was in Baniſhment, He had nothing left him, but a clear Conſcience, by which he had and did ſtill conquer all the Armies of misfortunes that ever ſeized upon him.

### LXV.

Alſo I have heard him ſay, That he was never beholding to Lady Fortune ; for he had ſuffered on both ſides, although he never was but on one ſide.

### LXVI.

I have heard him fay, That his Father one time, upon fome difcourfe of expences, fhould tell him, *It was but juft that every man fhould have his time.*

### LXVII.

I have heard my Lord fay, That bold foliciting and intruding men, fhall gain more by their importunate Petitions, then modeft honeft men fhall get by filence (as being loath to offend, or be too troublefome) both in the manner and matter of their requefts: The reafon is, faid he, That Great Princes will rather grant fometimes an unreafonable fuit, then be tired with frequent Petitions, and hindered from their ordinary Pleafures; And when I afked my Lord, whether the Grants of fuch importunate fuits were fitly and properly placed? He anfwered, Not fo well as thofe that are placed upon due confideration, and upon trial and proof.

### LXVIII.

I have heard my Lord fay, That it is a great Error, and weak Policy in a State, to advance their Enemies, and endeavour to make them friends by bribing them with Honours and Offices, ſaying, They are ſhrewd men, and may do the State much hurt: And on the other ſide, to neglect their Friends, and thoſe that have done them great ſervice, ſaying, they are Honeſt men, and mean the State no harm: For this kind of Policy comes from the Heathen, who pray'd to the Devil, and not to God, by reaſon they ſuppoſed God was Good, and would hurt no Creature; but the Devil they flatter'd and worſhipp'd out of fear, leſt he ſhould hurt them: But by this fooliſh Policy, ſaid he, they moſt commonly encreaſe their Enemies, and loſe their Friends; for firſt, it teaches men to obſerve, that the onely way to Preferment, is to be againſt the State or Government: Next, Since all that are Factious, cannot be rewarded or preferr'd, by reaſon a State hath more Subjects, then Rewards or Preferments, there muſt of neceſſity be numerous Enemies; for when their hopes of Reward fail them, they grow more Factious and Inveterate then ever they were at firſt: Wherefore the beſt Policy in a State or Government, ſaid my

Lord, is to reward Friends, and punifh Enemies, and prefer the Honeft before the Factious; and then all will be real Friends, and profer their honeft fervice, either out of pure Love and Loyalty, or in hopes of Advancement, feeing there is none but by ferving the State.

### LXIX.

I have heard him fay feveral times, That his love to his gracious Mafter King *Charles* the Second, was above the love he bore to his Wife, Children, and all his Pofterity, nay to his own life: And when, fince His Return into *England*, I anfwer'd him, That I obferved His Gracious Mafter did not love him fo well as he lov'd Him; he replied, That he cared not whether His Majefty lov'd him again or not; for he was refolved to love him.

### LXX.

I afking my Lord one time, What kind of Fate it was, that reftored our Gracious King, *Charles* the Second, to His Throne? He anfwer'd, It was a bleffed kind of Fate. I replied, That I had obferved a perfect con-

trariety between the Fortunes of His Royal
Father, of blessed memory, and Him; for as
there was a division amongst the generality of
the people, in the Reign of King *Charles* the
First, tending to His Destruction; so there
was a general Combination and Agreement
between them in King *Charles* the Second
His Restauration; and as there was a general
malice amongst the people against the Father
to Depose Him; so there was a general Love
for the Son to Enthrone Him. My Lord
answer'd, I had observed something, but not
all; for, said he, there was a Necessity for
the people to desire and Restore King *Charles*
the Second; but there was no Necessity to
Murder King *Charles* the First. For the
Kingdom being through so many Alterations
and Changes of Government, divided into
several Factions and Parties, was at last
hurried into such a Confusion, that it was
impossible in that manner to subsist, or hold
out any longer; Which Confusion having
opened the Peoples Eyes, the generality being
tyred with the evil effects and consequences
of their unsetled Governments under unjust
Usurpers, and frightned with the apprehen-

fion of future dangers, began to call to mind
the happy Times, when in an uninterrupted
Peace they enjoyed their own, under the
happy Reign of their Lawful Soveraigns; and
hereupon with an unanimous confent Re-
call'd and Reftor'd our now gracious King;
which, although it was oppofed by fome
Factious Parties, yet the generality of the
people outweigh'd the reft; neither was the
Royal Party wanting in their endeavours.

**LXXI.**

Afking my Lord one time, Whether it was
eafie or difficult to govern a State or Kingdom? He anfwer'd me, That moft States
were govern'd by fecret Policy, and fo with
difficulty; for thofe that govern, are (at leaft,
fhould be) wifer then the State or Commonwealth they govern. I replied, That in my
opinion, a State was eafily govern'd, if their
Government was like unto God's; that is to
fay, If Governours did Reward and Punifh
according to the defert. My Lord anfwer'd,
I faid well; but he added, the Follies of the
People are many times too hard for the
Prudence of the Governour; like as the fins

of men work more evil effects in them, then the Grace of God works good; for if this were not, there would be more good then bad, which, alas, Experience proves otherwise.

## LXXII.

Some Gentlemen making a complaint to my Lord, That some he employed in His Majesty's Affairs, were too hasty and over-busie. My Lord told them, That he would rather chuse such persons for His Majesties service as were over-active, then such that would be fuller of Questions then Actions. The same he would do for his own particular affairs.

## LXXIII.

Some condemning My Lord for having *Roman-Catholicks* and *Scots* in His Army; He answered them, that he did not examine their Opinions in Religion, but look'd more upon their Honesty and Duty; for certainly there were honest men and loyal Subjects amongst *Roman Catholicks*, as well as Protestants; and amongst *Scots* as well as *English*. Neverthelefs, my Lord, as he was for the King, so he was alfo for the Orthodox Church of *England,* as fufficiently appears by the care he took in ordering the Church-Government, mentioned in the Hiftory. To which purpofe, when my Lord was walking one time with fome of His Officers in the Church at *Durham,* and wonder'd at the greatnefs and ftrength of the Pillars that fupported that ftructure; My Brother, Sir *Charles Lucas,* who was then with him, told my Lord, that he muft confefs, thofe Pillars were very great, and of a vaft ftrength; But faid he, Your Lordfhip is a far greater Pillar of the Church then all thefe: Which certainly was alfo a real truth, and would have more evidently appear'd, had Fortune favour'd my Lord more then fhe did.

LXXIV.

My Lord being in Banifhment, I told him, that he was happy in his misfortunes, for he was not fubject to any State or Prince. To which he jeftingly anfwer'd, That as he was fubject to no Prince, fo he was a Prince of no Subjects.

LXXV.

In fome Difcourfe which I had with my

Lord concerning Princes and their Sujects; I declared that I had obferved Great Princes were not like the Sun, which fends forth out of it felf Rays of Light, and Beams of Heat; effects that did both glorifie the Sun, and nourifh and comfort fublunary Creatures; but their glory and fplendor proceeded rather from the Ceremony which they received from their fubjects. To which my Lord anfwer'd, That Subjects were fo far from giving fplendor to their Princes, that all the Honours and Titles, in which confifts the chief fplendor of a fubject, were principally derived from them; for, faid he, were there no Princes, there would be none to confer Honours and Titles upon them.

### LXXVI.

My Lord entertaining one time fome Gentlemen with a merry Difcourfe, told them, that he would not keep them Company except they had done and fufferd as much for their King and Country as he had. They anfwer'd, That they had not a power anfwerable to my Lords. My Lord replied, They fhould do their endeavour according to their Abilities:

No, said they, if we did, we should be like your Self, lose all, and get but little for our pains.

### LXXVII.

I being much grieved that my Lord for his loyalty and honest Service, had so many Enemies, used sometimes to speak somewhat sharply of them; but he gently reproving me, said, *I should do like experienced Sea-men, and as they either turn their Sails with the wind, or take them down; so should I either comply with Time, or abate my Passion.*

### LXXVIII.

A Soldiers Wife, whose Husband had been slain in my Lord's Army, came one time to beg some relief of my Lord; who told her, That he was not able to relieve all that had been loyal to His Majesty; for said he, My losses are so many, that if I should give away the remainder of my Estate, my Wife and Children would have nothing to live on: She answer'd, That His Majesty's Enemies were preferr'd to great Honours, and had much Wealth: Then it is a sign (replied my Lord) that your Husband and I were Honest Men.

### LXXIX.

A Friend of my Lord's, complaining that he had done the State much Service, but received little Reward for it; my Lord anſwer'd him, That States did not uſually reward paſt Services; but if he could do ſome preſent Service, he might perhaps get ſomething; but (ſaid he) thoſe men are wiſeſt that will be paid before-hand.

### LXXX.

I obſerving that in the late Civil Warrs, many were deſirous to be employed in States Affairs, and at the noiſe of Warr, endeavoured to be Commanders, though but of ſmall Parties, aſked my Lord the reaſon thereof, and what advantage they could make by their Employments? My Lord ſmilingly anſwer'd, That for the generality, he knew not what‧ they could get, but danger, loſs and labour for their pains. Then I aſk'd him, Whether Generals of Great Armies were ever enriched by their Heroick Exploits, and great Victories? My Lord anſwer'd, That ordinary Commanders gained more, and were better rewarded then great Generals. To which I

added, That I had obferv'd the fame in Hiftories, namely, That Men of great Merit and
Power, had not onely no Rewards, but were
either found fault withall, or laid afide when
they had no more bufinefs or employment for
them; and that I could not conceive any
reafon for it, but that States were afraid of
their Power: My Lord anfwer'd, The reafon
was, That it was far more eafie to reward
Under-Officers, then Great Commanders.

<h3 style="text-align:center">LXXXI.</h3>

My Lord having fince the Return from his
Banifhment, fet up a Race of Horfes, inftead
of thofe he loft by the Warrs, ufes often to
ride through his Park to fee his Breed. One
time it chanced when he went thorough it,
that he efpied fome labouring-men fawing of
Woods that were blown down by the Wind,
for fome particular ufes; at which my Lord
turning to his Attendants, faid, That he had
been at that Work a great part of his life.
They not knowing what my Lord meant,
but thinking he jefted; I fpeak very ferioufly,
(added he) and not in jeft; for you fee that
this Tree which is blown down by the Wind,

although it was found and strong, yet it could not withstand its force; and now it is down, it must be cut in pieces, and made serviceable for several uses; whereof some will serve for Building, some for Paling, some for Firing, &c. In the like manner, said he, have I been cut down by the Lady Fortune; and being not able to resist so Powerful a Princess, I have been forced to make the best use of my Misfortunes, as the Chips of my Estate.

### LXXXII.

My Lord discoursing one time with some of his Friends, of judging of other mens Natures, Dispositions and Actions; and some observing that men could not possibly know or judg of them, the events of mens actions falling out oftentimes contrary to their intentions; so that where they hit once, they fail'd twenty times in their Judgments. My Lord answer'd, That his Judgment in that point seldom did miss, although he thought it weaker then theirs: The reason is, said he, Because I judg most men to be like my self; that is to say, Fools; when as you do judg them all according to your self, that is, Wise men;

and since there are more Fools in the World then Wise men, I may sooner guess right then you : for though my judgment roves at random, yet it can never miss of Errors; which yours will never do, except you can dive into other mens Follies by the length of your own line, and found their bottom by the weight of your own Plummet, for the depth of Folly is beyond the line of Wisdom.

Besides, said he, You believe that other men would do as you would have them, or as you would do to them; wherein you are mistaken, for most men do the contrary. In short, Folly is bottomless, and hath no end ; but Wisdom hath bounds to all her designs, otherwise she would never compass them.

### LXXXIII.

My Lord discoursing some time with a Learned Doctor of Divinity concerning Faith, said, That in his opinion, the wisest way for a man, was to have as little Faith as he could for this World, and as much as he could for the next World.

### LXXXIV.

In some Discourse with my Lord, I told him

that I did fpeak fharpeft to thofe I loved beft.
To which he jeftingly anfwered, That if fo,
then he would not have me love him beft.

### LXXXV.

After my Lords return from a long Banifhment, when he had been in the Countrey
fome time, and endeavoured to pick up fome
Gleanings of his ruined Eftate; it chanced
that the Widow of *Charles* Lord *Mansfield*,
My Lords Eldeft Son, afterwards Duchefs of
*Richmond*, to whom the faid Lord of *Manf-
field* had made a joynture of 2000l. a Year,
died not long after her fecond marriage; for
whofe death, though My Lord was heartily
forry, and would willingly have loft the faid
Money, had it been able to fave her life; Yet
difcourfing one time merrily with his Friends,
was pleafed to fay, That though his Earthly
King and Mafter feem'd to have forgot him,
yet the King of Heaven had remembred him,
for he had given him 2000l. a Year.

# Some Few Notes of the Authoreſſe.

### 1.

T was far more difficult in the late Civil Wars, for my Lord to raiſe an Army for His Majeſties Service, then it was for the Parliament to raiſe an Army againſt His Majeſty: Not onely becauſe the Parliament were many, and my Lord but one ſingle Perſon; but by reaſon a Kingly or Monarchical Government was then generally diſliked, and moſt part of the Kingdom proved Rebellious, and aſſiſted the Parliament either with their Purſes or Perſons, or both; when as the Army which my Lord raiſed for the defence and maintenance of the King, and

his Rights, was raifed moft upon his own and his Friends Intereft : For it is frequently feen and known by woful Experience, that rebellious and factious Parties do more fuddenly and numeroufly flock together to act a mifchievous defign, then loyal and honeft men to affift or maintain a juft Caufe; and certainly 'tis much to be lamented, that evil men fhould be more induftrious and profperous then good, and that the Wicked fhould have a more defperate Courage, then the Virtuous, an active Valour.

## II.

I have obferved, That many by flattering Poets, have been compared to *Cæfar*, without defert; but this I dare freely and without flattery fay of my Lord, That though he had not *Cæfars* Fortune, yet he wanted not *Cæfars* Courage, nor his Prudence, nor his good Nature, nor his Wit; Nay, in fome particulars he did more then *Cæfar* ever did; for though *Cæfar* had a great Army, yet he was firft fet ont by the State or Senators of *Rome*, who were Mafters almoft of all the World; when as my Lord raifed his Army (as before

is mentioned) moſt upon his own Intereſt (he
having many Friends and Kindred in the
Northern parts) at ſuch a time when his
Gracious King and Soveraign was then not
Maſter of his own Kingdoms, He being over-
power'd by his rebellious Subjects.

III.

I have obſerved, That my Noble Lord has
always had an averſion to that kind of Policy,
that now is commonly practiſed in the world,
which in plain tearms is Diſſembling, Flattery
and Cheating, under the cover of Honeſty,
Love and Kindneſs : But I have heard him
ſay, that the beſt Policy is to act juſtly,
honeſtly and wiſely, and to ſpeak truly ; and
that the old Proverb is true ; *To be wiſe is to
be honeſt :* For, ſaid he, That man of what
Condition, Quality or Profeſſion ſoever, that
is once found out to deceive either in words
or actions, ſhall never be truſted again by wiſe
and honeſt men. But, ſaid he, A wiſe man
is not bound to take notice of all Diſſem-
blers, and their cheating Actions, if they do
not concern him ; nay, even of thoſe he
would not always take notice, but chuſe his

time; for the chief part of a wife man is to time bufinefs well, and to do it without Partiality and Paffion. But, faid he, The folly of the world is fo great, that one honeft and wife man may be overpowred by many Knaves and Fools; and if fo, then the onely benefit of a wife man confifts in the fatif-faction he finds by his honeft and wife actions, and that he has done what in Con-fcience, Honour and Duty he ought to do; and all fucceffors of fuch worthy Perfons ought to be more fatisfied in the worth and merit of their Predeceffours, then in their Title and Riches.

## IV.

I have heard that fome noble Gentleman, (who was fervant to His Highnefs then Prince of *Wales*, our now Gracious Sove-raign, when my Lord was Governour) fhould relate, that whenfoever my Lord by his prudent infpection and forefight did foretell what would come to pafs hereafter; it feemed fo improbable to him, that both him-felf and fome others believed my Lord fpoke extravagantly: But fome few years after, his predictions proved true, and the event did confirm what his Prudence had obferved.

v.

I have heard, That in our late Civil Warres there were many petty Skirmifhes, and Fortifications of weak and inconfiderable Houfes, where fome fmall Parties would be fhooting and pottering at each other; an action more proper for Bandites or Thieves, then ftout and valiant Soldiers; for I have heard my Lord fay, That fuch fmall Parties divide the Body of an Army, and by that means weaken it; whereas the bufinefs might be much eafier decided in one or two Battels, with lefs ruine both to the Country and Army: For I have heard my Lord fay, That as it is dangerous to divide a Limb from the Body; . fo it is alfo dangerous to divide Armies or Navies in time of Warr; and there are often more menloft in fuch petty Skirmifhes, then in fet-Battels, by reafon thofe happen almoft every day, nay every hour in feveral places.

VI.

Many in our late Civil-Warres, had more Title then Power; for though they were

Generals, or chief Commanders, yet their Forces were more like a Brigade, then a well-formed Army; and their actions were accordingly, not fet-battels, but petty Skirmifhes between fmall Parties; for there were no great Battels fought, but by my Lord's Army, his being the greateft and beft-formed Army which His Majefty had.

VII.

Although I have obferved, That it is a ufual Cuftom of the World, to glorifie the prefent Power and good Fortune, and vilifie ill Fortune and low conditions; yet I never heard that my Noble Lord was ever neglected by the generality; but was on the contrary, alwayes efteemed and praifed by all; for he is truly an Honeft and Honourable man, and one that may be relied upon both for Truft and Truth.

VIII.

I have obferved, That many inftead of great Actions, make onely a great Noife, and like fhallow Fords, or empty Bladders, found moft when there is leaft in them; which expreffes a flattering Partiality, rather then Honefty and Truth ; for Truth and Honefty lye at the bottom; and have more Action then Shew.

IX.

I have obferved, That good Fortune adds Fame to mean Actions, when as ill Fortune darkens the fplendor of the moft meritorious ; for mean Perfons plyed with good Fortune, are more famous then Noble Perfons that are fhadowed or darkned with ill Fortune ; fo that Fortune, for the moft part, is Fame's Champion.

X.

I obferve, That as it would be a grief to covetous and miferable perfons, to be rewarded with Honour, rather then with Wealth, be- caufe they love Wealth, before Honour and Fame ; fo on the other fide, Noble, Heroick and Meritorious Perfons, prefer Honour and Fame before Wealth ; well knowing, That as Infamy is the greateft Punifhment of un- worthinefs, fo Fame and Honour is the beft Reward of worth and merit.

XII.

I obferve, that fpleen and malice, efpecially in this age, is grown to that height, that none will endure the praife of any body befides themfelves ; nay, they'l rather praife the wicked then the good ; the Coward rather then the Valiant ; the Miferable then the Generous ; the Traytor, then the Loyal : which makes Wife men meddle as little with the Affairs of the world as ever they can.

### XIII.

I have obferved, as well as former Ages have done, That Meritorious perfons, for their noble actions, moft commonly get Envy and Reproach, inftead of Praife and Reward ; unlefs their Fortunes be above Envy, as *Cæfar's* and *Alexander's* were ; But had thefe two Worthies been as Unfortunate as they were Fortunate, they would have been as much vilified, as they are glorified.

### XIV.

I have obferved, that it is more eafie to talk, then to act ; to forget, then to remember ; to punifh, then to reward ; and more common to prefer Flattery before Truth, Intereft be- fore Juftice, and prefent fervice before paft.

### xv.

I have obferved, that many old Proverbs are very true, and amongft the reft, this: It is better to be at the latter end of a Feaft, then at the beginning of a Fray; for moft commonly, thofe that are in the beginning of a Fray, get but little of the Feaft; and thofe that have undergone the greateft dangers, have leaft of the fpoils.

### xvi.

I have obferved, That Favours of Great Princes make men often thought Meritorious; whereas without them, they would be efteemed but as ordinary Perfons.

### xvii.

I obferve, That in other Kingdoms or Countries, to be the chief Governour of a Province, is not onely a place of Honour, but much Profit; for they have a great Revenue to themfelves; whereas in *England*, the Lieutenancy of a County is barely a Title of Honour, without Profit; except it be the Lieutenancy or Government of the Kingdom of *Ireland*; efpecially fince the late Earl of

*Stafford* enjoyed that dignity, who fetled that Kingdom very wifely both for Militia and Trade.

### XVIII.

I have obferved, That thofe that meddle leaft in Wars, whether Civil or Foreign, are not onely moft fafe and free from danger, but moft fecure from Loffes ; and though Heroick Perfons efteem Fame before Life, yet many there are, that think the wifeft way is to be a Spectator, rather then an Actor, unlefs they be neceffitated to it ; for it is better, fay they, to fit on the Stool of Quiet, then in the Chair of Troublefome Bufinefs.

FINIS.

# Natures Pictures

DRAWN BY

# FANCIES PENCIL

TO THE LIFE.

.

WRITTEN BY THE

THRICE NOBLE, ILLUSTRIOUS, AND EXCELLENT PRINCESS,

The LADY MARCHIONESS of NEWCASTLE.

*In this Volume there are several feigned Stories of Natural
Descriptions, as Comical, Tragical, and Tragi-comical,
Poetical, Romancical, Philosophical and Historical, both in
Prose and Verse, some all Verse, some all Prose, some mixt,
partly Prose, and partly Verse. Also, there are some Morals,
and some Dialogues; but they are as the advantage, Loaves
of Bread as a Baker's Dozen; and a true Story at the
latter End, wherein there is no feigningss.*

*LONDON:*

PRINTED BY J. MARTIN AND J. ALLESTRYE, AT THE BELL,

IN SAINT PAUL'S CHURCH YARD.

1656.

A TRUE RELATION

OF THE

*Birth, Breeding, and Life,*

OF

# MARGARET CAVENDISH,

DUCHESS OF NEWCASTLE.

WRITTEN BY HERSELF.

WITH A

𝕮ritical 𝕻reface, &c.

BY

SIR EGERTON BRYDGES, M.P.

" What tafte, and elegance, and genius does,
  Still favours fomething greater than its place,
  However low, or high."—*Shakefp.*

" Though Fortune, vifible an enemy,
  Should chafe a virtuous pair, no jot of power
  Hath fhe to change their loves."—*Ibid.*

KENT :

𝕻rinted at the pribate 𝕻ress of 𝕷ee 𝕻riorȳ;

BY JOHNSON AND WARWICK.

1814.

# Sir Egerton Brydges'
# Preface.

UTO-BIOGRAPHY is fo at-
tractive, that in whatever man-
ner it is executed, it feldom fails
both to entertain and inftruct.
The Memoirs of *Margaret, Duchefs of Newcaftle*, written by herfelf, appear to me very
eminently to poffefs this double merit. Whether
they confirm or refute the character of the
literary and moral qualities of her Grace given
by Lord Orford, I muft leave the reader to
judge. The fimplicity by which they are
marked will, in minds conftituted like that of
the noble critic, feem to approximate to folly:
others, lefs inclined to farcafm, and lefs infected
with an artificial tafte, will probably think far
otherwife.

That the Duchefs was deficient in a cultivated judgment; that her knowledge was
more multifarious than exact; and that her
powers of fancy and fentiment were more
active than her powers of reafoning, I will
admit: but that her productions, mingled as
they are with great abfurdities, are wanting
either in talent, or in virtue, or even in genius,
I cannot concede.

There is an ardent ambition, which may
perhaps itfelf be confidered to prove fuperiority
of intellect. " I fear my ambition," fays the
Duchefs, "inclines to vain-glory; for I am
very ambitious; yet 'tis neither for beauty,
wit, titles, wealth, or power, but as they are
fteps to raife me to Fancy's Tower, which is
to live by remembrance in after-ages!" In
another place fhe exhibits traits of herfelf, fuch
as generally accompany genius. " I was
addicted," her Grace obferves, " from my
childhood to contemplation, rather then converfation; to folitarinefs, rather then fociety;
to melancholy rather then mirth; to write
with the pen then to work with the needle,
paffing my time with harmlefs fancies, their
company being pleafing, their converfation

innocent, in which I take fuch pleafure, as I neglect my health ; for it is as great a grief to neglect their fociety, as a joy to be in their company." Again, fhe fays: " my difpofition is more inclining to melancholy then merry; but not crabbed or peevifh melancholy, but foft, melting, folitary, and contemplating melancholy; and I am apt to weep rather than laugh."

Perhaps, however, it will be impoffible to acquit the Duchefs of vanity, as well as ambition, if it be vanity to indulge a too general and indifcriminate love of diftinction; and to expatiate with too much minutenefs about onefelf. Some of thefe minutiæ now afford amufement, arifing from other pretenfions than thofe with which they were written.

Her Grace was the companion of the Duke's misfortunes, the folace of his exile, the fharer of his poverty. In thefe gloomy days fhe had lefs opportunity of being acquainted with the fplendour of courts, and the characters and manners of men eminent on the theatre of practical life, than with the fcenes and actions of her own lonely imagination. We do not, therefore, find this Memoir full of anecdote,

or hiftory, or political delineation.  It is all
domeftic; and this domeftic painting is its
charm.

If the Duchefs herfelf were out of the
queftion, it is not uninterefting to have fuch
a circumftantial account of the reft of the
noble family of Lucas.  Whether their mode
of life be confidered as common to others of
their rank, or peculiar to themfelves, the
picture is pleafing and inftructive.  The
mother's character excites refpect and affection.  The burfting of the ftorms of civil war
upon thofe days of peace, and virtue, and
plenty, which fmiled fo treacheroufly on the
youth of the Duchefs, is truly affecting.  "In
fuch misfortunes," fays her Grace, "my
mother was of an heroick fpirit, in fuffering
patiently where there is no remedy; or to be
induftrious where fhe thought fhe could help.
She was of a grave behaviour, and had fuch a
majeftick grandeur, as it were continually hung
about her, that it would ftrike a kind of awe
to the beholders, and command refpect from
the rudeft."  "She lived to fee the ruin of
her children, in which was her ruin, and then
died!"—"Not onely the family I am linked to

is ruined, but the family from which I fprung, by thefe unhappy wars."

At pp. 11 and 12, the Duchefs has given with exquifite *naivetè* the account of her own going into the world, as maid of honour to the Queen, when the Court was at Oxford, and her fubfequent attachment and marriage to the Duke, then Marquis of Newcaftle. Not long after their marriage, the lofs of the battle of Marfton-moor drove them into exile. They moved from Paris to Holland, whence neceffity forced the Duchefs to come to England to folicit relief out of the Duke's immenfe eftates, which the prevailing Powers had feized.

Her Grace remained a year and half in England, during which fhe wrote her "*Poems*," and her "*Philofophical Fancies;*" to which fhe made large additions after fhe returned abroad. After her return alfo fhe wrote the volume from which this "*Life*" is extracted; and another book. Her "*World's Olio*" was, for the moft part, written before fhe went to England.

In this exile, and under the difappointment of her ineffectual efforts for relief, fhe fays,

" Heaven hitherto hath kept us, and though Fortune hath been crofs, yet we do fubmit, and are both content with what is, and cannot be mended; and are fo prepared, that the worft of fortunes fhall not afflict our minds, fo as to make us unhappy, howfoever it doth pinch our lives with poverty; for, if tranquillity lives in an honeft mind, the mind lives in peace, although the body fuffer."

What can be more amiable and virtuous, than a refort to the confolations of literature in fuch a ftate? After the enjoyment of high and flattering rank, and fplendid fortune, noble is the fpirit that will not be broken by the gripe of Poverty, the expulfion from home, and kindred, and friends, and the defertion of the world! Under the blighting gloom of fuch oppreffion to create wealth and a kingdom " within the mind," fhews an intellectual energy, which ought not to be defrauded of its praife.

After the Reftoration, peace and affluence once more fhone upon them amid the longloft domains of the Duke's vaft hereditary property. Welbeck opened her gates to her Lord; and the caftles of the North received with joy their heroic chieftain, whofe maternal anceftors, the baronial houfe of OGLE, had ruled over them for centuries in Northumberland. But Age had now made the Duke defirous only of repofe; and her Grace, the faithful companion of his fallen fortunes, was little difpofed to quit the luxurious quiet of rural grandeur, which was as foothing to her difpofition, as it was concordant with her duty. To fuch a pair the noify and intoxicated joy of a profligate court would probably have been a thoufand times more painful than all the wants of their late chilling, but calm, poverty. They came not, therefore, to palaces and levees; but amufed themfelves in the country with literature and the arts. This folitary ftate, this innocent magnificence, feems to have afforded contempt and jefts to the fophifticated mob of diffolute wits, who crowded round King Charles II. Thefe momentary buzzers in the artificial funfhine of the regal prefence, probably thought that they, who having the power to mix with fuperior wealth, in the bufy fcenes of high life, could prefer the infipid charms of lonely Nature, were only fit to be the butt of their ridicule! It is probable

that the memory of thefe witticifms might not
have entirely faded before the early years of
the late Lord Orford, who might have caught
the mantle of thefe fpritely oracles, and have
pronounced on the poor Duchefs's character
and amufements in a fimilar tone.

Still I muft not permit myfelf to be fo far
heated by my fubject, as to furrender the advantages of a juft but candid difcrimination.
Her Grace had, as I conceive, talents, as well
as virtues, which raifed her above the·multi-
tude, much higher than her rank.  Her powers,
with the aid of a little more arrangement, of
fomething more of fcholaftic polifh, and of a
moderate exertion of maturer judgment, might
have produced writings, which pofterity would
have efteemed both for their inftruction and
amufement.  But I muft admit that fhe wanted
the primary qualities of genius.   She was
neither fublime nor pathetic.  She had not
the talent of feizing that *felection* of circum-
ftances, of touching by a few fingle ftrokes
thofe chords, which, through the force of
affociation in our ideas, calls up at once whole
pictures !   Imitators, and they whofe poetical

faculties are not genuine, multiply images, by which, while they think they are excelling their models, deftroy the whole charm.

Her Grace wanted tafte; fhe knew not what to obtrude, and what to leave out. She pours forth every thing with an undiftinguifh-ing hand, and mixes the ferious, the collo-quial, and even the vulgar, in a manner which cannot be defended. In the "*Life*," how-ever, now reprinted, this great fault is lefs apparent than in any other of her compofi-tions.

But we muft not compare thefe compofi-tions with the more refined exactnefs of later times. In thofe days what female writer was there, who could endure the critical acumen of the prefent period? Who now reads Mrs. Katharine Phillips, better known by her poetical name of *Orinda?* And Mrs. Behn, who lived fomewhat later, is more remarkable for her licentioufnefs than for any better quality. Even of Mrs. Killegrew, the encomium beftowed by Dr. Johnfon[1] is

---

[1] In "The Life of Dryden."

generally thought to be undeſerved.  The
Counteſs of Pembroke, Lady Carew, Lady
Wrothe, and a few others ſucceeded; but
their productions are now unnoticed, except by a few black-letter literati.

# A True Relation of my Birth, Breeding, and Life.[1]

By Margaret, Duchess of Newcastle.

MY father was a Gentleman, which Title is grounded and given by Merit, not by princes; and 'tis the act of Time,[2] not Favour: and though my Father was not a

---

[1] [The notes are thofe of Sir Egerton Brydges, and I am not refponfible for them. The text of the Lee Priory Prefs reprint is full of typographical blunders, which, by careful collation with the rare copy in the Britifh Mufeum, have been corrected.]

[2] This remark, and fomething like this expreffion, had been already ufed by Lord Bacon, with regard to old nobility. If rank, ftation, or wealth, obtained by a low man, were commonly the refult of merit, the neweft honours would be the moft worthy of refpect; but as it

Peer of the Realm, yet there were few Peers who had much greater Eſtates, or lived more noble therewith : yet at that time great Titles were to be ſold,[1] and not at ſo high rates, but that his Eſtate might have eaſily purchaſed, and was preſt for to take ; but my Father did not eſteem Titles, unleſs they were gained by Heroick Actions ; and the Kingdome being in a happy Peace with all other Nations, and in itſelf being governed by a wiſe King, King James, there was no Employments for heroick Spirits ; and towards the latter end of Queen Elizabeths reign, as ſoon as he came to Mans eſtate, he unfortunately fortunately killed one Mr. Brooks in a ſingle Duel ; for

---

is too often otherwiſe, and wealth is more apt to follow narrow cunning, and perhaps fraud, than generous induſtry or ſkill, and titles, inſtead of being the recompenſe of generally-admitted worth or talents, too often flow from an individual act of whim or intereſt by a corrupt Miniſter, the diſtinctions which have been created by Time, are, on the whole, more worthy of eſteem and admiration, than thoſe which favour has procured to the preſent poſſeſſor.

[1] This relates to the reign of King James. The fact is a matter of general, not ſecret hiſtory, and may be found even in the pages of Hume, which are generally deficient in minute details.

my father by the Laws of Honour could do no lefs then call him to the field, to queftion him for an injury he did him, where their Swords were to difpute, and one or both of their lives to decide the argument, wherein my Father had the better; and though my Father by Honour challengd him, with Valour fought him, and in Juftice killed him, yet he fuffered more then any Perfon of Quality ufually doth in cafes of Honour; for though the Laws be rigorous, yet the prefent Princes moft commonly are gratious in thofe misfortunes, efpecially to the injured: but my Father found it not, for his exile was from the time of his misfortunes to Queen Elizabeths death; for the Lord Cobham [1] being then a great man with Queen Eliza-

---

[1] This was the Lord Cobham, whofe fubfequent misfortunes, condemnation, lofs of eftate, long imprifonment, and death in miferable poverty, as a Principal in what is called *Raleigh's Plot*, have been too often related to need repetition. See more efpecially " *Memoirs of King James's Peers*," 8vo. 1804. It feems aftonifhing, though the fact ftands on various authorities, that Cobham, weak as he was both in head and heart, fhould ever have been a favourite of the bold and magnanimous Queen.

beth, and this Gentleman, Mr. Brooks, a kind of a Favourite, and as I take it Brother to the then L. Cobham, which made Queen Elizabeth fo fevere, not to pardon him: but King James of bleſſed memory gracioufly gave him his Pardon, and leave to return home to his Native Country, wherein he lived happily, and died peaceably, leaving a Wife and eight Children, three Sons, and five Daughters, I being the youngeſt Child he had, and an Infant when he died.

As for my breeding, it was according to my Birth, and the Nature of my Sex; for my Birth was not loft in my Breeding, for as my Sifters was or had been bred, fo was I in Plenty, or rather with fuperfluity; Likewife we were bred Virtuoufly, Modeftly, Civilly, Honourably, and on honeft principles: as for plenty, we had not only, for Neceffity, Conveniency, and Decency, but for delight and pleafure to a fuperfluity; 'tis true we did not riot, but we lived orderly; for riot, even in Kings' Courts and Princes' Palaces, brings ruin without content or pleafure, when order in lefs fortunes fhall live more plentifully and delicioufly then Princes, that lives in a hurlie-

burlie, as I may terme it, in which they are
feldom well ferved, for diforder obftructs;
befides, it doth difguft life, diftract the appe-
tites, and yield no true relifh to the fences;
for Pleafure, Delight, Peace and Felicitie,
live in method and temperance.

As for our garments, my Mother did not
only delight to fee us neat and cleanly, fine
and gay, but rich and coftly; maintaining us
to the height of her eftate, but not beyond it;
for we were fo far from being in debt, before
thefe warrs, as we were rather beforehand
with the world; buying all with ready money,
not on the fcore; for although after my
fathers death the Eftate was divided between
my Mother and her Sonns, paying fuch a fum
of money for Portions to her Daughters,
either at the day of their marriage, or when
they fhould come to age; yet by reafon fhe
and her children agreed with a mutual confent, all their affairs were managed fo well,
as fhe lived not in a much lower condition
than when my father lived; 'tis true, my
mother might have increaft her daughters
Portions by a thrifty fparing, yet fhe chofe to
beftow it on our breeding, honeft pleafures,

and harmlefs delights, out of an opinion, that if fhe bred us with needy neceffitie, it might chance to create in us fharking quallities, mean thoughts, and bafe actions, which fhe knew my Father, as well as herfelf did abhor: likewife we were bred tenderly, for my Mother Naturally did ftrive, to pleafe and delight her children, not to crofs or torment them, terrifying them with threats, or lafhing them with flavifh whips, but inftead of threats, reafon was ufed to perfuade us, and inftead of lafhes, the deformities of vice was difcovered, and the graces and virtues were prefented unto us, alfo we were bred with refpectful attendance, every one being feverally waited upon, and all her fervants in generall ufed the fame refpect to her children, (even thofe that were very young) as they did to her felf; for fhe fufferd not her fervants, either to be rude before us, or to domineer over us, which all vulgar fervants are apt, and ofttimes which fome have leave to do; like-wife fhe never fuffered the vulgar Serving-men to be in the Nurfery among the Nurfe-Maids, left their rude love-making might do unfeemly actions, or fpeak unhandfome words in the prefence of her children, knowing that youth is apt to take infection by ill examples, having not the reafon of diftinguifhing good from bad, neither were we fufferd to have any familiaritie with the vulgar fervants, or converfation: yet caufed us to demean our felves with an humble civillity towards them, as they with a dutifull refpect to us, not becaufe they were fervants were we fo referved; for many Noble Perfons are forced to ferve through neceffitie; but by reafon the vulgar fort of fervants, are as ill bred as meanly born, giving children ill examples, and worfe counfel.

As for tutors, although we had for all forts of vertues,[1] as finging, dancing, playing on mufick, reading, writing, working, and the like, yet we were not kept ftrictly thereto, they were rather for formality then benefit, for my Mother cared not fo much for our dancing and fidling, finging and prating of feverall languages, as that we fhould be bred virtuoufly, modeftly, civilly, honourably, and on honeft principles.

----

[1] *Virtuofos,* accomplifhments.

As for my Brothers, of which I had three, I know not how they were bred, firſt, they were bred when I was not capable to obſerve, or before I was born; likewiſe the breeding of men were after different manner of ways from thoſe of women: but this I know, that they loved Virtue, endeavoured Merit, practic'd Juſtice, and ſpoke Truth; they were conſtantly loyal, and truly Valiant; two of my three Brothers were excellent Soldiers, and Martial Diſcipliners, being practiſed therein, for though they might have lived upon their own Eſtates very honourably, yet they rather choſe to ſerve in the Wars under the States of Holland, than to live idly at home in Peace: my Brother, Sir Thomas Lucas, there having a Troop of Horſe; my brother, the youngeſt Sir Charls Lucas ſerving therein: but he ſerved the States not long, for after he had been at the ſiege and taking of ſome Towns, he returned home again; and though he had the leſs experience, yet he was like to have proved the better Soldier, if better could have been, for naturally he had a practick Genius to the warlike arts, or Arts in War, as Natural Poets have to Poetry:

but his life was cut off before he could arrive
to the true perfection thereof; yet he writ
" A Treatife of the Arts in War," but by
reafon it was in characters, and the key thereof
loft, we cannot as yet underftand any thing
therein, at leaft not fo as to divulge it.[1]  My
other Brother, the Lord Lucas, who was
Heir to my Fathers eftate, and as it were the
Father to take care of us all, is not lefs Valiant
then they were, although his fkill in the
Difcipline of War was not fo much, being
not bred therein, yet he had more fkill in the
ufe of the Sword, and is more learned in
other Arts and Sciences then they were, he
being a great Scholar, by reafon he is given
much to ftudious contemplation.[2]

Their practice was, when they met together, to exercife themfelves with fencing,
wreftling, fhooting, and fuch like exercifes,
for I obferved they did feldome hawk or hunt,
and very feldom or never dance, or play on

---

[1] See an account of Sir Charles Lucas, in " Lord
Clarendon's Hiftory."

[2] His defcendant and reprefentative, the only furviv-
ing daughter of the late Earl of Hardwicke, now enjoys
the *Barony of Lucas*, as heir to this brother.

T

musick, saying it was too effeminate for Masculine Spirits; neither had they skill, or did use to play, for ought I could hear, at Cards or Dice, or the like Games, nor given to any vice, as I did know, unless to love a mistress were a crime, not that I know any they had, but what report did say, and usually reports are false, at least exceed the truth.

As for the pastimes of my Sisters when they were in the country, it was to reade, work, walk, and discourse with each other; for though two of my three brothers [1] were

---

[1] Sir Thomas Lucas of St. John's, near Colchester, married Mary, daughter of Sir John Fermor of Eston-Neston, in Northamptonshire, by whom he had Thomas Lucas of St. John's, near Colchester, Esq. who by Elizabeth, daughter and coheir of John Leighton of London, Gent. had three sons and five daughters, *viz.*

1. John Lucas of St. John's, near Colchester, afterwards *Lord Lucas*, who married Anne, daughter of Sir Christopher Neville, Kt., younger brother of the Lord Abergavenny, by whom he had John, his son and heir, born about 1624.

2. Sir Thomas Lucas, a captain in London, who married a daughter of Sir John Byron, Kt. by whom he had a son, Thomas.

3. Sir Charles Lucas.

4. Mary, wife of Sir Peter Killegrew, Kt.

5. Anne.

6. Elizabeth, wife of William Walter, Esq.

married, my Brother the Lord Lucas to a
virtuous and beautiful Lady, daughter to Sir
Chriſtopher Nevil, ſon to the Lord Abergavenny, and my brother Sir Thomas Lucas
to a virtuous lady of an ancient family, one Sir
John Byron's Daughter;[1] likewiſe, three of
my four ſiſters, one married Sir Peter Killegrew, the other Sir William Walter, the third
Sir Edmund Pye, the fourth as yet unmarried,
yet moſt of them lived with my mother, eſpecially when ſhe was at her country-houſe,
living moſt commonly at London half the
year, which is the Metropolitan city of England:[2] but when they were at London, they
were diſperſed into ſeveral houſes of their
own, yet for the moſt part they met every

---

7. Catherine, wife of Sir Edmund Pye of London, Kt.
8. Margaret, afterwards Ducheſs of Newcaſtle.*
*Arms.* Argent, a feſs between ſix annulets, gules.

[1] Siſter to the anceſtor of the preſent Lord Byron;
by which muſt be correĉted an error in the new Edition
of " *Collins's Peerage,*" which ſtates the Ducheſs to
have been the iſſue of this marriage.

[2] A beautiful piĉture of family harmony and affection; and curious as ſhewing the cuſtom of the greater
gentry to paſs the winter in London even then.

---

* Harl. MSS. 1542, f. 59.

day, feafting each other like Job's Children. But this unnatural War came like a whirl-wind, which fell'd down their Houfes, where fome in the Wars were crufht to death, as my youngeft brother Sir Charls Lucas, and my Brother Sir Thomas Lucas; and though my Brother Sir Thomas Lucas died not immediately of his wounds, yet a wound he received on his head in Ireland fhort'ned his life.

But to rehearfe their Recreations. Their cuftoms were in Winter time to go fometimes to Plays, or to ride in their Coaches about the Streets to fee the concourfe and recourfe of People; and in the Spring time to vifit the Spring-garden, Hide-park, and the like places; and fometimes they would have Mufick, and fup in Barges upon the Water;[1] thefe harm-lefs recreations they would pafs their time away with; for I obferved, they did feldom make Vifits, nor never went abroad with Strangers in their Company, but onely them-felves in a Flock together agreeing fo well, that there feemed but one Minde amongft

---

[1] This is alfo a very curious picture of manners.

them: And not onely my own Brothers and Sisters agreed so, but my Brothers and Sisters in law, and their Children, although but young, had the like agreeable natures, and affectionable dispositions; for to my best remembrance I do not know that ever they did fall out, or had any angry or unkind disputes. Likewise, I did observe, that my Sisters were so far from mingling themselves with any other Company, that they had no familiar conversation or intimate aquaintance with the Families to which each other were linkt to by Marriage, the Family of the one being as great Strangers to the rest of my brothers and Sisters, as the Family of the other.

But sometime after this War began, I knew not how they lived; for though most of them were in Oxford, wherein the King was, yet after the Queen went from Oxford, and so out of England, I was parted from them; for when the Queen was in Oxford, I had a great desire to be one of her Maids of honour, hearing the Queen had not the same number she was used to have, whereupon I wooed and won my Mother to let me go; for my Mother, being fond of all her Children, was

defirous to pleafe them, which made her confent to my requeft. But my Brothers and
Sifters feem'd not very well pleas'd, by reafon I had never been from home, nor feldome
out of their fight; for though they knew I
would not behave my felf to their, or my own
difhonour, yet they thought I might to my
difadvantage, being unexperienced in the
World, which indeed I did, for I was fo
bafhfull when I was out of my Mother's,
Brothers, and Sifters fight, whofe prefence
ufed to give me confidence, thinking I could
not do amifs whilft any one of them were by,
for I knew they would gently reform me if I
did; befides, I was ambitious they fhould
approve of my actions and behaviour, that
when I was gone from them, I was like one
that had no Foundation to ftand, or Guide to
direct me, which made me afraid, left I fhould
wander with Ignorance out of the waies of
Honour, fo that I knew not how to behave
myfelf. Befides, I had heard that the World
was apt to lay afperfions even on the innocent, for which I durft neither look up with
my eyes, nor fpeak, nor be any way fociable,
infomuch as I was thought a Natural Fool;

indeed I had not much Wit, yet I was not an Idiot, my wit was according to my years; and though I might have learnt more Wit, and advanced my Underſtanding by living in a Court, yet being dull, fearfull, and baſhfull, I neither heeded what was ſaid or practic'd, but juſt what belong'd to my loyal duty, and my own honeſt reputation; and, indeed, I was ſo afraid to diſhonour my Friends and Family by my indiſcreet actions, that I rather choſe to be accounted a Fool, then to be thought rude or wanton; in truth, my baſhfulneſs and fears made me repent my going from home to ſee the World abroad, and much I did deſire to return to my Mother again, or to my ſiſter Pye, with whom I often lived when ſhe was in London, and loved with a ſupernatural affection: but my Mother adviſed me there to ſtay, although I put her to more charges than if ſhe had kept me at home, and the more, by reaſon ſhe and my Brothers were ſequeſtered from their Eſtates, and plundered of all their Goods, yet ſhe maintained me ſo, that I was in a condition rather to lend then to borrow, which Courtiers uſually are not, being always neceſſitated by reason of great expenses Courts put them to. But my Mother said, it would be a disgrace for me to return out of the Court so soon after I was placed; so I continued almost two years, until such time as I was married from thence; for my Lord the Marquis of Newcastle did approve of those bashful fears which many condemn'd, and would choose such a Wife as he might bring to his own humours, and not such an one as was wedded to self-conceit, or one that had been temper'd to the humours of another; for which he wooed me for his Wife; and though I did dread Marriage, and shunn'd mens companies as much as I could, yet I could not, nor had not the power to refuse him, by reason my Affections were fix'd on him, and he was the onely Person I ever was in love with: Neither was I ashamed to own it, but gloried therein, for it was not Amorous Love, I never was infected therewith, it is a Disease, or a Passion, or both, I only know by relation, not by experience; neither could Title, Wealth, Power, or Person entice me to love; but my Love was honest and honourable, being placed upon Merit, which Affection joy'd at the fame of his Worth, pleas'd with delight in his Wit, proud of the refpects he ufed to me, and triumphing in the affections he profeft for me, which affections he hath confirmed to me by a deed of time, feal'd by conftancy, and affigned by an unalterable decree of his promife; which makes me happy in defpight of Fortune's frowns; for though Misfortunes may and do oft diffolve bafe, wilde, loofe, and ungrounded affections, yet fhe hath no power of thofe that are united either by Merit, Juftice, Gratitude, Duty, Fidelity, or the like; and though my Lord hath loft his Eftate, and banifh'd out of his Country for his Loyalty to his King and Country, yet neither defpifed Poverty, nor pinching Neceffity could make him break the Bonds of Friendfhip, or weaken his Loyal Duty to his King or Country.[1]

But not onely the family I am linkt to is ruin'd, but the Family from which I fprung, by thefe unhappy Wars; which ruine my

---

[1] The whole of this long paffage is in fentiment, and in the fpirit of the language, (though fome of the parts of it are awkwardly conftructed) highly amiable, eloquent, and affecting.

Mother lived to fee, and then died, having lived a Widow many years, for fhe never forgot my Father fo as to marry again ; indeed, he remain'd fo lively in her memory, and her grief was fo lafting, as fhe never mention'd his name, though fhe fpoke often of him, but love and grief caufed tears to flow, and tender fighs to rife, mourning in fad complaints ; fhe made her houfe her Cloyfter, inclofing herfelf, as it were therein, for fhe feldom went abroad, unlefs to Church ; but thefe unhappy Wars forc'd her out, by reafon fhe and her children were loyall to the King; for which they plundered her and my Brothers of all their Goods, Plate, Jewels, Money, Corn, Cattle, and the like, cut down their Woods, pull'd down their Houfes, and fequeftered them from their Lands and Livings ; but in fuch misfortunes my Mother was of an heroick fpirit, in fuffering patiently where there is no remedy, or to be induftrious where fhe thought fhe could help : She was of a grave Behaviour, and had fuch a Majeftic Grandeur, as it were continually hung about her, that it would ftrike a kind of an awe to the beholders, and command refpect from the rudeſt ; I mean the rudeſt of civiliz'd people, I mean not ſuch Barbarous people as plundered her, and uſed her cruelly, for they would have pulled God out of Heaven, had they had power, as they did Royaltie out of his Throne: alſo her beauty was beyond the ruin of time, for ſhe had a well favoured lovelineſs in her face, a pleaſing ſweetneſs in her countenance, and a well-temper'd complexion, as neither too red nor too pale, even to her dying hour, although in years, and by her dying, one might think death was enamoured with her, for he imbraced her in a ſleep, and ſo gently, as if he were afraid to hurt her : alſo ſhe was an affectionate Mother, breeding her children with a moſt induſtrious care, and tender love, and having eight children, three ſons and five daughters, there was not any one crooked, or any ways deformed, neither were they dwarfiſh, or of a Giant-like ſtature, but every ways proportionable ; likewiſe well featured, cleer complexions, brown haires, but ſome lighter than others, ſound teeth, ſweet breaths, plain ſpeeches, tunable voices, I mean not ſo much to ſing as in ſpeaking, as not ſtuttering, nor

wharling in the throat, or fpeaking through
the nofe, or hoarfly, unlefs they had a cold, or
fqueakingly, which impediments many have:
neither were their voices of too low a ftrain,
or too high, but their notes and words were
tuneable and timely: I hope this Truth will
not offend my Readers, and left they fhould
think I am a partial Regifter, I dare not com-
mend my Sifters, as to fay they were handfome; although many would fay they were
very handfome: but this I dare fay, their
Beautie, if any they had, was not fo lafting as
my Mothers, Time making fuddener ruin in
their faces than in hers; likewife my Mother
was a good Miftrifs to her fervants, taking
care of her fervants in their ficknefs, not
fparing any coft fhe was able to beftow for
their recovery: neither did fhe exact more
from them in their health then what they with
eafe or rather like paftime could do: fhe
would freely pardon a fault, and forget an
injury, yet fometimes fhe would be angry;
but never with her children, the fight of them
would pacify her, neither would fhe be angry
with others, but when fhe had caufe, as with
negligent or knavifh fervants, that would

lavishly or unnecessarily waste, or subtily, and thievishly steal, and though she would often complain that her family was too great for her weak Management, and often prest my Brother to take it upon him, yet I obferve she took a pleasure, and fome little pride, in the governing thereof: she was very skilful in Leafes, and fetting of lands, and Court-keeping, ordering of Stewards, and the like affairs: also I obferved, that my mother, nor Brothers, before thefe wars, had ever any Law-fuites, but what an Attorney difpatched in a Term with fmall coft, but if they had, it was more than I knew of, but, as I faid, my Mother lived to fee the ruin of her children, in which was her ruin, and then dyed : my brother Sir Thomas Lucas foon after, my brother Sir Charles Lucas after him, being shot to death for his loyall Service, for he was moft conftantly Loyal and Courageoufly active, indeed he had a fuperfluity of courage ; My eldeft fifter died fometime before my Mother, her death being, as I believe, haftned through grief of her onely daughter, on which she doted, being very pretty, fweet natured, and had an extraordinary wit for her age, she

dying of a Confumption, my fifter, her Mother,
died fome half a year after of the fame difeafe,
and though time is apt to wafte remembrance
as a confumptive body, or to wear it out like
a garment into raggs, or to moulder it into
duft; yet I find the naturall affections I have
for my friends, are beyond the length, ftrength,
and power of time: for I fhall lament the
lofs fo long as I live, alfo the lofs of my Lords
noble Brother, which died not long after I returned from England, he being then fick of an
Ague, whofe favours and my thankfulnefs, ingratitude fhall never disjoyne; for I will build
his Monument of truth, though I cannot of
Marble, and hang my tears and Scutchions on
his Tombe.   He was nobly generous, wifely
valliant, naturally civill, honeftly kind, truly
loving, Virtuoufly temperate; his promife
was like a fixt decree, his words were deftiny,
his life was holy, his difpofition milde, his behaviour courteous, his difcourfe pleafing, he
had a ready wit and a fpacious knowledge, a
fettled judgment, a cleer underftanding, a
rationall infight; he was learned in all Arts
and Sciences, but efpecially in the Mathematicks, in which ftudy he fpent moft part of

his time ; and though his tongue preacht not
Moral Philofophy, yet his life taught it, indeed he was fuch a perfon, that he might have
been a pattern for all Mankind to take :[1] he
loved my Lord his brother with a doting affection, as my Lord did him, for whofe fake I
fuppofe he was fo nobly generous, carefully
kind, and refpectfull to me ; for I dare not
challenge his favours as to my felf, having
not merits to deferve them, he was for a time
the preferver of my life, for after I was
married fome two or three years, my Lord
travell'd out of France, from the City of
Paris, in which City he refided the time he
was there, fo went into Holland, to a Town
called Rotterdam, in which place he ftayed
fome fix months ; from thence he returned to
Brabant, unto the City of Antwerp, which
city we paft through, when we went into
Holland, and in that City my Lord fettled
himfelf and Family, choofing it for the moft
pleafanteft, and quieteft place to retire himfelf
and ruined fortunes in : but after we had re-

---

[1] Sir Charles Cavendifh's character is drawn in equally
glowing colours by Lord Clarendon.

main'd fome time therein, we grew extremely
neceffitated, Tradefmen being there not fo
rich as to truft my Lord for fo much, or fo
long, as thofe of France ; yet they were fo
civill, kind and charitable, as to truft him, for
as much as they were able ; but at laft neceffity inforced me to return into England to
feek for reliefe ; for I hearing my Lord's
Eftate, amongft the reft of many more eftates,
was to be fold, and that the wives of the
owners fhould have an allowance therefrom,
it gave me hopes I fhould receive a benefit
thereby ; fo being accompanied with my Lords
only brother Sir Charles Cavendifh, who was
commanded to return, to live therein, or to
lofe his Eftate, which Eftate he was forced to
buy with a great Compofition before he could
enjoy any part thereof ; fo over I went, but
when I came there I found their hearts as
hard as my fortunes, and their Natures as
cruel as my miferies, for they fold all my
Lords Eftate, which was a very great one,[1]
and gave me not any part thereof, or any al-

---

[1] I think fhe eftimates it in her " *Life of the Duke* "
at upwards of £22,000 a year, which is equal at leaft to
£150,000 a year at this time.

lowance thereout, which few or no other was
fo hardly dealt withall; indeed, I did not
ftand as a beggar at the Parliament doore, for
I never was at the Parliamente Houfe, nor
ftood I ever at the doore, as I do know, or
can remember, I am fure, not as a Petitioner,
neither did I haunt the Committees, for I
never was at any, as a Petitioner, but one in
my life, which was called Gold-fmith's-Hall,
but I received neither gold nor filver from
them, only an abfolute refufall, I fhould have
no fhare of my Lords Eftate; for my brother,
the Lord Lucas, did claim in my behalf fuch
a part of my Lords Eftate as wives had allowed them, but they told him, that by reafon
I was married fince my Lord was made a
Delinquent, I could have nothing, nor fhould
have any thing, he being the greateft Traitor
to the State, which was to be the moft loyall
Subje&t to his King and Country: but I whif-
peringly fpoke to my brother to condu&t me
out of that ungentlemanly place, fo without
fpeaking to them one word good or bad, I returned to my Lodgings, & as that Committee
was the firft, fo was it the laft, I ever was at
as a Petitioner; 'tis true I went fometimes to

Drury Houfe to inquire how the land was fold, but no other ways, although fome reported I was at the Parliament Houfe, and at this Committee and at that Committee, and what I fhould fay, and how I was anfwered; but the Cuftomes of England being changed as well as the Laws, where Women become Pleaders, Attornies, Petitioners and the like, running about with their feveral Caufes, complaining of their feverall grievances, exclaiming againft their feverall enemies, bragging of their feverall favours they receive from the powerfull; thus Trafficing with idle words bring in falfe reports and vain difcourfe; for the truth is, our Sex doth nothing but juftle for the Preheminence of words, I mean not for fpeaking well, but fpeaking much, as they do for the preheminence of place, words rufhing againft words, thwarting and croffing each other, and pulling with reproches, ftriving to throw each other down with difgrace, thinking to advance themfelves thereby; but if our Sex would but well confider, and rationally ponder, they will perceive and finde, that it is neither words nor place that can advance them, but worth and merit: nor can words or place difgrace them, but inconftancy and boldnefs: for an honeft Heart, a noble Soul, a chafte Life, and a true fpeaking Tongue, is the Throne, Sceptre, Crown, and Footftoole, that advances them to an honourable renown, I mean not Noble, Virtuous, Difcreet, and worthy Perfons, whom neceffity did enforce to fubmit, comply, and follow their own fuites, but fuch as had nothing to lofe, but made it their trade to folicite; but I difpairing being pofitively denied at Goldfmiths Hall,—befides I had a firm faith, or ftrong opinion, that the pains was more than the gains, and being un-practifed in publick employments, unlearned in their uncouth Ways, ignorant of the Hu-mours and Difpofitions of thofe perfons to whom I was to addrefs my fuit, and not know-ing where the Power lay, and being not a good flatterer, I did not trouble myfelf or petition my enemies; befides I am naturally Bafhful, not that I am afhamed of my minde or body, my Birth or Breeding, my Actions or Fortunes, for my Bafhfulnefs is in my Nature, not for any crime, and though I have ftrived and reafoned with myfelf, yet that which is inbred, I find is difficult to root out, but I do not find that my Bashfulness is concerned with the Qualities of the Perfons, but the number, for were I enter amongft a company of Lazaroufes, I should be as much out of countenance, as if they were all Cefars or Alexanders, Cleopatras or Queen Didoes; neither do I find my Bashfulnefs rifeth fo often in Blushes, as contracts my Spirits to a chill palenefs, but the beft of it is, moft commonly it foon vanifheth away, and many times before it can be perceived, and the more foolifh, or unworthy, I conceive the company to be, the worfe I am, and the beft remedy I ever found was, is to perfuade myfelf that all thofe Perfons I meet are wife and vertuous; the reafon I take to be is, that the wife and vertuous cenfure left, excufe moft, praife beft, efteem rightly, judge juftly, behave themfelves civilly, demeane themfelves refpectfully, and fpeake modeftly, when fools or unworthy perfons are apt to commit abfurdities, as to be bold, rude, uncivill both in words and actions, forgetting or not well underftanding themfelves, or the company they are with; and though I never met fuch forts of ill bred creatures, yet Naturally I have fuch an Averfion

to fuch kinde of people, as I am afraid to
meet them, as children are afraid of fpirits, or
thofe that are afraid to fee or meet Devills;
which makes me think this Naturall defeét
in me, if it be a defeét, is rather a fear than a
bafhfulnefs, but whatfoever it is, I find it
troublefome, for it hath many times obftruéted
the paffage of my fpeech, and perturbed my
Naturall aétions, forcing a conftrainednefs or
unufual motions, but, however, fince it is
rather a fear of others than a bafhfull diftruft
of my felf, I defpaire of a perfeét cure, unlefs
Nature as well as Human governments could
be civilized and brought into a Methodicall
order, ruling the words and aétions with a
fupreme power of reafon, and the authority of
difcretion : but a rude nature is worfe than a
brute nature, by fo much more as man is better
than beaft, but thofe that are of civil natures
and gentle difpofitions, are as much nearer to
celeftiall creatures, as thofe that are of rude
or cruell are to Devils: but in fine, after I
had been in England, a year and a half, in
which time I gave fome half a fcore vifits, and
went with my Lords brother to hear Mufic

in one Mr. Lawes[1] his houfe, three or four
times, as alfo fome three or four times to
Hide Park with my fifters, to take the aire,
elfe I never ftirr'd out of my lodgings, unlefs
to fee my Brothers and Sifters, nor feldom
did I drefs my felf, as taking no delight to
adorn my felf, fince he I onely defired to
pleafe was abfent, although report did drefs
me in a hundred feverall fafhions : 'tis true
when I did drefs myfelf, I did endeavour to
do it to my beft becoming, both in refpect to
my felf and thofe I went to vifit, or chanc't
to meet, but after I had been in England a
year and a half, part of which time I writ a
Book of Poems, and a little Book called my
*Philofophical Fancies*, to which I have writ a
large addition, fince I returned out of England, befides this book and one other : as for
my book intitled *The Worlds Ollio*, I writ moft
part of it before I went into England, but
being not of a merry, although not of a froward
or peevifh difpofition, became very Melancholy, by reafon I was from my Lord, which

---

[1] Lawes was a celebrated mufical compofer, the friend
of Milton.

made my mind fo reftlefs, as it did break my
fleeps, and diftemper my health, with which
growing impatient of a longer delay, I refolved
to return, although I was grieved to leave Sir
Charles, my Lord's Brother, he being fick of
an ague, of which ficknefs he died : for though
his ague was cur'd, his life was decayed, he
being not of a ftrong conftitution could not, as
it did prove, recover his health, for the dreggs
of his Ague did put out the Lamp of his life,
yet Heaven knows I did not think his life was
fo near to an end, for his Doctor had great
hopes of his perfect recovery, and by reafon
he was to go into the Country for change of
aire, where I fhould have been a trouble,
rather than any ways ferviceable, befides, more
charge the longer I ftayd, for which I made
the more haft to return to my Lord, with
whom I had rather be as a poor begger, than
to be Miftrefs of the world abfented from
him ; yet, Heaven hitherto hath kept us, and
though Fortune hath been crofs, yet we do
fubmit, and are both content with what is,
and cannot be mended, and are fo prepared
that the worft of fortunes fhall not afflict our
minds, fo as to make us unhappy, howfoever

it doth pinch our lives with poverty ; for, if Tranquillity lives in an honeſt mind, the mind lives in Peace, although the body ſuffer : but Patience hath armed us, and Miſery hath tried us, and finds us Fortune-proof, for the truth is, my Lord is a perſon whoſe Humour is neither extravagantly merry, nor unneceſſarily ſad, his Mind is above his Fortune, as his Generoſity is above his purſe, his Courage above danger, his Juſtice above bribes, his Friendſhip above ſelf-intereſt, his Truth too firm for falſehood, his Temperance beyond temptation, his Converſation is pleaſing and affable, his Wit is quick, and his Judgment is ſtrong, diſtinguiſhing cleerly without clouds of miſtakes, diſſecting truth, ſo as it juſtly admits not of diſputes : his diſcourſe is always new upon the occaſion, without troubling the hearers with old Hiſtoricall relations, nor ſtuft with uſeleſs ſentences, his behaviour is manly without formallity, and free without conſtraint, and his minde hath the ſame freedom : his Nature is noble, and his Diſpoſition ſweet, his Loyaltie is proved by his publick ſervice for his King and Countrey, by his often hazard-ing of his life, by the loſſe of his Eſtate, and

the banifhment of his Perfon, by his neceffitated Condition, and his conftant and patient
fuffering ; but, howfoever our fortunes are,
we are both content, fpending our time harm-
lefsly, for my Lord pleafeth himfelf with the
Management of fome few Horfes, and exercifes himfelf with the ufe of the Sword; which
two Arts he hath brought by his ftudious
thoughts, rationall experience, and induftrious
practice, to an abfolute perfection: and though
he hath taken as much pains in thofe arts,
both by ftudy and practice, as Chimifts for
the Phylofopher's Stone, yet he hath this advantage of them, that he hath found the right
and the truth thereof and therein, which
Chimifts never found in their Art, and I
believe never will : alfo he recreates himfelf
with his pen, writing what his Wit dictates to
him, but I pafs my time rather with fcribling
than writing, with words than wit, not that I
fpeak much, becaufe I am addicted to contemplation, unlefs I am with my Lord, yet then
I rather attentively liften to what he fayes,
than impertinently fpeak, yet when I am
writing, and fad faind Stories, or ferious humours, or melancholy paffions, I am forc'd

many times to expreſs them with the tongue
before I can write them with the pen, by
reaſon thoſe thoughts that are ſad, ſerious,
and melancholy, are apt to contract and to
draw too much back, which oppreſſion doth
as it were overpower or ſmother the concep-
tion in the brain, but when ſome of thoſe
thoughts are ſent out in words, they give the
reſt more liberty to place themſelves in a more
methodicall order, marching more regularly
with my pen, on the ground of white paper,
but my letters ſeem rather as a ragged rout,
than a well armed body, for the brain being
quicker in creating than the hand in writing,
or the memory in retaining, many fancies are
loſt, by reaſon they ofttimes outrun the pen;
where I, to keep ſpeed in the Race, write ſo
faſt as I ſtay not ſo long as to write my letters
plain, inſomuch as ſome have taken my hand-
writing for ſome ſtrange character, & being
accuſtomed ſo to do, I cannot now write very
plain, when I ſtrive to write my beſt; indeed,
my ordinary hand-writing is ſo bad as few
can read it, ſo as to write it fair for the Preſs,
but however, that little wit I have, it delights
me to ſcribble it out, and diſperſe it about,

for I being addicted from my childhood to contemplation rather than converfation, to folitarinefs rather than fociety, to melancholy rather than mirth, to write with the pen than to work with a needle, paffing my time with harmelefs fancies, their company being pleaf-ing, their converfation innocent, in which I take fuch pleafure, as I neglect my health, for it is as great a grief to leave their fociety, as a joy to be in their company, my only trouble is, left my brain fhould grow barren, or that the root of my fancies fhould become infipid, withering into a dull ftupidity for want of ma-turing fubjects to write on : for I being of a lazy nature, and not of an active difpofition, as fome are that love to journey from town to town, from place to place, from houfe to houfe, delighting in variety of company, mak-ing ftill one where the greateft number is; likewife in playing at Cards, or any other Games, in which I neither have practifed, nor have I any fkill therein : as for Dancing, al-though it be a graceful art, and becometh un-married perfons well, yet for thofe that are married, it is too light an action, difagreeing with the gravity thereof; and for Revelling I am of too dull a nature, to make one in a merry fociety; as for Feafting, it would neither agree with my humour or conftitution, for my diet is for the moft part fparing, as a little boiled chickin, or the like, my drink moft commonly water, for though I have an indifferent good appetite, yet I do often faft, out of an opinion that if I fhould eat much, and exercife little, which I do, onely walking a flow pace in my chamber, whilft my thoughts run apace in my brain, fo that the motions of my minde hinders the active exercifes of my body : for fhould I Dance or Run, or Walk apace, I fhould Dance my Thoughts out of Meafure, Run my Fancies out of Breath, and tread out the Feet of my Numbers, but becaufe I would not bury myfelf quite from the fight of the world, I go fometimes abroad, feldome to vifit, but only in my Coach about the Town, or about fome of the ftreets, which we call here a Tour, where all the chief of the Town goe to fee and to be feen, likewife all ftrangers of what quallity foever, as all great Princes or Queens that make any fhort ftay : for this Town being a paffage or thorough-fare to moft parts, caufeth many times perfons of great quallity to be here, though not as inhabitants, yet to lodge for fome fhort time; and all fuch, as I faid, take a delight, or at left goe to fee the cuftome thereof, which moft Cities of note in Europe for all I can hear, hath fuch like recreations for the effeminate Sex, although for my part I had rather fit at home and write, or walk, as I faid, in my chamber and contemplate; but I hold neceffary fometimes to appear abroad, befides I do find, that feverall objects do bring new materialls for my thoughts and fancies to build upon, yet I muft fay this in the behalf of my thoughts, that I never found them idle; for if the fenfes brings no work in, they will work of themfelves, like filk-wormes that fpinns out of their own bowels; Neither can I fay I think the time tedious, when I am alone, fo I be near my Lord, and know he is well.

But now I have declared to my Readers, my Birth, Breeding, and Actions, to this part of my Life, I mean the material parts, for fhould I write every particular, as my childifh fports and the like, it would be ridiculous and tedious; but I have been honorably born and

Nobly match't; I have been bred to elevated thoughts, not to a dejected fpirit, my life hath been ruled with Honefty, attended by Modefty, and directed by Truth: but fince I have writ in generall thus far of my life, I think it fit, I fhould fpeak fomething of my Humour, particular Practice and Difpofition; as for my Humour, I was from my childhood given to contemplation, being more taken or delighted with thoughts then in converfation with a fociety, in fo much as I would walk two or three hours, and never reft, in a mufing, confidering, contemplating manner, reafoning with my felf of every thing my fenfes did prefent, but when I was in the company of my Naturall friends, I was very attentive of what they faid or did; but for ftrangers I regarded not much what they faid, but many times I did obferve their actions, whereupon my Reafon as Judge, and my Thoughts as Accufers, or excufers, or approvers and commenders, did plead, or appeal to accufe, or complain thereto; alfo I never took delight in clofets, or cabinets of toys, but in the variety of fine clothes, and fuch toys as onely were to adorn my perfon: likewife I had a naturall ftupidity towards the learning of any other Language than my native tongue, for I could fooner and with more facility underftand the fenfe, then remember the words, and for want of fuch memory makes me fo unlearned in foreign Languages as I am : as for my practife, I was never very active, by reafon I was given fo much to contemplation; befides my brothers and fifters were for the moft part ferious, and ftaid in their actions, not given to fport nor play, nor dance about, whofe company I keeping, made me fo too: but I obferved, that although their actions were ftay'd, yet they would be very merry amongft themfelves, delighting in each others company: alfo they would in their Difcourfe exprefs the generall actions of the world, judging, condemning, approving, commending, as they thought good, and with thofe that were innocently harmlefs, they would make themfelves merry therewith; as for my ftudie of books it was little, yet I chofe rather to read, than to imploy my time in any other work, or practife, and when I read what I underftood not, I would afk my brother, the Lord Lucas, he being learned, the fenfe or meaning thereof, but my ferious ſtudy could not be much, by reaſon I took great delight in attiring, fine dreſſing, and faſhions, eſpecially ſuch faſhions as I did invent myſelf, not taking that pleaſure in ſuch faſhions as was invented by others: alſo I did diſlike any ſhould follow my Faſhions, for I always took delight in a ſingularity, even in accoutrements of habits, but whatſoever I was addicted to, either in faſhion of Cloths, contemplation of Thoughts, actions of Life, they were Lawful, Honeſt, Honourable, and Modeſt, of which I can avouch to the world with a great confidence, becauſe it is a pure Truth; as for my Diſpoſition, it is more inclining to be melancholy than merry, but not crabbed or peeviſhly melancholy, but ſoft, melting, ſolitary, and contemplating melancholy; and I am apt to weep rather than laugh, not that I do often either of them; alſo I am tender natured, for it troubles my Conſcience to kill a fly, and the groans of a dying Beaſt ſtrike my Soul: alſo where I place a particular affection, I love extraordinarily and conſtantly, yet not fondly, but ſoberly and obſervingly; not to hang about them as a trouble, but to wait upon them as a ſervant, but this affection will take no root, but where I think or find

merit, and have leave both from Divine and
Morall Laws; yet I find this paffion fo troublefome, as it is the only torment to my life, for
fear any evill misfortune or accident, or ficknefs, or death, fhould come unto them, infomuch as I am never freely at reft : Likewife
I am gratefull, for I never received a curtefie
but I am impatient, and troubled untill I can
return it; alfo I am Chafte, both by Nature
and Education, infomuch as I do abhorre
an unchaft thought : likewife I am feldom
angry, as my fervants may witnefs for me, for
I rather chofe to fuffer fome inconveniences
than difturbe my thoughts, which makes me
winke many times at their faults; but when
I am angry, I am very angry, but yet it is
foon over, and I am eafily pacified, if it be
not fuch an injury as may create a hate;
neither am I apt to be exceptious or jealous;
but if I have the left fymptome of this paffion,
I declare it to thofe it concerns, for I never
let it ly fmothering in my breaft to breed a
malignant difeafe in the minde, which might
break out into extravagant paffions, or railing
fpeeches, or indifcreet actions; but I examin
moderately, reafon foberly, and plead gently

x

in my own behalf, through a defire to keep
thofe affections I had, or at leaft thought to
have; and truly I am fo vain, as to be fo felf-
conceited, or fo naturally partial, to think my
friends have as much reafon to love me as
another, fince none can love more fincerely
than I, and it were an injuftice to prefer a
fainter affection, or to efteem the Body more
than the Minde; likewife I am neither fpite-
full, envious, nor malicious; I repine not at
the gifts that Nature, or Fortune beftows upon
others, yet I am a great Emulator; for though
I wifh none worfe than they are, yet it is
lawful for me to wifh my felf the beft, and to
do my honeft endeavour thereunto; for I
think it no crime to wifh myfelf the exacteft
of Natures works, my thred of life the longeft,
my Chain of Deftinie the ftrongeft, my mind
the peaceableft; my life the pleafanteft, my
death the eafieft, and the greateft Saint in
Heaven; alfo to do my endeavour, fo far as
honour and honefty doth allow of, to be the
higheft on Fortunes Wheele, and to hold the
wheele, from turning, if I can, and if it be
commendable to wifh anothers good, it were
a fin not to wifh my own; for as Envie is a

vice, fo Emulation is a Virtue, but Emulation is in the way to Ambition, or indeed it is a Noble Ambition, but I fear my Ambition inclines to vain-glory, for I am very ambitious; yet 'tis neither for Beauty, Wit, Titles, Wealth, or Power, but as they are fteps to raife me to Fames Tower, which is to live by remembrance in after-ages: likewife I am, that the vulgar calls, proud, not out of a felf-conceit, or to flight or condemn any, but fcorning to do a bafe or mean act, and difdaining rude or unworthy perfons; infomuch, that if I fhould find any that were rude, or too bold, I fhould be apt to be fo paffionate, as to affront them, if I can, unlefs difcretion fhould get betwixt my paffion and their boldnefs, which fometimes perchance it might, if difcretion fhould croud hard for place; for though I am naturally bafhful, yet in fuch a caufe my fpirits would be all on fire, otherwife I am fo well bred, as to be civill to all perfons, of all degrees, or qualities: likewife I am fo proud, or rather juft to my Lord, as to abate nothing of the qualitie of his Wife, for if honour be the marke of Merit, and his Mafters royall favour, who will favour none but thoſe that have Merit to deſerve, it were a baſeneſs for me to neglect the Ceremony thereof: Alſo in ſome caſes I am naturally a Coward, and in other caſes very valiant; as for example, if any of my neereſt friends were in danger, I ſhould never conſider my life in ſtriving to help them, though I were ſure to do them no good, and would willingly, nay cheerfully, reſign my life for their ſakes: likewiſe I ſhould not ſpare my Life, if Honour bids me dye; but in a danger where my Friends, or my Honour is not concerned, or ingaged, but only my Life to be unprofitably loſt, I am the verieſt coward in Nature, as upon the Sea, or any dangerous places, or of Thieves, or fire, or the like; Nay the ſhooting of a gun, although but a Pot-gun, will make me ſtart, and ſtop my hearing, much leſs have I courage to diſcharge one; or if a ſword ſhould be held againſt me, although but in jeſt, I am afraid: alſo as I am not covetous, ſo I am not prodigall, but of the two I am inclining to be prodigall, yet I cannot ſay to a vain prodigallity, becauſe I imagine it is to a profitable end; for perceiving the world is given, or apt to honour the outſide more than the inſide, worſhipping fhow more then fubftance; and I am fo vain, if it be a Vanity, as to endeavour to be worfhip't, rather than not to be regarded; yet I fhall never be fo prodigall as to impoverifh my friends, or go beyond the limits or facilitie of our Eftate, and though I defire to appear to the beft advantage, whileft I live in the view of the public World, yet I could moft willingly exclude myfelf, fo as Never to fee the face of any creature, but my Lord, as long as I live, inclofing myfelf like an Anchoret, wearing a Frize gown, tied with a cord about my wafte: but I hope my readers will not think me vain for writing my life, fince there have been many that have done the like, as Cefar, Ovid, and many more, both men and women, and I know no reafon I may not do it as well as they: but I verily believe fome cenfuring Readers will fcornfully fay, why hath this Lady writ her own Life? fince none cares to know whofe daughter fhe was, or whofe wife fhe is, or how fhe was bred, or what fortunes fhe had, or how fhe lived, or what humour or difpofition fhe was of? I anfwer that it is true, that 'tis to no purpofe to the Readers, but it is to the Authorefs, becaufe I write it for my own fake, not theirs; neither did I intend this piece for to delight, but to divulge; not to pleafe the fancy, but to tell the truth, left after-ages fhould miftake, in not knowing I was daughter to one Mafter Lucas of St. Johns, near Colchefter, in Effex, fecond wife to the Lord Marquifs of New-caftle; for my Lord having had two Wives, I might eafily have been miftaken, efpecially if I fhould dye and my Lord Marry again.[1]

---

[1] It is remarkable that this has, notwithftanding, been the cafe. See "The Lounger's Common-Place Book," vol. iii. p. 398.

FINIS.

CHISWICK PRESS:—PRINTED BY WHITTINGHAM AND WILKINS, TOOKS COURT, CHANCERY LANE.